Bubbles A Broad

Bubbles A Broad

Sarah Strohmeyer

LARGE PRINT

Lg Pt
Str

This large print edition published in 2004 by
RB Large Print
A division of Recorded Books
A Haights Cross Communications Company
270 Skipjack Road
Prince Frederick, MD 20678

Published by arrangement with Penguin Putnam, Inc.

This book is a work of fiction. Names, characters, places and incidents either are products
of the author's imagination or are used fictitiously. Any resemblance to actual events or
locales or persons, living or dead, is entirely coincidental.

The treatments contained in this book are to be followed exactly as written. The publisher
and author are not responsible for your specific health or allergy needs that may require
medical supervision. The publisher and author are not responsible for any adverse reac-
tions to the treatments contained in this book.

Publisher's Cataloging In Publication Data
(Prepared by Donohue Group, Inc.)

Strohmeyer, Sarah.
    Bubbles a broad / Sarah Strohmeyer.

        p. (large print); cm.

    ISBN: 1-4193-0356-2

1. Yablonsky, Bubbles (Fictitious character)—Fiction. 2. Steel industry and
trade—Fiction. 3. Women journalists—Fiction. 4. Beauty operators—Fiction.
5. Pennsylvania—Fiction. 6. Large type books. 7. Humorous fiction. 8. Mystery fiction.
I. Title.

PS3569.T6972 B824 2004b
813/.6

Printed in the United States of America

To Charles, who is every inch the Stiletto

AUTHOR'S NOTE AND ACKNOWLEDGMENTS

The title *Bubbles A Broad* is the brainchild of Pittsburgh fan Shirley Tucker, who cleverly turned it from two words to three. Thanks to July Maltenfort for the story of "Peanut Butter Knees." Thanks also to the many Bubblesheads who offered help, beauty tips and suggestions on how to handle this and that during the writing of *A Broad*. Marna Ehrech's energized crystals made me a believer.

As always, the Naughty Girls of Middlesex, who merit a book of their own, were a source of support. So too was my husband, Charles, and Anna and Sam, who are very good sports about losing me every summer.

CHAPTER 1

Mrs. Carol Weaver, rhododendron expert of the Lehigh Garden Club, demon on the tennis court and wife to the late Steel vice president Halsey Weaver, was not the type to slum it on our side of town unless her maid needed a lift home.

So what was she doing on my West Goepp Street doorstep far from her exclusive Saucon Valley mansion on a sleeting Sunday night? More important, where did she find that matching cashmere sweater set and pearls?

But those weren't the only questions I had for her.

"Aren't you supposed to be in prison?" I asked. "Didn't you, like, kill a bunch of people?"

"Not a bunch. One." Carol hugged her bony shoulders. "And I didn't do it. Now, are you going to let me in, Bubbles? Or are you going to call the cops and blow the biggest news story of a lifetime?"

What could I do? It was November, almost Thanksgiving, and it seemed unseasonably cruel to let this murderess—albeit a polite and peppy murderess—freeze to death on my fading green AstroTurf welcome mat. Also, the next morning began my first week of try-outs for an official, full-time, paid-with-benefits staff position at the *News-Times*.

This was not the night to be turning away biggest news stories of a lifetime.

"All right," I said, ushering her inside. "But not for long. You need to leave before the cops find you here."

"I've been discreet," she said, stepping in delicately.

I checked the neighbors and, sure enough, Mrs. Hamel's ruffled white curtains quickly closed. Discreet held no coin on West Goepp.

Carol looked damn good for a fifty-year-old woman who'd spent the last eight months in the State Correctional Institution in Jakeville. I hadn't a clue as to how she had managed to find a pill-free sweater set or keep her roots fresh in the slammer. I wanted to examine her nails, but caught myself. That was a sore point—especially between us.

Like a queen surveying her subjects before bending to the guillotine, Carol maintained a regal, composed air. I don't know if her aim was to calm my jumpy nerves—a cold-blooded murderer in my living room!—but it worked. Temporarily at least.

She settled into my couch and wrinkled that button nose of hers in disgust, thereby making *me* feel like the criminal. My coffee table was strewn with potato chip bags and empty A-Treat bottles, along with an ashtray overflowing with G's Basic cigarettes. (G is my daughter Jane's boyfriend. A guy so lazy that he shortened his name to one letter—G—for, as he puts it, "God or Genius, depending.")

I hustled about with a dark green garbage bag, tossing in my crusty, black plastic tray of Lean Cuisine lasagna and mumbling about whether I could get her some hot tea, as though tea was something we actually drank in this house.

"Hot water," she replied, shivering.

"You want some?"

"No. I'm in it."

"Oh." I put down the garbage bag and sat on the cleared coffee table. "I guess that's why you're here, say?"

My gaze wandered over to my purse, which held my spiral-bound Reporter's Notebook. It's not every day that a murderer escapee wanders into the house of a beautician-turned-budding-reporter offering the news story of a lifetime.

"I'm here because I need a real reporter, one who's not too jaded to get at the truth." Carol crossed her legs and straightened her posture. "I've been reading your articles on Henry Metzger, Bubbles, and I have to admit, I've been impressed."

For some reason this flattered me. Carol used to be married to the head flak at Lehigh Steel, referred

3

to around here as simply, Steel. Weaver was the guy who issued press releases filled with lies about what a progressive company Steel was, how it treated its workers fairly and was constantly pushing for innovative, nonpolluting ways to turn out iron bars.

Funny. Iron bars is what Henry Metzger, the former chairman of Steel, should have been behind all along. His crimes were too numerous to list—though I managed to expose a few in my investigative pieces for the *News-Times*.

"Thank you," I said, shifting on the coffee table and realizing that my skirt was sticking to the residue of spilled A-Treat. "But you broke out of prison to tell me that?"

"I broke out of prison because someone's trying to kill me." Carol leaned forward. "You're my last resort."

I was back to being uncomfortable again. "Can't you find other last resorts? Like ones with palm trees and Caribbean addresses, far, far away from my house?" Couldn't she sit in another chair so she wasn't in full view of the street outside?

As if she had read my mind, Carol hopped up and started checking windows and once or twice trying the front door lock. While Carol's back was turned, I made a dash for my handbag. Flipped open the notebook and clicked the pen attached.

"Remember when we first met?" she said, staring out the window. "It was shortly after you caught your husband cheating while you were supposed to be at work. What was that jerk's name?"

4

"Dan Ritter. Though, uhm, he calls himself Chip. You know, to sound more WASPy when he married Wendy."

"Right." Carol made a clucking noise. "They're all the same, aren't they, these men? They get to a certain age, attain a certain degree of success, wake up one day, turn over in bed and decide that the wife looks like their mother. They get scared and become repulsed. They . . ."

I cut through the Oprahesque psychoanalysis. "Is that why you killed your husband? Because he was cheating on you?" You can't hide stuff like adultery from beauticians. The House of Beauty had been buzzing about the Weavers' marital woes for weeks before one word of it hit the press.

"I didn't kill Hal. I loved Hal, and even though I'd heard rumors that he was sleeping around, I never saw evidence of that. He still loved me." Carol sucked in a deep breath. "We had a terrific sex life."

I must have seemed skeptical because Carol added testily, "I'm being honest, can't you tell? I'd think that after holding someone's hands for two hours a month you'd get to know a person, Bubbles."

That was a direct reference to the fact that Carol had been a regular customer of mine at the House of Beauty. She had searched me out because I was the only manicurist in town who still did acrylic nails the old-fashioned way. I didn't drill holes into the natural nails, I filed, and if it was a French

5

manicure you were looking for, I never painted on the white. It was applied with a careful streak of dental enamel. The resulting nails were stronger than a bear's canines.

So strong that when Carol soaked the tips in cyanide and then raked them across her husband's back in a sexual, homicidal frenzy, not one nail broke. This was a fact harped on repeatedly by the Lehigh PD's Homicide Division, which was positively clueless when it came to manicures.

I tried to explain that natural nails were actually sharper than Carol's rounded acrylic ones, but the detectives had already formed a theory—that Carol's nails were murder weapons. Murder weapons I had meticulously constructed and buffed with a tasteful pink gloss.

"If you didn't kill your husband, Carol, then who did?"

"How about Henry Metzger?"

"Good luck getting to the bottom of that pit. Henry Metzger is dead. Shot before my very eyes."

"But Henry Metzger may have ordered the hit and a faction at Steel took up his cause."

"What cause?"

"That's the key question, isn't it? That's what you need to find out." She parted my blinds, peeking out and then shutting them tighter. "My husband told me once he knew a secret that could bring down Steel. He must have been right because he was killed by Steel's upper management to keep quiet."

I wrote this down. Carol was making an impassioned claim, but like many members of the state's penal club, she was conveniently glossing over a few illogical details.

"I've heard of Steel's goons breaking the legs of union leaders," I said, "but scratching vice presidents to death? It's . . . it's too feminine."

"That's exactly what Steel wants you to think." She put her hands on her hips. "That's why they took pains to make sure there was cyanide on my nails when the cops arrived that morning. I don't know how those evil SOBs at Steel managed to pull that trick, but let me tell you right now, they can get away with anything they want in this town. Including framing an innocent wife for murder."

"What about your daughter? Can't she help?"

"Kiera is twenty and pregnant. Far too young and immature for motherhood, if you want my opinion. Certainly *she* doesn't. Kiera won't speak to me. Hasn't since the arrest."

The only sounds in the room were of rain beating against the aluminum siding and my pen scratching along the tablet.

"Tonight after I got out, I stood outside my daughter's house in the rain and stared into her windows, hoping to see some sight of her. Isn't that weird?"

"Not really. My mother does that all the time." I took one last note. "Drives me crazy. She keeps claiming she doesn't want to be a bother. 'It's

7

okay. You don't have to ask me in,' she says. 'I *like* the cold. The rain's *good* for my arthritis.'"

Carol frowned. "This is a bit different, Bubbles. My daughter's due to give birth near Christmas. She'll need her mother there, to help her get some rest and cook her warm dinners. This kid hasn't a clue of how much work motherhood involves."

That last line got me. Whatever I've said about Mama, about her retro sixties fashion trends, penchant for dangerous octogenarians in fake Kmart leather and her ability to embarrass me with her painfully personal comments made to strangers, I will always be grateful to her for the weeks she spent with me after Jane was born. Dan the Man was useless, of course. Passed out at dirty diapers and became nauseous at one whiff of sour milk. Mama had been a godsend.

"I pray every night that I'll be reconciled with Kiera. But that will be impossible if I'm dead. It sounds awful to say, but deep down I'm grateful my cellmate Marta was almost murdered tonight and not me."

The pen slipped across the tablet as my stomach did a quick somersault. "Your cellmate was almost murdered?"

"That's right."

"And your reaction was to break out of prison and rush right over to my house?" I just wanted to get this straight. "Because this is the kind of fact pattern cops find very interesting when they're booking someone for harboring a fugitive."

"Hear me out." Carol tented her fingers. "Marta stole from a care package I received in the mail yesterday . . . postmarked from Saucon Valley. The package contained Moravian spice cookies with extra cloves just the way I like them. So whoever sent them knows me well."

"Why didn't you eat them?"

"I'm on Atkins. Anti-carb."

Forget anti-carb. Carol should look into becoming anti-dote, what with her toxic history.

"Marta is a born thief. She found the package under my bunk, ripped it open and managed to get through three cookies before she started feeling queasy. I escorted her down to the infirmary and then hid myself in the infirmary laundry and was carted out. I didn't want to wait around for her to die and then be blamed for her death, too."

"So you don't know if she died?"

"No, I don't. At least I didn't hear anything on the car radio. But do you see why I need you, Bubbles?" Her voice turned urgent and her face was as pale as the white plastic mini blinds behind her. "You have to find who killed my husband and who set me up. You have to find the person who is trying to kill me before . . . before my daughter . . ." She wiped away tears and coughed to hide the emotion fighting to surface. "Please, Bubbles. I promised myself I wouldn't get hysterical, but I don't know where else to turn."

However, I was stuck on one word. *Radio.* Where did Carol hear a car radio? And, come to think of it, how did she get away . . . and so fast? The State Correctional Institution was stuck in a cornfield out by Jakeville; it wasn't exactly convenient to a regular bus route. Then there was her sweater set and her constant window checking. . . .

My sucker-alert alarm went off. I might be blond and big busted with a Two Guys Community College diploma on my bedroom wall—but I didn't need a degree from Slippery Rock to know when I was being played.

"Who's been helping you?" I tapped my pen against the tablet. "Why do you need me if you have a friend who sprung you from jail?"

Carol's expression turned to shock, then hurt and, finally, indignation.

"Skip it." She threw up her hands. "I thought you'd be different from the other reporters I've written to, Bubbles. I hoped you hadn't turned cynical yet, that you were still the warmhearted girl who used to listen to all my troubles over the manicure table. I see I was very, very wrong."

With a series of quick movements she unlocked my front door, opened it and slammed it shut, running into the night. I heard a car start up and then pull out. At least I had been right about that—Carol had an accomplice.

Immediately I was plagued with self-doubt. What an insensitive slug I was. What if Carol were telling the truth? What if she'd been framed by the same folks who were trying to kill her? What if, through no fault of her own, she'd been sentenced to jail, estranged from her own daughter and therefore unable to hold her first grandchild? I knew first-hand how cruel Henry Metzger had been. Who was to say he had been the only creep at Steel?

Nah. I waved that away. What was this, the Lifetime channel? Only my mother's nutsy friend Genevieve could swallow a conspiracy theory that complicated, and I bet even she'd have reservations.

Like a lot of socialite criminals, Carol had probably bought her own lie that she was innocent. Who, me? Carol Weaver, former president of the Junior League, a housewife with ironed towels and homemade chicken pot pies, guilty of murder? Surely, there must be some mistake.

So she had escaped and tried to rope me into believing her spin. When it was clear that I'd be skeptical, too, she cut her losses and split, no doubt to try her luck with other reporters.

For an hour I sat on my couch, absently eating potato chips and trying to decide what to do. Mr. Salvo, my immediate boss and night editor at the *News-Times*, was off, this being the second Sunday of doe season.

He was deep in the Pocono woods waiting for an innocent whitetail to step in front of his thirty-ought-six. Deer season is serious business in Pennsylvania. Kids get off school like it's a religious holiday. Elvis could rise from the dead, walk into my kitchen, suck down all my mayonnaise, and I still wouldn't dare call Mr. Salvo at deer camp.

11

Without Mr. Salvo to contact, I thought of my buddy Mickey Sinkler, a detective down at the Lehigh Police Department. He was off duty tonight, and all I got was his home answering machine. Probably at deer camp, too.

So I sat with the phone on my lap and read over my notes. They didn't make sense. I'd never heard of Steel executives getting bumped off. Fired, you bet. Or sent to Williamsport. But not murdered.

I decided to take my inability to reach anyone as a cosmic clue. I needed to sleep on what had happened tonight and hope for a clearer head in the morning.

Before I went to bed, I called Jane at Dan's and listened to her whine about how Dan wouldn't let G stay over at his house, even in the guest room, for fear of infestation from fleas and other vermin.

Then I locked the doors, turned off the lights and laid out my clothes—black stretch skirt, high-heeled lace-up boots and a tasteful tiger-print top—for my first assignment as a tryout—the Lehigh Historical Society's annual breakfast. Classy, say?

Now perfectly prepared for the next morning, I slathered on moisturizer, tweezed a few stray eyebrow hairs, rested my head on the pillow and thought about Steve Stiletto, my Associated Press photojournalist boyfriend. A dead ringer for Mel Gibson before he went super-Catholic wacko. A hunk with a heart.

Despite having been shot in the shoulder one month before, Stiletto was over his mystical "chaste" phase and was healing fast. He was even well enough to drive to New York, where he was finishing plans to oversee a new AP bureau in England at the end of the month. He wanted me to join him there, and I had to admit the offer was tempting.

Misty moors (I didn't really know what a moor was, though it sounded awfully romantic). Stiletto showing me the sexy beaches in the south of France. He was determined to whisk me there so we could spend our first night of intimacy over-looking the Mediterranean surf, with the moon rising and the warm waves lapping outside our window, the two of us in nothing but a tangle of sheets and hot kisses.

Oh, my God. I put my hand to my chest, where a rapid beat thumped. Just the idea of sex with Stiletto drove me crazy with desire. It made my legs ache and my body yearn, like I was about to go mad if I couldn't have it.

So why didn't I run away with him? What was wrong with me?

It wasn't like I was afraid of transatlantic plane travel or eating stuffed sheep stomachs. I didn't fear being homesick or meeting rude French people who might pooh-pooh my Payless collection.

Stiletto told me the other night that he knew why I was keeping him at arm's length . . . and I knew he knew. He knew in the kind of way that made me squirm uncomfortably and think un–Lithuanian/Polish good Catholic girl thoughts

13

about him and his longish brown hair and blue eyes, his six-pack abs and the way he slipped his hand behind my neck to pull me to him to kiss me and that damn chastity vow that had gone on way, way too long and petrified me to a refrozen virgin who didn't know how to blow a . . .

Christ. I threw the pillow over my head and tried to recall this week's ShopRite triple coupon items. Green Giant canned green beans. Buy one get one free. I was asleep before I even got to cereals.

I awoke at 4 A.M., frightened sick with a sudden realization. Not that if I didn't buy cranberries advertised three packages for a dollar fifty during the holiday season, I'd never get them fresh again the whole year. But that someone was in the house.

They were downstairs.

In my slumbered haze I'd heard a door close and then footsteps. Slow and heavy. Ever since I'd been attacked late at night in my own bed by one Daniel Brouse, I'd never slept with the baby-like assurance that a woman's house is her Barbie Dream Home, and I was now more alert than a Boy Scout.

Brouse was in prison. Stiletto was in New York. Jane was at Dan's. And G didn't step. He shuffled. Shuffled to the refrigerator, mostly. It definitely wasn't G.

Instinctively I rolled out of bed, assembled the covers over the pillows, grabbed my robe and pushed up my bedroom window that leads to the fire escape. (The same one Brouse had crawled

14

up.) Outside was damp and freezing, and I was loath to kneel on the wet, cold, rusted metal as I carefully closed the window shut.

Within seconds the shots rang out. Five of them. *Zip. Zip. Zip. Zip. Zip.* White-yellow sparks fired in the dark and into my pillows with dead-on accuracy. I was so startled, it had happened so fast, that I nearly fell backward off the metal stairs.

I hastily scrambled down the fire escape and ran to the front porch. I leaped over the low brick wall that separated our porch from the Hamels' and banged on their door like a madwoman. The rain was falling hard, making it difficult to hear footsteps. I needed the Hamels to open up. I needed them to open the door now.

I thought of running to my car, but he would get me there. I peered into the night, hugging my robe and wishing someone, anyone, was out. Then I heard footsteps inside, and an immense feeling of relief swept over me.

Until I realized the footsteps were inside *my* house. He was trudging down *my* stairs.

He was coming after me.

CHAPTER 2

Detective Mickey Sinkler averted his eyes as I wrapped myself in a thick pink towel and stepped out of the steamy bathroom. We'd known each other since grade school, when Mickey earned fame among the nose-picking set for snorting cafeteria Jell-O with a straw. We had gotten ourselves into scrapes ever since, including a low point where I'd fallen off the Fahy Bridge right in front of him. Still, he was so shy about my near nakedness that his big satellite dish ears were bright red.

"Thanks for staying, Mickey," I said, moving past him down the hall to my bedroom. "I don't think I could have taken a shower alone."

"Man. If you'd only said that when we were in high school."

I ignored the yellow crime scene tape and turned the knob on my bedroom door. Mickey grabbed my damp wrist.

"Where do you think you're going?" he demanded.

"In here. I've got to get dressed."

"No way, Bubbles. This is a crime scene now. You'll contaminate it."

"Do you mind? My towel is falling down."

Mickey blushed again and let go of my wrist. "Sorry."

"The technicians have been all over this house, Mickey. They've brushed and powdered and poked and photographed every one of my possessions, including my underwear drawer. Now, if you'll excuse me, I need to get to work."

Before he could snag me again, I swiftly opened the door and slammed it in his face, locking it behind me. But I wasn't prepared for the effect of seeing my bed with tiny holes in it, little pieces of fluff everywhere.

Thank heavens I'd gotten out in time. Thank heavens it had only been a BB gun! That would have really, really stung. And me with an assignment this morning. Think of the amount of makeup I would have needed to hide the red pellet marks.

My pulse raced at the thought of heavy foundation and BB marks. Almost in response, Mickey rapped on the door, causing me to jump about a foot. "Don't touch anything, Bubbles. Retrieve your clothes and come out."

"In a minute," I called back, slipping into a pair of stretchy pink underwear, a matching bra and a brand-new pair of no-name-brand panty hose. (Two pairs for a buck at The Dollar Store.) I stepped into the skirt and laced up the boots, trying my best to act professional, but was overcome with a new feeling. Hot fury.

Who in the hell did he think he was, this shooter? I briskly combed back my hair, rewrapped it in the towel and proceeded to make up my face. Entering my room in the middle of the night. Pelleting me without even turning on the light. I dabbed on Cream Bisque foundation and smeared the dots together, catching the reflection of my shot-up bed in the mirror.

I mean, those were brand-new pink percale sheets from Kmart. And from the Martha Stewart collection, too!

I had been so grateful when Mr. Hamel opened the door to my frantic pounding that I had flung my arms around him. I didn't notice until later that he was wearing only his T-shirt and boxers, his gray hair sticking up like stubborn weeds. Unfortunately, whoever was after me had gotten away, fleeing my house through the back door and escaping through the neighbors' backyards.

"Bubbles!" Mickey called. "Are you all right? What are you doing?"

"Makeup."

"Aww, crap. I'll be here till Tuesday."

"You still think it was Carol Weaver who broke in here, Mickey?"

"Won't have a better idea until the prints come back and the ballistics," he said through the door.

"They have ballistics tests for BB guns?"

"I don't know. Not like I walk the squirrel beat, but think about it. Who else would've taken potshots at you if not Carol Weaver?"

18

I had told Mickey pretty much everything Carol had said. As I predicted, he hadn't been swayed by her protestations of innocence. She'd been singing the same song since her arrest, claiming some "vast Steel conspiracy," as he put it.

"The Hillary Clinton of lockup, she was," he said.

As for the tainted cookies, Mickey said interviews with other inmates at Jakeville indicated that Carol had foisted them on Marta—who appeared to be making a slow and painful recovery in the prison infirmary. Mickey's version was quite a contrast to Carol's claim that Marta had ripped open the box and stolen them.

I puffed powder on my face to set it. "Carol seemed so nice. And, except for her understandable nervousness, so normal."

"She could be bipolar," Mickey said. "That'd explain her hot and cold behavior."

I painted on thick black eyeliner. "You mean she's an Eskimo?"

"What? No. Bipolar. It's a mental illness marked by severe mood swings and paranoia." He let out a sound of exasperation. "Are you almost done?"

Puh-leeze. I hadn't even begun eye shadow. As I shimmered my lids blue, my thoughts turned to Carol's pregnant daughter. Even if Carol had been the BB assassin, her daughter needed to know that Carol was thinking of her. I had to find Kiera and relay Carol's wish that she could be with her. It was my duty as a mother.

Commotion erupted outside the door. I heard Mickey saying, "Hey, hold on there. What the. . . ." The lock jiggled and with a great loud boom it was forced opened.

I slapped my arms across my nearly naked chest. "Mickey Sinkler!"

But it wasn't Mickey. Standing in the doorway by the lock he had just busted was a tall figure in a worn leather jacket and jeans. Stiletto.

I managed to open my mouth just in time for Stiletto to kiss it, softly and gently, as he brought me to him. He radiated concern and what I detected to be a surprising amount of fear. He smelled so good, of leather and rain, that I wanted to melt.

"I wish I'd gotten here sooner," he said huskily, looking down at me and smiling at my near nakedness. "I raced from New York after Sandy called. Tell me what happened. Right from the beginning."

This is what I love most about Stiletto. He's one of those one-hundred-percent listeners who holds your hands and asks good follow-up questions as though your life, your very breath, was the most important essence on Earth. (Actually, this is a total lie. What I love most about Stiletto is how his tight jeans crease suggestively and the way his Adam's apple bobs up and down when he talks——but lately I've been trying to be more cerebral.)

I told him, sitting at the edge of the bed, dropping hairs and DNA and eyelashes and ruining the crime scene in all sorts of ways. When I was done, Stiletto got up and shut the door.

"Carol Weaver will try to track you down again. You know that," he said. "Are you prepared? Do you have a game plan?"

I wanted to ask Stiletto how he was certain Carol would come after me, but didn't want to come off like an amateur. "I get out the tape recorder instead of the Reporter's Notebook?"

Mickey Sinkler opened the door, visibly pissed. "Enough. You two have got to scram. Jesus. On the bed no less."

Stiletto turned slowly, thinking. "This place is not safe. Bubbles might be in the crosshairs of a serial killer."

Serial killer? I poked my head through the tiger-print shirt. I hadn't really thought of Carol Weaver as a serial killer.

"Now, calm down, Stiletto." Mickey made a calming motion with his hand. "It was only a BB gun."

"I don't care if it was a squirt gun, someone broke into Bubbles's house and entered her bedroom in the middle of the night." Stiletto was mad, but in control. "There's nothing to be calm about."

Stiletto had one hand on the splintered door-jamb and another on his hip. It was some male, testosterone animal thing, the way Stiletto's chest was broadened and his legs spread.

No matter how many protein shakes he had

downed or weights he had lifted, Mickey was no match.

"Let me ask you something," Stiletto asked. "Have you caught this lunatic yet?"

Poor Mickey shifted feet. "You mean Carol?"

Stiletto gave him an of-course-I-meant-Carol look.

"Uh, er, no."

"You have any idea who her accomplice was?"

Mickey and I locked gazes over Stiletto's shoulder. I had failed to confide in Mickey about my suspicion that Carol had had assistance. "Accomplice?" he said.

Stiletto folded his arms. "I find it a hard to believe that Carol Weaver escaped from a prison in the boonies of Whitehall and was able to trek twenty miles across town here by herself within an hour of escape. Don't you?"

"Twenty miles, is it?" Mickey looked helpless.

"Twenty-one to be exact. I clocked it." Stiletto shook off his frustration. "I'm sorry, Mickey. I shouldn't take out my anger on you. Shouldn't make you the punching bag." In clear contradiction, he lightly punched Mickey on the shoulder.

Mickey rubbed the spot where Stiletto had barely touched him and grunted a reply. He'd never been a big Stiletto fan since once upon a time he'd wanted to be my boyfriend first.

As for me, I didn't appreciate being talked about in the third person like I was a three-year-old. Still, the two of them preoccupied with each other gave me a chance to finish putting on my makeup, and that was protection in its own special way.

I squeezed between the men and walked down the rose-carpeted hall to the bathroom. It took me eight minutes to blow-dry my hair and apply the last bit of lipstick. When I was done, it was 7:45. I had fifteen minutes to get to the Moon Inn for the Lehigh Historical Society annual breakfast.

I flirted with the idea of blowing off the assignment and spending the day with Stiletto. After all, he had made such an effort to be here, and certainly the newspaper would excuse me this once. I couldn't imagine anyone objecting to an "I can't make it into the office today because someone took me for target practice."

No. No. No. Wasn't it that kind of slack-jawed behavior that had led to my eight years of failed courses at the Two Guys Community College? I nodded to my reflection in the mirror. This was the new me. Bubbles Yablonsky, star reporter. Disciplined. Hardworking. Cerebral. *Extremely* cerebral.

Hey, you've got to fake it to make it.

"It's decided," Stiletto said, when I exited the bathroom. "You're coming to live with me."

I stopped dead. Standing a foot or so behind Stiletto, Mickey shook his head, slightly amazed, I assumed, by the ability of some men to get whatever they want.

"I don't know . . . ," I began.

"I do," Stiletto said. "Think about it, Bubbles. Picture yourself coming home tonight. The house is dark. The sun sets around five, so the neighborhood is pitch black except for a few broken streetlights. You let yourself in with the key and flick on the—"

"Okay," I interrupted, not eager to envision the scene, "I get your point. But what about Jane? She has school."

"Dan," he said. "Dan's not one of my favorite people, but you're the first to say he's not a bad father. I'm sure he would insist on having her stay at his house until the killer is found."

"BB shooter," Mickey corrected, adding, "I think Stiletto's right. He has security over in Saucon Valley and wait staff. Even if he's not there, someone else will be home."

"I'll be there." Stiletto's voice was low and steady, Clint Eastwood–like. "No one would dare shoot at Bubbles in my bed."

I gulped, that odd quivering sensation rippling up and down my legs.

"I guess," I said weakly.

"Brilliant." Stiletto checked his watch. "Now, don't worry, Bubbles. I'm going to call my housekeeper, Eloise, and ask her to meet me here. We'll get your things and Jane's so the two of you don't have to come back. I know this is a big week for you." He kissed me on the forehead. "And you shouldn't have anything else on your plate but writing the best story possible. Whoever shot at you isn't going to risk crawling out of her rock during the day."

He practically pushed me down the stairs. "Give 'em hell, Yablonsky."

I was about to dash out the door when the phone caught my eye. Dan. I had to fill him in on our change of plans. Usually Dan makes me wait on hold when I call his office, but not this time.

"Sounds reasonable," he said, when I told him I'd be staying with Stiletto and Jane would be staying with him. "I don't like Jane going back to that hellhole you live in anyway."

Before I could reply using a play on the words "hell" and "hole," Dan's voice softened and he sounded like the man who used to give me loving back rubs during the years I was working two jobs to put him through law school.

"You take care of yourself, Bubbles," he said with sincerity. "That monster who shot at you in your own bed deserves to get it between the eyes."

I mumbled that I'd be stopping by later in the day to explain everything to Jane in person, hung up the phone, opened the door to my front step and found myself face to face with two monsters far more frightening than Carol Weaver and her mysterious accomplice ever could be.

"You don't look shot up" were the first words out of my mother's mouth.

Wider than she is tall, given to dressing like either Jackie O or Jacqueline Susann depending on her prescription of the month, my sixty-something fireplug of a mother couldn't stand to miss excitement. And I define excitement here broadly. In Mama's world, Mr. Hamel mowing the lawn with his shirt off and flabby chest bared could cause heart trouble.

This morning Mama was definitely leaning in the Jacqueline Susann direction. She was in a tight black, long-sleeved T-shirt with faint grease spots that read *Mama's Gourmet Pierogies. We Stuff 'Em Good* in white lettering stretched across her ample bosom. The cream-colored slacks she was wearing did her Polish-sausage thighs no favors despite the all-in-one girdle she wore underneath.

Her hair, naturally gray, sometimes jet black, occasionally red, once-in-a-blue-moon blond, today was brunette and enhanced by an extension she had attached with a black hair band. That combined with her dark-lined eyes and bright pink cheeks made for a package that I'm sure she imagined implied "LA sophisticate," but that to most mentally balanced people would blare "circus clown."

"Bubbles looks like death," whispered my mother's friend Genevieve, a hulking rectangular mammoth in a tweed coat, her usual accessory of a rusted musket slung over her shoulder. "Check out her eyes."

I sighed. Such a simple task. Covering an annual breakfast of the historical society. Fourth graders with IQs below seventy could do it. Yet it would be a miracle if I arrived before the last round of coffee.

"The eyes is makeup," I said. "And, no, I'm not shot up."

"That's what Mrs. Stottlemyer said, that you'd been blown to tiny bits in your own bed. And she would know," Mama said. "She's got a cell phone."

I stood there clearly in one big blond bit. Mama and Genevieve squinted dubiously.

Finally Genevieve snorted. "I have to admit, LuLu, that daughter of yours looks all in one piece. A bit anorexic, perhaps. But one piece nonetheless."

Mama still wasn't convinced, but she was frightened. I knew this because she launched into a series of unintelligible Pennsylvania negatives. "Don't spare the particulars on my account, Bubbles. My husband wasn't incinerated in the ingot mold and I didn't not hear about it 'cause I'm a woos. Not like I can't take gore."

I told them exactly what happened. "Now, if you two don't mind," I said, noticing that my watch now read 8:05, "I have to go to work."

The women didn't budge. They took up the entire top step. "What's Stiletto's Jeep doing here, then?" Mama asked. "Don't tell me he's sleeping over now. I thought you and me had a talk about that. You know, how a woman's virtue is . . ."

"Like an unbruised apple, I know, I know." How would I explain my reasons for being late to Mr. Salvo? I'm sorry, Mr. Salvo, but my mother wouldn't let me get into my car without explaining the rules of female economics—that men have needs which women manipulate in exchange for goods and services.

In fact, I was so fixated on getting past these two old broads that I forgot to think ahead of what I was saying. "Stiletto's here to get my stuff. I'm moving in with him for safety sake, until they find the shooter. Now, if you would kindly move aside."

I skipped down the front cement steps. The day was cloudy and gray, giving the neighborhood a shabby and neglected look. The brick and aluminum-sided row homes that lined West Goepp were unusually sparse of holiday decorations, except for a few tattered cardboard turkeys and wide-eyed Pilgrim children dressed in drab brown. Last night's rain had pooled on the thickly repainted porch railings.

"You're moving into Stiletto's?" Mama's voice behind me was sharp and high.

I closed my eyes. I was thirty-five. I was the mother of a teenager entering college—God willing. I did not need a lecture about dented fruit. "Yes," I said between clenched teeth.

"*Yes!*" Mama and Genevieve hollered. There was a loud slap. I turned to find them high-fiving each other behind my back.

"Took you long enough," Genevieve said. "We been waiting four months to get back into that spread of his."

As the stepson of the awful—and awfully rich— Steel baron Henry Metzger, Stiletto had inherited his sizeable wealth and Saucon Valley mansion. Mama visited it once when Metzger was alive. The in-ground swimming pool, clay courts and rolling green lawns hadn't impressed her one whit. But to this day she spoke in awe of Metzger's genuine leather Barcolounger with the heated footrest, built-in massage and handy-dandy cup holder.

"Hey, you think Stiletto still got that wide-screen TV his dad had?" Mama's eyes were saucers of wonder. "Oh, Genny, wait till you see it. You can watch two channels at once."

"Wheel and QVC?"

"Vowels and Viagra."

Genevieve crossed herself. "Saints be praised."

"Hold it, you two." I emitted a piercing whistle between my teeth. "Stiletto is being very gracious. Just because I'm moving in doesn't mean that . . ."

I hesitated. Maybe Mama and Genevieve's visits weren't such a bad idea. They might buy me some time. Time to bone up on my long forgotten—if I ever knew them—sexual maneuvers. Time to buy frilly underwear that no married or celibate women own. Time to research birth control.

"We'd have to bring our own food, though," Mama added thoughtfully. "That spicy stuff he eats gives me the winds."

CHAPTER 3

The Moon Inn was Lehigh's most cherished historical treasure, dating back to 1760 and restored by the historical society two hundred years later. Built by the Moravians out of local stone, it boasted a unique mansard tile roof and was famous for hosting George and Martha Washington on numerous occasions.

These facts had been drilled into my brain since elementary school. I could have Alzheimer's, not even know my own name, yet I'd remember that the Moon Inn was built in 1760, boasted a unique mansard tile roof and hosted George and Martha Washington on numerous occasions.

I found an unbelievable parking spot right on the cobblestone section of Main Street where I stopped and locked the Camaro. I looked around. No one had followed me the few blocks from West Goepp. I doubted anyone would attack me here. Not in front of the Lehigh Historical Society. Not in front of all these ladies.

Yes, ladies. Because these were not regular women, or at least not any regular women I knew.

These were ladies, some old, most middle aged, a few young. (Even weirder.)

They wore long skirts and jaunty hats and sensible flats. They wore brown Pendleton wool jackets and plaid slacks and haircuts that required minimal care and faces without a dollop of makeup except for a polite smear of pink on the lips. I mean, what's the point of being a girl, I thought as I watched them file into the Moon Inn's formal entrance.

"Not exactly the place to bum a cigarette," I muttered, locking the door.

As soon as I said that I caught a whiff of tobacco. Me and cigarettes have had a love-hate relationship ever since I discovered them in high school. I love them. My body hates them, as does my conscience.

Whenever I fall off the wagon and succumb to my Virginia Slim addiction, I spend the following days calculating just how much damage I've done to my lungs and combing the back pages of the women's magazines searching for a miracle fix-it that can erase the effects of my bad behavior.

But this morning my inner evil twin was brimming with justifications. Just one, what could it hurt? Haven't you been through enough in the past twenty-four hours? I mean, if you can't have a cigarette after someone breaks into your house and tries to pellet you, when can you have one?

Good enough for me. I trotted around the corner, my nose leading the way. Sure enough, slouched against the kitchen door was my smoker dressed in what appeared to be a chef's uniform. I was about to ask if she could spare one, when I halted.

Hold on. I knew her. And though I couldn't place her face or her name, I was suddenly filled with dread. Whoever she was, she wasn't a friend. The white. . . .

It hit me like a knockout punch. Holy crow. Lorena Ludwig.

I spun around and clicked my way back to the front entrance, hoping she hadn't spied me. The white uniform had triggered my memory and what a bad memory it was.

The last time I saw Lorena was two years ago. She'd been wearing a wedding dress and standing in the middle of the House of Beauty, our two-sink salon on the South Side. Actually, Lorena wasn't so much standing as throwing fists. Fists which I was ducking, though I could hardly blame her for trying to land one on me.

It was all my fault. I'd been rushing when I mixed up my chemicals. I won't tell you what they were since I'd hate for you to make the same mistake. Suffice it to say, what I thought was my homemade recipe for glitter gel—you know, to give the bride a certain "sparkle" on her wedding day—turned out to be, well, the worst disaster of my hair-care career.

I had rubbed the gel in my hand and was circulating it through Lorena's hair when I noticed a peculiar odor. Like barbecue. It was emanating from Lorena's scalp. Her hair was sparkling all right. It was also coming out in clumps. Large brown clumps.

I could still hear Lorena's wild cursing to this day. "What the fuck is this? This ain't glitter. This sucks donkey."

Of course I apologized profusely and immediately rinsed out her hair, but the harm had been done. Lorena was bald. Not completely bald, just bald in random patches. The rest of her wet hair hung loosely, the last clinging glitter sparkling hopefully.

"You're going down, Yablonsky." And that's when Lorena leaped out of her chair and lunged toward me. The next thing I felt were her manicured hands around my neck and the sensation of drowning.

Sandy, my best friend and proprietor of the House of Beauty, was on her, tugging at the dress. Lorena and I hit the floor and rolled about. Her matron of honor tried to get in on the act, yanking my hair, while Sandy was forced to pull on Lorena's train, eventually ripping it right off.

The cops were called and Lorena was charged with assault. I agreed to drop the charges if Lorena promised not to sue me or the House of Beauty. Sandy threw in every free beauty product she could find to sweeten the deal. Lorena gathered up the shampoos and conditioners, the face masks and skin toners, and stormed out of the House of

Beauty, her hair in patches, her wedding dress scuffed and ripped.

And that was the last I saw of her.

Until now.

"Shoot." I entered the Moon Inn and tiptoed into the antique yellow meeting room with its doily-covered tables laden with coffee, rolls and fresh-squeezed orange juice. Waiters in tidy white coats poured coffee from silver pots and brought in trays of croissants, but not one of the servers was Lorena. Perhaps she was a sous-chef, relegated to chopping carrots in the kitchen.

The historical society women were gathered around five tables, chatting in low tones. In one case, a member with short gray hair giggled into her linen napkin. A youngish woman in a brown turtleneck and camel-colored slacks saw me and came over, extending her hand warmly.

"Susan Morse," she said, flicking back her incredibly shiny brown mane. How did she get it so shiny, I'd like to know. Beer maybe. "You must be from the paper. You are . . . ?"

"Bubbles." I was relieved she hadn't said my name so Lorena could hear. "Bubbles Yablonsky."

Susan handed me an agenda. "We're about to get started. The big issue is whether or not to apply for federal funding to research Lehigh's historical Underground Railroad. But, uhm, wasn't there supposed to be a photographer here, too?"

A photographer? Dangy. I slapped my forehead

like a cartoon character. One of my fatal flaws as a reporter is that I constantly forget to submit photo slips to request a photographer at an event. Mr. Salvo always has to remind me. I suppose he didn't this time because, as a tryout, I was expected to perform as a regular reporter. Kind of like a little test. A little test I had kind of a little failed.

"Let me call the paper and see where he is," I lied, hoping to catch a slacker lolling around the photo department. "Is there a phone . . ."

"*He?*" Susan Morse cocked her head. "I spoke to a Mr. Salvo last night and he said he was sending a *she*."

"A she?" So, Mr. Salvo had come to my rescue after all. What a champ. But . . . "I don't think we have any woman photographers on the paper. Kind of sexist that way."

"Sure sounds like a she. A Lorena . . . Oh, perhaps this is her now." Susan brushed past me.

I was too scared to face her. Couldn't be.

"Is this the society shindig?" a voice husky with cigarettes barked. "Oh, shit. I can see right now I'm gonna need coffee." She whistled to the waiter. "Hey. Monkey boy. How's about bringing a pot over here."

The historical society women stopped chatting to look at who had whistled for a waiter. Blood drained from my face. The voice, the words, the tone. They were unmistakably Lorena. Lorena Ludwig. Queen Bitch Bride from hell.

Where to hide? I pondered crawling under one of the cotton-covered tables. Could I slip under one and not be noticed? I imagined my rear end poking out of the doily and cringed.

"Your reporter," I heard Susan say in a stiff-upper-lip manner, "said there were no lady photographers on your newspaper staff."

"Yeah, well." Laugh. Grunt. "I'm no lady, I'm a tryout. Fresh from Two Guys, you might be interested to know, Sues. So where is this so-called reporter anyway?"

I was about to make a mad dash around the tables and through the kitchen door when Susan's hand clamped on my shoulder. "Here she is. Bubbles?"

"Bubbles?" Lorena said.

I rotated slowly, dread filling up every empty space inside me. Involuntarily, I found myself raising my hands to protect my face.

Lorena stared, the gears clicking in her head. Not every day you run into a woman named Bubbles who once ruined your wedding.

"Do I know you?" Lorena asked.

I shrugged and tried to avoid examining her hair, though I couldn't help it. Frizzy brown, it had grown back, I was thankful to see. Lorena had it piled in a ponytail, which offset her high cheek-bones and olive skin. Her eyebrows had been tweezed to nonexistence and re-created through dramatic, angled pencil lines. The white jacket she'd been wearing was off. In its place was a

36

black, hip-length leather coat from JCPenney. (I know because I almost bought one on sale.)

She reeked of cigarettes.

"Two Guys, maybe," I whispered. "You have Tony Salvo as a professor?"

"Nuh-uh." She shook her head, her ponytail flapping the sides of her face. "That's not it."

Susan Morse must have left us because suddenly she was in the front of the room, clanking a silver spoon against a water goblet for order. I had never been so overjoyed for a historical society meeting to get underway as I was at that moment.

Sidling away from Lorena, I sat on an embroidered chair and buried my face in my Reporter's Notebook. I prayed that Lorena would become equally immersed in her job, but no such luck. I could feel her eyes boring into the back of my head, searching, searching, searching to place me. Feeling, as I had felt, that while she couldn't name or place me, whatever I had done to her . . . it had been bad.

"As many of you need to get on with your day," Susan began politely, "we put the item of most controversy at the top of the list. Whether to excavate what some archaeologists claim was a cave near the Monocacy Creek used as part of the Underground Railroad.

"It has been theorized that enslaved people were transported at night in boats with muffled oars up the Lehigh, to the Monocacy and then to the cave which, as many of you know, once opened onto a natural tunnel. The enslaved walked through the tunnel to waiting carriages downtown, carriages that would take them farther north to Canada.

"I happen to be in favor of this project, though it will require considerable funding. . . ."

A wrinkled hand shot up. Susan gestured to it. "Yes, Eunice."

Eunice stood. She was an older woman, pushing sixty, and if I didn't know better, I'd say she flashed Susan Morse one hell of a dirty look. Dirty looks like that would have gotten your face dunked in the toilet of Northeast Junior High. And flushed.

"This is going to cost a lot of money. Money that could be spent on more worthy projects," Eunice began. "So let's go over the facts before we start chasing windmills."

Windmills, I thought, writing this down. Weren't we discussing railroads? This historical society stuff was going to be harder than I thought.

"The fact is that while there was a tunnel that led from the Monocacy Creek, it was never part of the Underground Railroad. Professor Foley disproved this local legend during a privately funded excavation he conducted in 1968. Some of us weren't around then to have known about that. Some of us weren't even born." Eunice shot Susan a superior look.

I waited for a flash. A click. Any indication that Lorena was on the job. Shifting slightly in my chair, I snuck a peek out of the corner of my eye.

Lorena was staring at me like Count Dracula window shopping at the blood bank, a camera dangling limply about her neck.

"Wed-ding," she mouthed, reaching up and gripping a lock of hair. "You!"

Pretending not to understand, I pointed at my ear, shrugged again and returned to my notes. The tables were shaping up to be a pretty attractive option.

"Now, if you want to talk about worthwhile projects, how about the Putz Haus on Church Street," Eunice said. "There is a whole host of problems— roofing, plumbing, I could go on—that need to be repaired. Not sexy and trendy and headline grabbing like the cave, but money well spent."

"Don't you turn your back on me," Lorena yelled. "Don't you go disrespecting me, Bubbles Yablonsky."

I groaned. My tryout. This was my tryout. *No. No. No.* I wrote violently. I wrote my name and address and the alphabet backward. Anything to pretend that I was so into my work I hadn't heard her.

"Oh, right. Like you didn't hear me," Lorena shouted even louder. "How about I rip out your ears and stuff them in my mouth, then you'll hear me."

My wrists shook.

"Excuse me," Eunice said, addressing Lorena. "But I believe I had the floor."

"I don't want the floor," Lorena retorted. "I want

Bubbles. No—wait. Correction. I want her ass."

A collective gasp rose from the ladies, faster than the steam off their tea. My throat tightened and my pulse raced. It was a nightmare come true. Worse than the dream of being naked for the final exam you missed in the classes you never took.

I focused straight ahead, but I wasn't fooling anyone. The ladies knew who Lorena was talking about. All eyes were on me.

"Madam chairwoman," Eunice appealed to Susan. "I know you'd like a distraction from my latest tirade, but this is ridiculous."

Susan stood. "If there is a problem, perhaps you two should leave."

"No problem," I piped up.

"Yes, problem." Lorena's camera equipment hit the floor with a thud. "And if Bubbles won't take it outside, then we'll just get down and dirty right here."

Crap. I shoved my notebook in my purse. Then I stood and faced Lorena. Lorena was so mad her eyes were black marbles. Her fists were clenched, about to spring.

"Lookit, Lorena," I said. "This is not the time or the place. . . ."

"Not the time or the place, huh? What are you, Emily Post? You want to talk about time and place, let's go back two years. Time? One hour before my wedding. Place? Your salon, the House of Beauty." Lorena was making no attempt to keep her voice down.

40

"Please, Lorena."

"Burned off my hair, she did," Lorena shouted to the room. "On my wedding day. My fiancé took one look at me and said, 'No way.' Called off the wedding right there, in front of my whole family."

Again another round of gasps.

I winced, too. Hadn't heard that part of the story.

Susan was rushing out to the hall. I heard her pick up the phone and dial.

"I'm so sorry. . . . ," I started. "I didn't know. . . ."

"You know what I got for my trouble, for her burning off my hair and ruining my wedding and sending me home single and wasted?" Lorena smacked her fist into her hand. "Zit cream. Free zit cream. I didn't need zit cream, I needed a husband."

There was a uniform murmur of agreement that a husband was better than zit cream.

Susan returned, furious. "I want you both to leave," she said. "I've just called the newspaper and filed a complaint. This is outrageous. Two professionals acting in this—"

"Aww, keep your panties on, Prunella," Lorena cracked. "Not like you're so perfect."

Eunice applauded, but no one paid attention. I felt like sinking into the floor. I wanted a T-shirt that said, "I'm not with butthead!" and a big foam finger pointing to Lorena.

"What is that supposed to mean?" Susan said, getting up on her own high horse. "Who do you think you are?"

"I *know* who I am. The question is, who are you *pretending* to be, Mrs. Susan Morse." Lorena's wrath had suddenly changed direction, like a blowing storm. "Back in the day, you were Susan 'Slutty' Pendergast. Lover of all things male and hard. I know 'cause it's written on the third stall of the Two Guys women's bathroom. Your alma mater."

It was difficult to tell which revelation would cause more scandal among the Lehigh Historical Society crowd—that Susan Pendergast Morse was a cheap tramp or that she had graduated from a community college housed in a former discount department store. All heads were bent, lips flapping madly.

Yet nothing that was said matched what followed next. From out of nowhere a fist swung and it wasn't Lorena's. Susan Morse delivered an uppercut that would have sent Sugar Ray Leonard to the mat. Lorena was down for the count, right on the Moon Inn's refurbished wide pine floors.

"Scuff marks!" exclaimed a woman at table two.

I tried to rouse Lorena, who was soggy with confusion. Blood was dripping from her lip and her eyes were wobbling around in her head.

"For your information my undergraduate degree is from Cedar Crest, not Two Guys," Susan cursed, standing over her. "You ignorant sloth."

The sloth comment had pushed Lorena too far. Or maybe it was the subtle Two Guys slam. Either way, Lorena grasped onto me and pulled herself up, her eyes flames of hate, blood running down her chin.

"Don't, Lorena," I urged. "It's not worth it. Think of the tryout."

"The tryout can suck donkey." Lorena pulled off her coat and whipped it above her head, letting it sail into a dangling white paper Moravian star, which went flying.

Lorena and Susan assumed crouching positions and began circling each other ominously.

The historical ladies scuttled about, retrieving flower-stenciled dishes, silverware, plates of rolls, butter and sugar bowls. They blew out candles and rescued cut glass vases of red and orange autumn mums. Then they huddled in a far corner. The wait staff lined the walls and the chef even came out to watch the action, drying his hands on a kitchen towel and wearing an absurd look of glee.

I figured for sure the spectators would start chanting, "fight, fight, fight, fight," as we had at so many similar Liberty High School gatherings on Pine Street. But the only rallying call was from an elderly dowager in a purple suit to "Save the Haviland!"

Lorena lunged for Susan's turtleneck. Susan caught Lorena's hands, brought her knee up and socked her in the wazoowey.

"Ow!" Lorena moaned, doubling over.

I took this opportunity to grab Lorena from behind, linking my arms through her elbows.

Lorena kicked and swore while Susan wound up her arm for another strike.

"Duck!" I screamed, throwing Lorena down, causing Susan to miss and wobble for balance.

"You're in for it now," Susan said menacingly, once she had recovered.

"Mrs. Morse, Mrs. Morse," pleaded the head-waiter. "No!"

Too late. Susan cocked her arm, leaped and dropped herself onto Lorena for a full body slam. Wham! I literally heard the air gush from Lorena's lungs as I was forced to let go of her.

Lorena passed out promptly.

"How could you do that?" I asked Susan. "Lorena was helpless on the floor. You nearly killed her."

"Mind your own beeswax, bubblehead." As if to bring home the point, Susan picked up a Lehigh beeswax candle that had toppled from the sideboard. "Next time, get your newspaper to send real reporters instead of dipshits like you two."

And with that she stood, straightened her turtle-neck, flattened her hair and stomped off. Onlookers were mute in silent awe. I don't like to think ill of people, but at that moment I despised Susan Morse in particular and the entire Lehigh Historical Society in general.

I knelt by Lorena, who was wheezing and gasping for breath as she regained consciousness. She couldn't speak she was so stunned. All she could do was wiggle her finger in a signal for me to bend closer to her.

"I'm going to get you for this, Yablonsky," she whispered hoarsely. "I don't know when or how, but you're gonna pay. Just as soon as I'm done with this tryout."

Which, by my estimation, was right about now.

CHAPTER 4

Iknew it was bad when the publisher was called to Dix Notch's office.

Dix Notch is the *News-Times* corporate suck-up. The managing editor, who is of the opinion that the purpose of newspapers is to print advertising and not articles by Two Guys grads who happen to be hairdressers just trying to make it in a new business.

Mr. Salvo, my immediate boss, former Two Guys professor and constant ally, was still off playing cards, smoking stogies and drinking beer in a tent on the shores of the Tobyhana Creek. An activity whimsically referred to in these parts as deer camp.

I sat across from Notch in his muted green office as he picked through forms on his mahogany desk. Though it was almost winter, his balding head bore the stigma of a diehard golfer. It was sunburned red to match his power tie.

"Here it is," he said proudly, pulling out a pink letter. "Termination of tryout form. Reasons thereof. Are you ready, Penelope?"

Penelope, his loyal puppy of a secretary, nodded

eagerly. She was sitting on the broad leather couch, her legs crossed, steno pad in hand. Notch told me he'd brought her in because he wanted to get every word down on record, a record that would be attached to my termination of tryout form and deposited in my permanent file.

And just in case the publisher, Bill Graham, stuck up for me once again, Notch requested that he, the publisher, perform the termination personally.

"Graham's got to fire you, so it'll stick. That man always overrules me just because you manage to pull some rabbit out of the hat at the last minute," Notch had said. "Either that or he's got a weakness for blondes."

Needless to say, Penelope hadn't been in the room to "permanently record" *that* statement.

"All righty then." Notch licked the tip of his pen. "Length of scheduled tryout. One week."

I checked my nails and pondered torture. Put it in perspective, I told myself. Not like I was being held prisoner by barbarians. No one was driving spikes in my eyes or thumbscrews into my thumbs. I had tolerated living with Dan the Man for five or so years. I could take Notch gleefully reciting my failures as a reporter.

"Length of actual tryout." Notch checked his watch. "Two hours. Let's be generous."

Penelope giggled.

"You know, Mr. Notch," I said, "you're right. I did not act in a very professional manner."

"That's true. Unless, of course, the manner of your profession is women's wrestling."

Again a snigger from Penelope.

"But in all fairness, I was coming off only a few hours' sleep."

Notch continued writing, pausing once or twice for a sip of coffee from his Lehigh Rotary Club mug. I raised my voice to better catch his attention.

"I was working under unusual circumstances. Carol Weaver showed up at my house last night and then someone, maybe her, shot up my bed with a BB gun and I—"

"Oh, for Jimminy's sake," he said, slamming down the pen. "What is it with you, Yablonsky? Where do you come up with these mini-dramas?"

"But it's true," I protested. "I'm sure Lawless will find out about it . . . if he ever gets . . ." I wanted to say "his lard ass" but decided no. "Into the office. Really. The cops think the shooter might have been Carol Weaver. And you know who she is."

Notch turned to Penelope. "Can you see what I've had to put up with all these months? BB gun? Come on. That's rich."

"I *know*," Penelope agreed. "How have you managed for as long as you have?"

Notch couldn't answer her because there was a knock at the frosted glass door and Bill Graham entered looking very disappointed. He wasted no words. He didn't even sit, just stood there with his hands in his charcoal suit pocket, dapper and efficient . . . and distant. I stood and tried to look remorseful.

"I had expected by the end of the week to be signing your notification of employment, Bubbles. Not this."

Notch sprung from his swivel chair and carried the pink termination slip to Mr. Graham. Mr. Graham took it from him, holding the pen over it like a dagger.

"I've gone out on a limb for you, right from the get go when Steel filed that lawsuit."

I cringed. Even if I had been in the right, no freelance reporter wants to embroil their paper in a multimillion-dollar lawsuit with the city's most powerful company. Not on the first big story he or she writes.

Mr. Graham started to sign his signature and stopped. "I suppose I should have listened to you, Dix. You advised me all along against backing her."

Notch, glorious at his desk, raised a knowing eyebrow. I wished I had Lorena's glitter gel so I could sear it off his head.

"Before you terminate me completely," I said, "what could I have done differently? Lorena made the ruckus. I was trapped." Lorena had been swiftly packed off an hour before with strict instructions never to lighten the photographers' darkroom again.

"How about getting up and walking out?" Mr. Graham suggested. "What you *don't* do is throw yourself into the fight and embarrass the news-paper in front of a group of readers. They must think this paper is staffed by chimpanzees, the way you girls behaved."

I opened my mouth to say that I did not throw myself into the fight, that I was stopping it, but Notch cut in.

"Like a brawl at Eddy's pool hall," he offered.

"Exactly." Graham swiftly scribbled his name and handed the slip back to Notch. "Here you go. It is done."

I could have cried. All my hard work to become a newspaper reporter—the schooling, the moon-lighting, the boring strawberry festivals and zoning board meetings, then nearly getting killed in Dutch country and coal country—all that hard work had been worthless. Dix Notch's original proclamation—that I would never make it in this business—had come true. Come true with flying colors.

And the worst of it was, it was so incredibly, unbelievably, clearly unfair.

I picked up my purse and the fake rabbit fur coat and shuffled to the door—a kind of high-heeled-boot shuffle. Penelope flashed me a triumphant look.

"So, looks like page one is shaping up," Mr. Graham said to Notch, getting back to business. "That Carol Weaver story is hot."

I stopped at the door, pretending to busy myself with putting on my coat.

"You can go, Yablonsky," Notch said.

"This zipper's stuck," I lied.

"Cops establish any connection between the break-in and shooting on West Goepp last night and her escape?" Graham asked.

"I . . . I don't know," Notch stammered, fearful, I was positive, of exposing his pet Lawless to be the lazy reporter he truly was. "Lawless has been calling the house all morning. The people there are refusing to talk to him."

Liar, liar. Ugly pants on fire. That was my house and no one called me.

"Well, has he thought about going there in person?" Graham's voice was thick with sarcasm. "Or would that be too much to ask, that Lawless actually leave the newsroom for a story?"

"He doesn't have to go anywhere," I said. "He could just ask me."

"Speaking of leaving . . .," Notch said.

Mr. Graham swung around, looking at me with new interest. "Hold on, Bubbles. Do you know these people on West Goepp?"

"Sure do," I said. "They're me."

"There she goes again." Notch dropped his pen. "Even her grammar skills are pathetic."

"*You?*" Mr. Graham said, ignoring him. "What do you mean you?"

"Carol Weaver showed up at my house last night." I nodded to Notch. "I used to do her nails, you know."

Notch groaned.

51

"After we spoke, she left. I went to bed and then I woke up at four or so. There was a noise downstairs, so I fled through my bedroom window. That's when I saw the shooter enter my bedroom and fire the shots into my bed, thinking I was lying there."

Graham, Notch and Penelope said nothing. Penelope continued taking notes like a robot.

Notch put his hands on his hips. "Jesus, Bill. This woman—"

Graham interrupted him. "Why didn't you call the paper?"

"Didn't know anyone came in before eight. And, besides, I had to get to that Lehigh Historical Society breakfast. It was the first day of my tryout."

"You certainly had time to let Lawless know as soon as you got here."

Notch stepped back, bracing for my next statement.

"Lawless wasn't in yet," I said breezily. "He usually doesn't come in until eleven."

"I see," said Mr. Graham, dryly.

"And I did tell someone." I smiled. "I told Mr. Notch."

"Bullshit," Notch said. "Her communication skills are so poor that I had no idea what she was rambling about."

All of us turned to Penelope, still blissfully scribbling away.

"Penelope?" Mr. Graham asked. "Did you hear Bubbles say all this?"

Penelope lifted her pen and shot a glance at Notch. Notch shook his head, put his hands in his pockets and turned to the window.

"Yes," she said, biting her lip as though it had hurt her to say it.

"And Mr. Notch didn't believe me, did he?" I pressed.

"No," she whispered. "He thought you were making it up."

Graham cleared his throat. He was not about to chew out Notch in front of us. "Okay. I guess it doesn't matter who told who when."

Darn.

"Before you leave, though, make sure you stop by Lawless's desk and tell him everything. We had an exclusive in our own newsroom and didn't even realize it." Graham snapped a suspender and managed a jovial smile. "All's well that ends well, I suppose."

I would have rather signed away all rights to pursue reporting than hand Lawless a neatly packaged story without him so much as scooting his chair for it. What else could I do for the fat toad? Get him a sandwich and a glass of iced tea on my way out of the *News-Times*, banned from this place forever?

I thought fast. "I'm sorry, Mr. Graham. I can't do that. I can't discuss this with Lawless or any reporter."

"Why not?" Mr. Graham frowned.

"Uhm, because. Just because." Worked in grade school. Why not now?

"If this is out of spite . . ."

"No," I said. "Not really. I can't because Carol Weaver came to me with a news tip. She'd been reading my stories about Henry Metzger and she wanted to kind of solicit my services as a reporter to uncover what she claims is a setup. A setup involving Steel and the murder of her husband. She trusts me. . . . And me alone."

"Interesting word choice," Notch said, "solicit."

Graham set his jaw. Accustomed to plenty of negotiations with drivers unions and the writers' guild, he knew a strategic bluff when he saw it.

"And where else could you sell your story, but to the *News-Times*?"

I opened my big blues wide. "I've heard the *Allentown Morning Call* pays well. And, of course, I did that feature for the *Philadelphia Inquirer* once. I'm sure they wouldn't pass on a story about how a Steel wife was framed to take a murder rap when Lehigh Steel had her husband killed because he knew too much."

Graham bit. "Is *that* what she told you?"

"More bull," Notch said, leaving the window. "Carol Weaver killed her husband because Hal Weaver was sleeping around. He had a midlife crisis, took up with some tootsie and Carol saw the writing on the wall. Her pampered life as a Steel wife was coming to an end. She was pissed."

We had all forgotten about Penelope, who was writing furiously. She shook her hand to keep it from cramping.

I took a few steps into the office. "And who was this tootsie?"

"*I don't know,*" Notch whined. "I don't spend my every waking hour sifting for gossip like you hairdressers."

"One of the secretaries to the vice presidents," Graham answered seriously. "I heard it at the tennis club. She ended up marrying Weaver's best friend this summer, another Steel VP, though I don't know which one. There are only something like fifty-seven."

We were silent for a bit. Penelope scratched on the pad until Notch said, "Oh, you don't need to write this down, Penelope. You can go."

"Thank God." She got up, massaging her hand as she made it to the door.

When she'd left I said, "If what happened was as simple as you say, Mr. Notch, a straightforward domestic crisis, then how come an intruder tried to kill me hours after Carol Weaver left my house?"

"With a BB gun?" Notch said. "Not likely. Not unless you're a household pest, Yablonsky—and the jury's out on that one."

Didn't understand what I had said, eh?

Graham quickly caught his slip. Strike one. "I think she's got a point, Dix."

"Let her sell her point to the *Call*. That is if she can." Notch sat back at his desk. "I know a quagmire when I see one and the Weaver story will suck us out of time and money. That's why Lawless didn't waste the effort."

Strike two. Graham, who until now had treated Lawless's laziness with sarcasm, shifted into open disgust. "Do you mean to tell me, Dix," he began, "that Carol Weaver approached Lawless, too?"

Notch squared his shoulders. "She's written him several times from prison. You and I both know, Bill, that lots of prisoners write claiming to be innocent, trying to convince the cops-and-courts reporter to dig up enough left-field stuff to get them an appeal. If Lawless responded to every letter, he'd never get anything done."

"He never gets anything done anyway," Graham snapped. "No wonder we haven't won a Pulitzer or, Christ, even a state AP award for spot news reporting on his beat. What does that man need to do a little digging . . . a freaking backhoe?"

Strike three. Notch was out.

"I shouldn't be doing this," Mr. Graham said. "Not after what happened this morning." He snatched the pink letter off Notch's desk and folded it carefully. "Bubbles, your termination is suspended until Friday."

I clapped my hands. "Thank you."

"If you can reel the Carol Weaver story in by then, you'll have more than earned a full-time position here. I have the feeling cops and courts might have an opening soon."

This was too, too good to be true. One minute I was fired, the next I was slated for cops and courts. Lawless's job. The best beat on the newspaper.

"You'll never do it. Not in a week," Notch grumbled. "Like I said, it's a quagmire."

"You don't have much time," Mr. Graham agreed. "So if I were you, I'd start hustling."

"Right." I swung my purse over my shoulder. "I'll go down to the courthouse and bone up on Carol Weaver's case. Maybe I can track down this so-called tootsie."

"Be careful," Mr. Graham said. "I'd rather have you alive than on the staff."

Maybe *he* would, but not me, I thought, practically running out of Notch's office and through the newsroom.

"Bye, bye," Penelope singsonged from her computer. "We'll miss you . . . not."

I stopped and spun on my heels. "Turns out, Penelope, that I am finishing my tryout after all." I picked up a pen from her desk and wrote a phone number on a Post-it. "If you need to reach me, I'll be here. Steve Stiletto's. I've moved in."

Penelope gaped at the number. "Steve Stiletto? You're joking."

"Call there tonight and see."

"You lucky stiff," she shouted as I danced down the stairs. "I *hate* you."

Life is wonderful, even the day after someone shoots up your bed. I was invigorated and determined to dig the truth out of Carol Weaver's story. I threw open the front door to the outside and jogged to the parking lot.

This was the last step, the very last step I had

to take to become a full-time reporter. Me, Bubbles Yablonsky. Me who didn't graduate from high school, who got knocked up at seventeen. Me who . . .

I nearly fell over when I arrived in the *News-Times* parking lot.

My car! What had they done to my car?

CHAPTER 5

"Of all the people to become a news photographer, I'd never have imagined Lorena Ludwig," my House of Beauty boss and best friend, Sandy, observed.

We were studying my disfigured car, which I had driven four blocks from the *News-Times* and hidden in her salon's back parking lot, the one she shares with Uncle Manny's Bar and Grille. "Talk about bad luck. It's like destiny."

"Or stalking."

"And you're sure this is her doing."

I pulled up a lock of hair and hummed *dum-dum-de-dum*. "Coming back to you?"

"Please. I still have nightmares of flying hair and wedding bouquets. It was all the result of bad karma, anyway. Lorena had no business wearing white." Sandy readjusted an orange cardigan over her shoulders as a stiff November breeze blew. "You know what they called her in high school, don't you?"

"Jail bait?"

"Peanut Butter Legs—because hers spread so smooth and creamy."

"Fire in the hole!" Genevieve lowered her goggles and turned up a skyrocketing orange and red flame from her blowtorch.

I gripped Sandy's arm and shielded my eyes from the heat as Genevieve applied the flame to the driver's side door of my car. My dear, precious three-toned Camaro began to smolder.

"Stop!" I cried. "It's too dangerous."

Genevieve lowered the flame and rose stiffly, flakes of pink and gray metal paint dusting her husky-sized denim overalls. "C'mon, Sally. I was just getting started."

"It can't take it, Genevieve. There's so much rust, what if there's a gas leak? The Camaro will explode."

"Hadn't thought of that," she said, smiling. "That'll get Manny's attention, say?" She turned up the flame and leaned down for another go.

"The fire marshal," Sandy shouted, adding cleverly, "we don't have a permit. The government will come after us."

"Damn government." Genevieve extinguished the torch. "Well, at least I got off the 'F' word."

"That's true," Sandy said. "It's not so bad. Animal rights advocates would like it." Sandy poked me to remember my manners.

"Thank you, Genevieve, for setting fire to my car. Let me see what it looks like now."

Genevieve stepped to the left and revealed what Sandy had just described as my destiny. In Day-Glo pink reflective lettering large enough to be detected by an orbiting space satellite, the spray-painted words on the side of my Camaro read BUBBLES . . . LIKE A DONKEY. The middle part was the "F" word that Genevieve had managed to burn down to the smoking metal.

"No thanks needed," Genevieve said, licking her finger and rubbing off a smudge. "Anytime you need a moonshine blowtorch, you know who to call."

When I saw my vandalized car in the *News-Times* parking lot, I knew this was a job for Genevieve. Only Genevieve had a complete laboratory of End-Times chemicals in her basement and assorted moonshine-powered welding and sanding tools. Every family should have a survivalist as a friend. Saves tons on mechanics.

The back door opened and Mama stepped out with a steaming cup of tea. "How about the other side?" she asked. "You get that off, too?"

Genevieve shook her gray head. "Whoever did this must have used that bootleg paint NASA puts on shuttles. Doesn't melt easily under extreme heat, won't chip on reentry. That's got me to thinking you . . . know . . . what, LuLu." Her bushy gray eyebrows raised conspiratorially.

"Aliens?"

"Hey," Genevieve put down the blowtorch, "you said it. I didn't."

Of course, aliens. Why hadn't I thought of that? Actually I had, because Lorena was out of this world, that was for sure.

61

I walked around the front to the passenger side.

BUBBLES SUCKS DONKEY. In the same Day-Glo pink. I stared at it dumbly.

"Too bad about the back." Genevieve assessed the Camaro's rear.

ASK ME ABOUT DONKEY SUCKING was scrawled on the trunk. Over the left rear light a *HEE* and on the right a *HAW* were etched in the same paint.

"The cops are going to pull you over 'cause of the 'hee-haw.' It's a safety hazard," Genevieve said.

"I think it's nifty, the hee-haw part," Mama said. "Wonder how it will look at night with the lights on."

I buried my face in my hands. I was about to investigate a story that might have me interviewing all fifty-seven elusive, executive, snotty vice presidents at Steel. Easily the most powerful, the most prominent men in town. And I had to drive around in a car like this? It was humiliating.

Which was exactly what Lorena's goal had been, to humiliate me just as I had—however accidentally—humiliated her. Twice.

"Did you know that in high school Lorena once snuck into shop class and welded mood rings together to forge brass knuckles?" Sandy said. "They'd turn blackish purple when she slugged someone."

Already this tryout was testing more than my reporting skills; it was playing Russian roulette with my sanity.

Sandy told me it wasn't safe for me to be hanging

around out in the open, what with my bed getting shot up with BBs and my car defaced. So after Mama and Genevieve left to get back to the pierogie shop, she took me inside to her two-sink, turquoise salon and sat me down at the front counter, where she surveyed me with concern.

"Why don't you forget this reporting stuff," she said. "Come back to the salon where you belong."

Poor Sandy. She was such a proper creature. Always contributing the maximum amount to her IRA, never forgetting to return a movie to the video store or make her six-month dental appointment. This unpredictable world of journalism was not her style one bit.

As a best friend she'd been more than supportive of my new career ambitions, but she could not comprehend why I'd want a job where you got shot at and sued by misquoted subjects, where you were forced to punch the clock on Sundays and slave a straight twenty-four hours on Election Day.

Or worse—where you had to work in a newsroom off limits to holiday decorations of any sort. No pumpkins, no reindeer, no fluttering flags, shiny red paper hearts or bright green cardboard clovers.

Sandy paid no mind to the unspoken rule of Western Civilization that Christmas decorations must never be put up until after Thanksgiving. A Lehigh girl born and raised, she'd strung multicolored bulbs the week before Halloween and already the windowsills were covered with fake snow and clusters of singing elves. A huge Santa and a blinking Rudolph waited, unplugged, in the back store room—her only deference to Thanksgiving etiquette.

"It's not so bad, this journalism," I said. "I just have to get past the tryout and get on staff. When I get my first paycheck, I'm taking you and Martin and Jane and Mama out for a big, big dinner at Trainor's."

"That's the spirit," she said, patting me on the shoulder. "Concentrate on the positive. And think of this. Not every woman gets to go home to Steve Stiletto. Not to say you don't deserve it after what you went through."

I groaned and rested an elbow on her front counter.

"You still shook up from this morning, say? That must have been awful, someone breaking into your house. Thank God Jane wasn't there."

"That's not it," I said, hesitatingly. "It's . . . Stiletto."

"Uh-oh." Sandy lit a Basic cigarette and pulled out an empty Diet Pepsi can from the trash to use as an ashtray. "Don't tell me you still haven't recovered from the Bon Jovi trauma. You've got to get over that, Bubbles. Just because you choked when you met your idol doesn't mean you're going to freeze with Steve."

"Sannnn-dee!" screeched a shaky voice. "How much longer?"

64

What could easily pass for a gray blob of art-class clay spoke from the far end of the salon. Miniature and ancient Mrs. Domenici sat hunched in Sandy's chair, her dark hair wrapped in perm rollers, a blue plastic cape around her neck.

"What's she doing here?" I asked. "I didn't even see her when I came in."

Sandy held up a finger and checked her watch. "Eight more minutes, Mrs. Domenici," she shouted back.

Mrs. Domenici nodded and continued doing nothing but gazing straight ahead, recalling, perhaps, the sunny days in Sicily running barefoot among the vineyards, or whatever it is that women as old as Mrs. Domenici do in those chairs. Not reading. Not watching TV. Just sitting.

"She's going on a trip," Sandy said. "She called me last night because she's leaving tomorrow and she was desperate." Sandy shrugged. "So it's my day off. What could I do?"

"Where are you going, Mrs. Domenici?" I asked.

Mrs. Domenici said nothing.

"You have to holler," Sandy said. "After seven kids and twenty-one grandkids she's screamed herself deaf."

"*Where are you going, Mrs. Domenici?*"

Mrs. Domenici answered me via the mirror. "To visit my oldest daughter, Jeanette."

That was nice.

"She must be pushing one hundred. Though,

I'll tell you what." Sandy tapped an ash. "Her memory is better than yours and mine. We were talking about what happened to you and she came up with the name of Carol Weaver's maid."

"Really?" I could use that kind of information. "Who?"

"Who was Carol Weaver's maid?" Sandy shouted.

Mrs. Domenici put a hand to her ear. "Huh?"

Sandy repeated, even louder.

"Norma Lubrecht. She goes to my church. She took over cleaning for Alice Califaro after Alice retired last winter and moved to Florida to live with her sister." Mrs. Domenici chewed on something invisible.

"What's Norma doing now? Still cleaning houses?" I screamed.

"She's bagging at Schoenen's, that is when she's not running around directing our Christmas pageant at St. Jude's," Mrs. Domenici said. "Can't for the life of her find a virgin to play Mary."

Not surprising considering the girls in this town, I thought.

"You should volunteer," Sandy suggested.

"What's that supposed to mean? I haven't been a virgin since seventeen."

That was when Sandy and I, then high school idiots, crashed a Lehigh University fraternity party for kicks. Sandy ended up puking off the second-floor balcony while I found myself on the sticky floor under Dan the Man, beer dripping over my

66

face from the Schaeffer cans strapped to either side of his head.

"That's my point, isn't it? You may not *be* a virgin, but you *feel* like a virgin." Sandy ground out her ash, checked her watch again and leaned close to me. "Be honest, Bubbles. Has Dan or any man made you . . . you know?"

I gave her a look. Sandy may have been my best friend from forever, but as with all good Pennsylvania girls, not even lifetime friends discussed *that*. At least not at eleven-thirty on a Monday morning in broad daylight and crystal clear sobriety.

"Made me dance the light fandango?" I offered.

Sandy rolled her eyes. "You and your euphemisms. What were you, raised in a monastery?"

"I was raised by LuLu Yablonsky in a fatherless household. You draw your own conclusions."

"My conclusion is this. You don't know what earth-rocking sex is. Dan was no Romeo to begin with, and after he left, you were so down on yourself you slept with complete losers like the Radio Shack guy. You weren't looking for pleasure, Bubbles, you were looking for acceptance and reaffirmation. I don't mean to get personal. . . ."

"Little late for that." Sandy was starting to tick me off.

"But there is sex and there is *sex*. Once you've had the latter you'll never settle for the former."

I'd heard this before from Sandy, who, despite

67

her prim jean skirts and pastel cotton tops, secretly envisioned herself as Pennsylvania's answer to Emmanuelle.

"It's a mental defect," I explained. "Every time I think about Stiletto and me, you know, doing it, my palms start to sweat, my heart races and I get so hot, you know?"

"Oh, I know," Sandy answered knowingly, her smile a clear imitation of the *Mona Lisa*'s.

"And just when I'm about to explode with desire and frustration and pure, dirty lust . . ." My legs were aching again, already. "I imagine myself in bed with Stiletto for the first time, with me trying to live up to all those fancy, foreign women he's slept with, and I . . . I just freeze. My mouth goes dry, along with the rest of my body."

"Rejection." Sandy drummed her fingers on the table. "That's what you're afraid of, rejection. You ever tell Stiletto about what happened with Bon Jovi?"

"Are you kidding? I'd rather dye my hair brown first."

"You better tell him." Sandy jumped up to turn off Mrs. Domenici's buzzer. "Or else you and Stiletto will bomb in bed."

I slumped. While Sandy went off to attend to Mrs. Domenici, I weighed her prediction. Dan used to call me frigid on nights when I would have rather cleaned the mildew from my refrigerator door than have sex with him. And maybe he was right. I was a sex dud. Despite my love of

68

tight clothes and all material sheer, of spiked heels and big hair, inside I had nothing to offer in the bed department but some warmth in the winter. And I wasn't getting better with age, either.

To tell you the truth, I never understood the sex obsession. All that pumping and grunting and sweating. Sandy and her baker husband, Martin, apparently had a hot and heavy affair every night. Possibly because they'd never had kids and probably because Martin baked her fresh croissants every morning and served them to her in bed. Now *that's* orgasmic.

And, yes, Stiletto was different. Stiletto exuded sexuality. Just the way he walked, not self-consciously strutting, but confidently striding, transmitted a secret signal to women in his path. They would swiftly check out the four major touch points that defined hunkability—height (tall, but not freakish), chest (broad and not too hairy), hips (slim) and eyes (warm, alluring). Stiletto met all four, and then some.

In addition there was his intriguing dossier. Stiletto had been around, literally. He'd covered wars in Pakistan and India, battles in Bosnia and skirmishes in Africa. Women swooned when he described the glowing, mystical sunrise over the Taj Mahal (a story he told with sincere emotion) or how he risked his life to save a group of starving orphans from a Sarajevo ghetto, dodging bullets as he hustled them to Hungary in the middle of the night.

Most importantly, Stiletto loved me. Me and me alone. He'd shown me his devotion. He'd said so, several times, thereby allowing me to break my chastity vow. He'd even held off the advances of redheaded hotshots like Esmeralda Greene, an AP reporter who used to model underwear and who would have given herself to him in a snap of her bra strap.

Jump him, you say. Rip his clothes off! Quick. Before he gets away.

But wait—here was my problem. Like Sandy said—it all came down to Jon Bon Jovi and a horrible five-minute encounter at the Allentown Fair.

I shuddered at the memory and looked up. Mrs. Domenici and Sandy were staring at me.

"What about that big story you're working on?" Sandy said. "Why are you sitting there moping about Bon Jovi?"

Right. Once again sex had muddled my thoughts. I reached for the phone book and dialed the Northington County Courthouse in Eastman, requesting my former House of Beauty client Angie Rand, the best clerk of the Criminal Courts office. When Angie got on, I asked her if she could dig out the Carol Weaver file from closed cases.

"Don't have to dig far," she said. "Got it right here on my desk."

I paused while trying to invent a million reasons why Carol's file would be at the ready.

70

"Of course," I said, "what with her escaping from Jakeville and all."

"Maybe that's why Lawless wanted it so much," she said. "Glad I didn't let him sign it out. Knowing him, he'd probably get mustard all over it or forget to bring it back."

Forget nothing, I thought, hanging up, grabbing my fake rabbit fur and running out the door. Lawless wanted to hide it.

Hide it from me.

CHAPTER 6

So, this was the game Notch and Lawless were playing. When the going gets tough, the fat and lazy wiggle out of their chairs and waddle down to the courthouse to fight for their jobs. Notch must have hauled Lawless into his office and said, Lookit, boy, it's a crunch crisis. That Yablonsky bimbo is after your cops-and-courts beat, so you've got to play dirty if you want to keep yourself in HoHos.

What other tricks did Lawless have up his sweat-stained sleeve? Tacks under my tires? Krazy Glue on my steering wheel? Stealing my notes?

This is what I wondered as I headed east on winding Route 22 to Eastman, ignoring the best I could stares from onlookers on their front steps as the Donkey Sucking mobile passed by. Who knew there could be so many witty plays on donkey synonyms? Especially punctuated by the clever horn.

"Hey, hon, move your ass!" Honk. Honk.

You get the idea.

The Northington County Courthouse, built in 1766, looks like the U.S Capitol. Only smaller and in Eastman, PA, instead of Washington, DC. Has its own bell tower, too. Of course there were a lot fewer criminals in 1766, what with hog stealing being the major crime in the Lehigh Valley back then, so the courthouse had to be expanded two centuries later.

Unfortunately the addition was built in 1978 at the height of Bad Institutional Architecture. Dull gray limestone, narrow windows and unimaginative layout. Just like my high school.

I parked the Camaro out back and took the official entrance in, turning over my purse, keys, belt and fake gold hoop earrings to the guard at the door. After passing inspection, I gathered my stuff and made my way down the corridor to the clerk's office.

Angie winked and buzzed me in. She had a new haircut that was too short and too feathery for her age, which was mid-fifties. If she'd stuck with me as a hairdresser, I would have permed it for more fullness, less fuss.

"Here's the sign-in sheet. New security procedures." She handed me a clipboard. "You just missed Lawless. Seems he got wind that banana cream pie was the dessert special in the basement cafeteria today so he stuck around."

"And was he his usual pleasant self?" I signed my name, business and destination clearly so Lawless could read it when he returned from the cafeteria to spy.

"First he complained about the parking, how

there wasn't enough of it. Then he bitched that the security guard was an idiot and we were too slow." Angie took the clipboard from me. "Asked two or three times if you'd been by."

"We got a kind of competition going on to see who can get the better story."

Angie opened the filing cabinet, where she quickly retrieved the Carol Weaver file. "If you're taking bets, put me down for fifty on you. This was the first I've seen Lawless in at least three years, and that's despite two murder trials."

If I were a tattletale, I'd repeat this remark to Mr. Graham. With all the inventions of cell phones and laptops, reporters can get away with their own form of murder these days. Why show up for the trial when you can watch it on cable TV from the corner bar?

But I'm not a tattletale. Or am I?

"Wanna go into the back room?" Angie asked. "I could use a cigarette break, and technically we're supposed to watch reporters while they go through the papers."

"Sure."

Angie signaled to her coworkers that she was taking five, grabbed her red leather cigarette case, her open Diet Coke and escorted me to the rear room.

The conference room was supposed to be for lawyers meeting with their criminal clients, so it permitted smoking, to cut down on the homicide rate. She opened a window, letting in the cool air while I perused the folder. It was huge.

Court documents never were my specialty. There were so many pages of gobbledygook, including presentencing reports and postsentencing reports, lengthy requests for extensions, briefs about letting certain evidence in or keeping certain evidence out. Highly confusing and ultimately boring.

I read the only document that interested me—the police report—and studied the police sketch of Carol Weaver's house. The master bedroom where Hal had been found was in a suite at the end of the second-floor hall. Two walk-in closets, full bath with steam shower and views toward an apple orchard. Park Place real estate, as Mama put it.

What I did not read was the coroner's report. I winced as I turned pages of grainy black-and-white photos of Hal's slashed back along with detailed descriptions invoking the colors "pink" and "blackish." I won't even mention stomach contents.

"This is what you want." Angie removed a sheet from the bottom of the file.

It contained the particulars, that on the morning of February 15, Hal Weaver had been found dead in his bed by his wife, Carol. Carol seemed hysterical when the police arrived after her incomprehensible 911 call. Her nineteen-year-old daughter, Kiera, had been sleeping downstairs at the time and did not hear Hal come in the night before, which Carol estimated had been after midnight.

I turned to Angie. "Where had he been all evening?"

"Doesn't say." She raised an eyebrow. "Read on."

Tests taken at the scene showed scant trace of cyanide in Hal Weaver's body, largely because cyanide does not stay in the system for long. Toxicology tests determined the presence of cyanide in the scratches on his back and under the acrylic nails of Carol Weaver's hand. Subcutaneous poisoning by cyanide, the coroner wrote, would be fatal within hours after exposure, whereas poisoning via inhalation could be a matter of minutes.

Carol, fifty-five, and Hal, fifty-seven, had been married for thirty years and separated for three months. Interviews with Hal's friends and colleagues indicated that he had been planning a divorce, citing a permanent unraveling of their marriage. In short, Hal and Carol had stopped having sex years before. He had taken to sleeping in apartments provided by Steel for visiting executives on extended stays from out of town.

When arrested, Carol claimed that she had nothing to do with her husband's death. She said her husband had been acting strangely lately, suffered from severe depression and that she had taken to sleeping in a separate bedroom during his rare visits home to be with their daughter Kiera.

She was aware that on Valentine's Day her

husband had spoken to Ken Bailey, their family lawyer, about proceeding with a divorce. She admitted to being firmly opposed to a permanent separation and said that, after his meeting with Bailey, her husband agreed to give their marriage another chance.

Based on the forensic evidence, especially the cyanide traces under her nails, Carol was arrested and charged with one count of murder in the first degree. On March 28 she pleaded to a reduced charge of manslaughter with a minimum sentence of twenty years in jail.

From the corner of my eye I could see Angie regarding me.

"What?" I said, taking notes on the file.

"Nothing jumps out at you as odd?" She exhaled a blue stream.

"That he was out all night and no one knows where?"

"And?" she coached.

I turned back to the file. "The sentence?"

"One minute Carol Weaver passionately denies any involvement, the next she plea bargains to manslaughter." Angie flipped through the affidavit, holding her smoking hand aloft. "I mean, no trial? She could have argued that her nails picked up the cyanide when she turned over her husband in bed."

"You think she's innocent?"

"Listen, Bubbles, I've been a clerk of courts for two decades. I've sat through endless hearings, closing arguments and lying experts. Let me tell you right now, the evidence against Carol Weaver was crap."

I thought about what Carol had told me, that she and her husband had a great sex life, that he still loved her. It didn't jibe with the police report, which implied that the two had no physical relationship at all. And Angie had a point.

Why plea when you had a chance to win? Why plea when you were convinced Steel was responsible for your husband's death?

"Notice who her lawyer was?"

I looked back. Kenneth Bailey. Lehigh's most famous divorce lawyer, as Hal Weaver must have known since he had met with him the day before his death. Beloved by Steel executives who'd grown tired of their unfashionable and aging wives, Bailey could reduce alimony, put the home in the ex-husband's name and saddle the wife with full custody of the kids. How did I know this?

"Dan, my ex, clerked with Bailey," I said. "Bailey taught him all about how to leave a wife."

"You should ask Dan about it, then." Angie ground out her cigarette angrily. "Ask him why Bailey took on a homicide case, representing a woman who had allegedly murdered his own client, who had been seeking a divorce the day he got killed. Ask him why Carol copped to a ridiculous plea agreement."

"Why don't I just ask Bailey myself?" After all,

isn't that what a go-getter reporter like me should do?

"Can't. He's dead."

I jotted this down. This case was getting more and more interesting. "Foul play?"

"Doubtful. He slipped on his driveway during that freak snowstorm last April, on the same morning he was supposed to file postsentencing exculpatory evidence on Carol's case. Hit his head and popped an aneurysm. He was eighty, though, so it wasn't out of the ordinary."

At first I thought Angie said "escalpatory," which might explain his skull injury. Then I remembered that exculpatory meant evidence that could clear you of a crime.

"Who took over her case, then? Someone from Bailey's firm?"

"Bailey was his firm." She pointed to a framed photo on the wall of the Northington County Bar Association from ten years ago. Bailey was at the bottom, looking gray and tired even then. "After he died, his wife closed up the office, which he had relocated to the basement of their house, sold the whole estate and moved to Florida. Carol was assigned a public defender, since she was broke by then, but I don't know if she even talked to the guy."

"So what happened to the evidence Bailey was supposed to file?"

Angie shrugged. "Never made it to my court. Too weird, say?"

"It's not weird," I said, emotion stirring inside me. This is how civil rights lawyers must feel, why they devote their whole lives to clearing innocent inmates on death row. "It's . . . it's a conspiracy."

Like Carol said, I thought.

"There've been many nights I tossed and turned over Bailey's death, the lack of evidence to merit an indictment against Carol and why she copped to the plea." Getting flustered, Angie took a swig of Diet Coke and waved the mess away. "The girls in the office say I'm obsessed. They want me to shut up about it."

Good, I thought. I love obsessed clerks who've been told to shut up. "I want to hear," I said. "Why do *you* think Carol copped to the plea?"

Angie's eyes brightened. "Because copping to the plea would end the case and give her daughter a huge settlement not only from the life insurance company, but from Lehigh Steel. It was a mother thing."

"I know all about mother things."

"Ah-hah! But you don't know," she crossed her arms and leaned toward me, "that Carol's daughter, nineteen and still living under Daddy's roof, mind you, never once came to court. Not once."

What did that mean? That Kiera so despised Carol for what she'd done she wouldn't support her in court? Or did it mean that Kiera was too self-centered to care? Or that the entire matter was too disturbing for a teenager to deal with?

"In fact, besides the press—not Lawless, of

course—and lawyers from the Weavers' insurance company, only one person came to every hearing, whether it was a status conference, a rescheduling matter or a two-minute conference call about where to order lunch."

"Who?" I asked, almost forgetting to take notes.

"Hal Weaver's mistress. Back then an executive secretary at Steel and a nicer woman you'd never want to meet." Angie looked off. "I felt so sorry for her. She was so sad and she always sat in the back row, quiet as a flower, fidgeting with her hands, as though she was worried Carol Weaver would get off."

"Mistress? How do you know she was Hal's mistress?"

Angie fluttered her eyelashes. "Twenty years as a court clerk, you know these things. That woman was beyond distraught. She really loved Hal, I think. Really did."

Or perhaps not.

If I had murdered my lover and his wife was taking the rap, I'd have fidgeted nervously in court, too. Especially if I had been forced by my bosses at Steel to commit the crime.

I didn't want to interrupt Angie's reverie but I had to ask. "Do you remember her name?"

"Of course. I validated her parking every day." Angie smiled. "Susan Pendergast. Now Susan Pendergast Morse. Know her?"

Know her? I thought. I wanted to kill her myself less than five hours ago.

★ ★ ★

I searched through the bottom of my purse and found a dollar ten in gunk-covered change. Plunking the money into the courthouse payphone, which reeked of spicy lawyer cologne, I called Peanut Butter Legs at home. She was listed as living on Union Boulevard in Lehigh and I was sure she'd be in, seeing as she'd been kicked off the tryout and all.

Lorena didn't pick up until I started leaving a message on her answering machine.

"Saw on my caller ID it was the courthouse payphone number and assumed it was an ex wanting me to post bail. Yet again." She exhaled, blowing rudely into the phone. "If you're calling to apologize, *Blond-skee*, it's too little, too late."

"Apologize? I should be calling you with a body-work estimate on my Camaro."

"I have no idea what you're talking about." Blatant lie.

"Lorena. You are the only human I know who repeatedly uses the phrase, *suck donkey*. My car is ruined thanks to you."

"Really? That's too bad. Is it embarrassing?"

I was about to answer, "Of course!" when I stopped. This is exactly what Lorena Ludwig wanted, to hear me moan and complain about the pain she'd caused me. I wasn't playing. I had contacted Lorena for another purpose besides fresh paint.

That I'd get later.

"Listen, Lorena, let's forget about this for now."

"Forget about what? There's nothing to forget." More exhalation of smoke into the phone. In the background I heard the distinctive high-brow voice of Viki Buchanan delivering one of her famous, self-righteous lectures.

"Is *One Life to Live* on so early?"

"It's taped. From last week. Now that I got time to kill, thanks to you, I'm catching up. Viki's on one of her tirades. Asa's threatening to steal her daughter."

"Which one?"

"The real one. Jessica."

"Jessica's not the real one. Jessica's the one Viki thought she had when she was her alternate personality Nikki Smith high on drugs."

"You're wrong."

"Am not. I've been watching *OLTL* since I was six."

"Park it, Blondsky. No one knows *One Life to Live* like yours truly. I got *OLTL* tattooed on my ass."

I winced. Not an image to savor so soon after breakfast.

We spent the next two minutes debating the lineage of Jessica and other trials of Llanview, Pennsylvania, both of us finally agreeing that nowhere in our home state had we ever met a big, rich Texan like Asa Buchanan. Or men who lounged about in three-piece suits and ties at home, for that matter.

And what was with the sherry drinking these

people were always doing smack in the middle of the day? Why weren't they stumbling into tables and falling asleep on those overstuffed couches? If you had only one life to live, why would you live it in a place like Llanview, which wasn't even on the map?

Exhausted by our *One Life to Live* vent and prompted by the recorded operator's voice to deposit another quarter, I finally hit the lowest common denominator. "Lookit, Lorena, I may have a way for you to get back at Susan Morse and get back your tryout at the *News-Times*."

"I like the revenge part. Talk fast."

I filled her in on my past twenty-four hours, from Carol Weaver's visit to my five-minute termination to the revelation that Susan Morse had been Hal Weaver's mistress. It was a risk, admittedly, especially considering Lorena's violent temperament, but I had to tell her everything.

I confided partly because I decided any woman who thought Max Holden was an overrated soap character might have decent taste. But mostly I did it because I felt guilty. First about ruining Lorena's wedding and nixing her marriage and then about nixing her chances to get on the paper as a photographer.

I mean, us Two Guys alums, we got to stick together during and after fistfights. Alumni networking, I think they call it.

And that was the last reason I told her everything. Lorena had mentioned that Susan Morse was a Two Guys alum. Susan had skirted that, noting proudly that she was a Cedar Crest graduate. I wanted Lorena to tell me where she came up with Two Guys.

"Where did you get that Susan went to Two Guys? Was that a joke?"

"No. That wasn't a joke," Lorena replied, annoyed. "Susan graduated the year before me, three years ago. She once brushed up against me in the hall and didn't say excuse me. Can you believe that? I've had it out for her ever since."

I made a mental note to apologize profusely if I so much as breathed on Lorena. "Okay. Thanks."

"Ahem." Lorena wasn't about to let me off that easy. "And what, may I ask, is my quid pro quo?"

"Quid pro quo?"

"Yeah. Old Dutch phrase. Translation? I've scratched your back, now give me money or my fist in your face."

I've been to Pennsylvania Dutch Country. I didn't remember that translation.

"If I find Susan and this story moves along and I need photos, I'll call you, Lorena. That way I'll present the article to Dix Notch as a whole package. My story and your art, together. Deal?"

"It doesn't suck too much," Lorena conceded. "That is if you deliver."

With that cozy conclusion, we hung up on each other and I called Wendy, my ex-husband's new wife, the twig-thin cheeseball heiress. Wendy was her usual snippy self, as though the mere act of answering the phone had been beneath her.

"Please tell Jane," I said oh-so-politely, "that I'll stop by later today to explain about the BB shooting this morning and to bring her clothes which—"

"No rush," Wendy interrupted. "Steve Stiletto's maid, Eloise, dropped off a suitcase about a half hour ago and I'm picking up Jane early from school to take her shopping before the cocktail party this evening. One of Chip's client affairs."

"On a Monday?" Who goes to parties on a Monday? Monday was meatloaf and football night.

"To celebrate his win. Chip got a jury to pay big on a negligent bowling ball case stemming from a tort at the Galaxy Lanes. His client used to commute by hitchhiking. He can't anymore, now that the bowling ball wouldn't let go of his thumb. Thirty-three percent of half a million for a torn ligament's not bad."

I tried to absorb this. After working two jobs to put Dan through law school and then suffering more poverty, not to mention student loan payments, during his piddly small claims cases, never did I imagine Dan was the kind of lawyer who could bring in half a million for a stuck thumb.

"And Jane needs a better outfit for her interview with Bo Wimble on Wednesday morning. I'm afraid Doc Martens and ripped black jeans just won't wash with the Ivy League."

"Who's Bo Wimble?"

"Oh my God. You really are out of it, aren't you? Bo Wimble is the local Princeton rep, a golfing partner of Chip's. Chipper convinced him to interview Jane one-on-one over breakfast, before school. Isn't that super?"

Chipper?

"What happened to Joan Smullen from the university?" I said. "I thought she was supposed to do the interview."

"She doesn't even shave her legs. Like I told Chip, Professor Smullen would mostly likely fill Jane's head with the joys of lesbian love and then make a pass at her before the interview's end."

I nearly dropped the phone. What an image! What a thing to say! "I've spoken to Professor Smullen and she seems—"

"Oops. Gotta go. Caterer just pulled up. Stop by before five, Bubbles. And use the back entrance by the kitchen. The front will be strictly for guests."

Like hell, I thought, slamming the phone. Wendy was exerting too much influence over Jane. First it was the purple and ivy bedroom with the color TV and personal stereo. Then it was her attempt to force Jane into strapless dresses and country club debutante dances. Now it was Bo Wimble.

Definitely like hell.

CHAPTER 7

Two Guys Community College isn't Lehigh University, the famous engineering school across town. Where Lehigh has an impressive grass courtyard and imposing stone gates marking its entrance, Two Guys has a silhouette of two guys in black bell bottoms and afros on a graffitied sign left over from when the school was a department store in the seventies.

And where a three-toned Camaro with ASK ME ABOUT DONKEY SUCKING on it might alarm campus security if it were parked next to the Saabs and Alfa Romeos in Lehigh University's parking lot, at Two Guys it fit in like camouflage at a gun show.

I pulled next to a Pacer that had WASH ME written in its dusty back bumper. Three spaces down was a Jeep that had JUST DIVORCED painted on its rear window.

I was home. At least I thought I was home, until I got out and found two teenagers in flannel shirts and jeans staring at my car.

"Boy," said one, "I never heard about that. . . . And I grew up on a farm."

88

I moved the Camaro to the deserted parking lot behind the store. Maybe pressuring Lorena to fork over the cash for the paint job wasn't too much to ask. Burned hair or no.

Inside Two Guys I snaked my way through the various aisles. The old store still held the aromas of its glory days, polyester sweaters and plastic shoes, chewy pretzels with yellow mustard and sickly parakeets in the pet department. Reminded me of being a kid on Thursday night shopping sprees with Mama, getting lost in the racks of five-dollar dresses.

At the end of Aisle Five, in an area formerly known as Sheets and Towels, was a tiny cubicle marked GUIDANCE. My former guidance counselor, Mary Cathobianco, was bent over a desk piled high with folders, catalogues and test results.

I knocked on the door frame. "Mrs. Cathobianco?"

Still as tired and wrinkled as she was when I was a student, Mrs. Cathobianco looked up, a second passing before she recognized me. "Bubbles. Come in. I was just going to call you."

I sat on a metal folding chair where I'd spent many an hour pleading for just one more chance. After eight years of flunking everything from Funeral Cosmetics to Accounting for Almart employees, I'd worn Mrs. Cathobianco's patience wafer thin. Her final offer—Mr. Salvo's Journalism 101 course—had been my salvation.

"Call me?" I said.

"Yes. Have you seen our latest flyer?" She opened a drawer and pulled out a glossy paper that folded into three sections.

On the front, in big white letters and trademark Two Guys poor grammar it said: "Feel Like a Failure? A Flop? A Dope? Then you gotta meet Bubbles Yablonsky."

I opened it and there was an old picture of me twirling my hair, gazing out the window. It was accompanied by a snappy paragraph about how I'd been knocked up in high school, then left by my husband to raise a baby daughter. How I had only a GED and an inability to earn any grade over 59.

"Eight years later," it said, and . . . and there was my byline on a *News-Times* article.

"If you don't succeed. Try, try again at Two Guys Community College. Two Guys' Biggest Loser Ever Bubbles Yablonsky could make it. Surely you can too!"

I felt a lump in my throat. "Oh, Mrs. Cathobianco . . . I can't believe I'm Two Guys' Biggest Loser ever."

Mrs. Cathobianco smiled. "You should be proud, Bubbles. You earned it."

"May I keep the flyer?"

"Certainly." She capped her pen. "Now how may I help you? Don't tell me you need more course work."

"I'm looking for info on a student who graduated three years ago, Susan Pendergast. Now Susan

Morse. She's a member of the Lehigh Historical Society." I shut the door and told her the basics. "I don't need Susan's grades or the results of her IQ tests, nothing too personal. I'd just like to get a glimpse of her course work. Chemistry classes. Poisoning with cyanide. That kind of thing."

Mrs. Cathobianco was already at her ancient computer, checking names. "Usually I don't run these kinds of checks. Student records are confidential. But since you are Two Guys' Biggest Loser Ever, I'll bend the rules. Anyway, now my curiosity is piqued."

"Thanks."

She arrived at a page and put her finger to the screen. "Seems she was in our master's program. Says here that a Susan Pendergast graduated three years ago with an M.R.S."

I cleared my throat. "An M.R.S.? I thought that was a joke."

"Not at Two Guys. Our Matronly Required Studies program is very rigorous. We teach both practical and theoretical, culminating in fieldwork for three months."

"What is it?"

Mrs. Cathobianco clicked down farther. "Essentially, it's expanded and intensified home economics. You know, in this day and age we don't have generations of domesticated women passing down the old skills, from bleaching shower grout and studying the miracles of Borax to catching a financially secure husband."

I walked around to examine her computer screen. "And that's what Susan studied? Shower grout?"

"With PA certification. Pennsylvania housekeeping is a specialty. Only the most qualified can meet its standards. You've really got to master your toothbrush as the ultimate cleaning tool." She hesitated. "It says here Miss Pendergast excelled in the practical—laundry whitening, husband catching and coupon clipping—and aced her thesis on 'The Versatile Cassava: It's Not Just for Dessert.'"

Then she frowned.

"What's wrong?" I asked.

"Seems Miss Pendergast was a tad weak on the theoretical." She pointed to a word I didn't recognize. "Schadenfreude, for example, the German expression for taking joy in a neighbor's pain. It's required for Pennsylvania certification but Miss Pendergast nearly failed it. Fortunately, she made up for the low grade by doing okay in the Art of Surreptitious Gossip."

My toe started involuntarily tapping, bothered as I was by what I sensed might be home girl discrimination. "How come I never knew about this M.R.S. stuff? I would have loved to have caught a wealthy husband."

Mrs. Cathobianco spun away from her computer, her eyes full of guidance-counselor sympathy. "I'm sorry, Bubbles, but you were in the Study A Broad program. You didn't qualify."

"Abroad? I've never gone past Perth Amboy. How could I have been abroad?"

"Oh, Bubbles, a girl doesn't have to go far to be a broad."

"What does that mean?"

She bit her lip, as I'd seen her do before when she was trying to couch bad news, such as that I was destined for expulsion or that Dan's tuition check had bounced. "Let me explain it more clearly. Miss Pendergast was in the Domestic Studies Program and you were in the A Broad because, well, because you are a . . . broad."

I blinked.

"A chick. Babe. Broad. That's you." Mrs. Cathobianco had given up on being delicate. "Lady. Matron. The missus of the house. That's Miss Pendergast, as is proven by her recent marriage and acceptance into organizations such as the Lehigh Historical Society."

"I see." I sullenly returned to my side of the desk. "And how did you determine this?"

"Your entrance exams. Listing Diet Pepsi, Tastykakes and Basic cigarettes as three of the major food groups automatically sent you A Broad."

"You remember my entrance exams?"

"Remember them?" Mrs. Cathobianco laughed. "My God. We photocopied that answer and posted it in the staff lunchroom."

This was slightly hard to take, the idea that the esteemed staff of Two Guys had been munching on their tuna sandwiches and having a good laugh at my expense. Then again, why wouldn't Diet Pepsi, Tastykakes and Basic cigarettes be the three major food groups?

Some people just don't get it.

I thanked my former guidance counselor and left the building, mulling strategy. Could it be that Susan Morse, M.R.S., had set her hooks into Hal Weaver with a goal of replacing Carol with herself? Any woman with a degree in how to catch a husband was no match for a middle-aged wife whose tricks were long out of the bag, so to speak.

Okay, I was really daydreaming now, but what if, after meeting with Ken Bailey on February 14 and deciding against divorce, Hal had broken off his affair with Susan? Here Susan had invested all her academic learning into becoming Mrs. Hal Weaver No. 2 and for what? A few rolls in the hay? That wouldn't have satisfied her. She'd be ticked that she didn't win the big prize. The job promised after graduation. The M.R.S. on her letterhead.

So she gets revenge. Has one last night with the guy, poisons him with time-delayed cyanide scratches. He goes home and passes out in bed, probably feeling woozy when he hits the sheets, and never wakes up.

But how could Carol have had traces of cyanide on her fingertips?

And then it struck me. Nail polish. Carol had been running late on her last visit to me for a nail fill. I remember discussing how it would take only a few minutes to apply a clear or light pink polish to her nails, but Carol was in a hurry and said she'd apply the polish at home.

Could that polish have been tainted with cyanide? Could Susan have been the tainterer? Was there such a word as tainterer? Maybe she was a tainteress?

I was deep in thought about tainting and tainterers when I stepped out the back door of Two Guys into the bright light of day and spied a strange man studying my Camaro's bumper.

Granted, there was a lot to study. Donkey this. Donkey that. But it was the way he was studying, circling the car slowly, checking over his shoulder once or twice.

A chill rippled through me and it wasn't the afternoon winter wind. Hugging my fake rabbit fur to keep my knees from knocking, I slipped behind a large green Dumpster and watched him.

He was as plain and frumpy as could be. Military-short hair, Coke-bottle glasses, stout body in plain brown pants and a navy pullover sweater so tight that it strained across his paunch.

Oh, no, I thought. What if he was from the Department of Motor Vehicles? Didn't Mama or Genevieve say that the HEE and the HAW were violations on the taillights?

A five-hundred-dollar fine. Or what if he impounded the car until the violations were repaired?

Then he did something quite odd. Reaching into his pocket and glancing around the lot—with those glasses he must have been nearly blind—he knelt down and felt up under my wheel well. Was he planting a bomb? Or checking the rust? What was there to check? Rust fell off in hunks weekly.

He stood, clapped off the dirt and grime, put his hands in his pockets and strolled away. As casual as could be. Whistling a tune. "The Theme from *M*A*S*H*," I think it was.

Well, I'll be. I watched him step into a nondescript navy Crown Victoria and drive off. When he had pulled out to Nazareth Street, I jogged over to the Camaro, reached to where he'd put his hands and felt around. Nothing.

Just rust.

What had he been up to?

Mama refused to shop at Schoenen's, the darling of Lehigh's grocery stores, where women in tennis whites paid eleven dollars for heirloom bottles of cider d' pommes. (Apple cider vinegar is sold generically for seventy-nine cents a bottle at ShopRite, FYI.)

Sure the produce was lush, green and fresh, and the clerks addressed you formally. (Hello, Mrs. Smith-White? Is Amanda entering Moravian Prep upper campus so soon?) But one dollar and seventy-five cents for a head of iceberg? Come on! Mama couldn't take it. Did they think we were fools? And not even double coupons on Wednesdays.

My last disastrous visit happened when the store clerk refused to sell Mama saffron without a ten-dollar deposit before checking out, arguing that saffron, at least Schoenen's saffron, was more expensive per ounce than gold. This prompted Mama to open her change purse and scatter dollar bills on Schoenen's newly waxed floor, shouting in Polish that she might as well stick her money where the sun don't shine. Which, untranslated, came out as Gdansk.

So it was with much trepidation that I parked the Donkey Sucking mobile next to a Land Rover and entered Schoenen's. Immediately I was regarded with mild disfavor, even from the clerks passing items over the beeping scanners. The only women like me in the store—that is to say, women with high-school educations and annual incomes that exempted them from paying taxes or living worry free—were involved in the unglamorous end—checking, stocking and bagging.

Norma Lubrecht, Carol Weaver's former maid, was outside on break. What luck! Grabbing a premade turkey and avocado wrap from the deli department for $3.99 (Don't tell Mama!) and a Diet P., I checked out and made my way to the picnic table out where a woman I assumed to be Norma sat savoring the last grounds of her coffee in the not-too-warm November sun.

"Mrs. Domenici says hello," I said, sitting down and sliding in.

Norma Lubrecht regarded me over her red

97

plastic cup. I was surprised to find her so young, not more than twenty-five, and very attractive—except for her makeup faux pas. Her wavy, streaked blond hair was pulled back into a pony-tail and held with a simple green band that matched her simple green Schoenen's uniform.

Against her blond hair and light complexion, her brows were too dark brown, a color of which she must be very fond. Her lids were various shades of tan, amber and chestnut. Her brown eyes were lined in taupe and her lips were the tone of tree bark. The overall effect recalled images of Cher in her 1970s Cherokee Nation phase.

"How is Mrs. Domenici?" Norma asked, finishing her coffee.

"She's going on a trip." I opened the plastic container and took out half of the wrap. No bacon. No mayo. Who were these shriveled Schoenen's tyrants?

"No kidding." Norma put down her coffee cup. "You one of her grandkids?"

"Not really." I introduced myself as Bubbles Yablonsky, hairstylist to the South Side of Lehigh, and reporter. I bit and swallowed turkey while she took this in. "What I'm here to ask you about is your former boss, Carol Weaver. She showed up at my house last night. . . ."

"She did?" Norma fingered a large gold cross at her neck. "She's supposed to be in jail."

"That's what I told her. Anyway, Carol claims that she's been set up, that there was a conspiracy to put her in prison, and she wants out before her daughter gives birth at Christmas."

"Christmas, hah!" Norma patted her mouth with a paper napkin, shook out the cup and screwed it on top of her Thermos. I tried to discern what the "hah" meant. That Carol had a better chance of being born in a manger than getting out by Christmas? Or, hah, Christmas was an overrated holiday that pressured families to drown in debt.

"That baby won't be born at Christmas," Norma said. "More like Thanksgiving. That's probably why Mrs. Weaver came home. Kiera is helpless without her."

"Oh?"

Norma folded her thin arms on the table. "You ever meet that girl?"

"I've heard stories."

"Slob." Norma sucked lunch tidbits from her teeth. "Underwear. Socks. Sticky bowls of leftover ice cream. Soda cans. Cigarette butts hidden in an ashtray underneath her bed."

Spooky. It was as though Norma had been to *my* house.

"I put my foot down. I told Mrs. Weaver that enough was enough. I didn't care if Mr. Weaver had moved out and the whole family was in the dumps. The way I saw it, either Kiera picks up before I clean, or I quit."

"And?"

"And the next day Mr. Weaver was found dead and I was out of a job."

I finished half of the sandwich and gulped the Diet Pepsi, remembering too late about Norma's slob meter. She judged me with distaste.

"You think the two are related?"

"I know they're related. They're mother and daughter."

"No." I wiped my mouth with the back of my arm. "Do you think your ultimatum and Mr. Weaver's death were related?"

"I don't think so. Why would they be?" Norma checked her watch. "I gotta get back to work. You got a specific question or are you fishing?"

Fishing, I wanted to answer honestly. "Did you know that Mr. Weaver was having an affair?"

"Aren't they all?" Norma didn't miss a beat. "You ask any wife in Saucon if her husband is having an affair and she'll answer, 'Who, my husband? You must be joking.'" Norma put her hand to her chest in mock indignation. "You ask any cleaning woman in those humongous houses and she won't think twice. Goes with the territory. Makes these aging old businessmen feel young again."

Norma leaned close. "Like my old boyfriend used to say, men can't go without sex, you know. Not for long. Course, with my old boyfriend, it wasn't like you wanted to go without sex for long, if you know what I mean."

"Oh, I know what you mean." I tried not to think about Stiletto and whether he had been able to go without sex for long.

"And Mrs. Weaver and her husband had had separate bedrooms for months," she added.

Norma Lubrecht must still be irked by Kiera's messiness if she was ratting on her former employer so freely. "I gather you didn't like working for the Weavers."

"That was my first job cleaning houses. Not my thing, especially scrubbing out other people's toilets." Norma looked eager to go. She was inching toward the edge of the bench and eyeing the store in case the shift police emerged. "And the Weavers owed me close to two hundred when I left. I couldn't bring myself to ask for the cash, not with Mr. Weaver being found poisoned. I'm still pissed about it, though. I needed the money to pay rent."

"I hear you." I dropped the uneaten part of my dry, dry sandwich back in the plastic container. "One last thing. Do you know where Kiera lives now?"

"Sure, where she's always lived. At 35 Rock Creek Lane in Saucon. She got the house. Just like she stands to get all the Weaver money, stocks, cash and silver." Norma crumpled her brown paper bag. "Her mother may be in jail and her father dead, but if Mrs. Weaver ever slips out of the picture, Kiera is gonna make out like a queen."

Which also explained why Norma so readily dumped on Kiera—jealousy.

CHAPTER 8

Outside Schoenen's I sacrificed the last of my crumb-covered change to the pay phone. Norma's "men can't last without sex" comment had struck a nerve. A long forgotten nerve that appeared to have been disabled somewhere between my crush on David Cassidy and realization of Dan's infidelity.

"Hey, babe," Stiletto answered. The line was staticky and there was the sound of traffic. He must have been in his Jeep, top down. "How are you holding up?"

I hadn't realized how tired I was until he asked. Up since four, all that adrenaline coursing through my veins, then the fight with Lorena. I was pooped. Either that or I was suffering from the tranquilizing effects of a turkey sandwich.

"Chipper than a LA cheerleader on speed," I lied. "Listen, uhm, you're still on board about me staying at your house, right?"

"On board? I've been thinking about it all day." There was a note of sultriness among the static. "Eloise has the night off, so it'll be just the two of us. Finally." He paused and then lowered his voice. "I hope you're ready."

Ready? I was about to make a public spectacle of myself right there at the Schoenen's pay phone I was so ready. The metal telephone cord was wrapped tight enough around my index finger to cut off all circulation, which was okay because all blood had rushed to other parts of my body right when Stiletto had said, "Hey, babe."

But what if Stiletto meant something else by "ready"? What if ready meant position no. 35 in that Karma Sutra he told me about? What if ready meant that I was perfectly buff, shaved, moisturized, cellulite-free and raring to go? What if ready meant birth control?

My lord. I was nowhere near ready for tonight.

"Uh-huh," I said in as confident a voice as I could muster.

"Great. By the way, I heard about what went down with Notch today. I've never met this Lorena chick . . ."

"You're lucky."

Stiletto laughed. "Anyway, don't worry. The paper's not going to lose you because some whack case got in a fistfight. Graham recognizes talent even if Notch treats you like dirt. Your future is gold there."

"Thanks." Stiletto had never been on the working end of high heels, though. He had no idea how difficult it was to be a hairdresser in a newsroom. "By the way, you ever hear of a vice president at Steel by the name of Morse?"

"Brian Morse?"

"Could be. The one I'm looking for married a woman named Susan Pendergast. She used to be a secretary at Steel."

Stiletto's mind was quick. "Jesus Christ. Is that the woman you punched out this morning?"

"*I* didn't punch her out, Lorena did. Or tried to. And it's just a coincidence." An incredibly annoying coincidence. "Susan Morse may have been Hal Weaver's mistress. She showed up at all the court hearings for his murder case and I'm thinking she's as good a suspect as Carol."

"I had to deal with a Brian Morse today when I went to Steel to research the Mahoney case," Stiletto said, shouting to overcome a weakening signal. "He was a *shwrimga brr*."

The static had drowned out his words. "A what?" I shouted back, even though my end was fine.

"A *shrwomr mbrr* and not one help on the Mahoney case," he answered.

The Mahoney case was the last investigation Stiletto was conducting to document the evils perpetrated by his stepfather, Henry Metzger. Stiletto had hated his stepfather for years and was all too happy to spend Metzger's money not on himself, but on the numerous families who had suffered at the hands of the former Steel chairman's cruelty. Metzger had been famous for letting safety standards slide so workers were routinely maimed or killed. In some shady circles, he was infamous for murder.

In the weeks after Metzger was shot to death in

104

the mansion Stiletto subsequently inherited, Stiletto had spent hours researching Metzger's victims, contacting them or their families and paying reparations. This required sorting through Metzger's personal records, a task Stiletto didn't mind while he was recovering from his own gunshot wound, but that now was becoming a complete pain.

With the British AP assignment fast approaching, Stiletto was running out of time. He'd asked for Steel's cooperation, including that executives turn over their own files, but they had dragged their feet. From what little I could distill from the static, Morse was also not being a good sport.

Stiletto got back into range. "I assume you know that Morse has Hal Weaver's position now. Head of corporate communications."

"Really?" I didn't know that actually.

"I'll check him out for you, see what I can find. In the meantime . . ." More static. *Scrrrrrch.* "Where do you want me to put your stuff? There are ten bedrooms . . . including mine."

Zing. There went that nerve again. And strangely it was affecting my hearing. "Sorry, Stiletto. The line's getting impossibly staticky. Bye!"

I hung up, my heart beating fast. The way I saw it, I had approximately eight hours to get ready after more than a decade of sexual neglect. The negligee and sharp razor were no problem. It was the cellulite that was nagging me.

That and the Karma Sutra.

★   ★   ★

I had a couple of hours to kill before I had to meet Jane at Dan's, so I broke the rules by running back to my house to get supplies.

Hunting around my lingerie drawer (read underwear, bra and Journey T-shirt drawer) I found an old red teddy Dan had purchased for me on our second anniversary. It smelled of oak, stale perfume and dust. I shoved it in my purse anyway.

Foraging for birth control was a complete waste. My one attempt at conscientious protection had been a diaphragm, which was about as comfortable as walking around with a Frisbee in my pelvis. The only squiggly thing it ever protected me from was a centipede on my shower curtain. Diaphragms make excellent bug trappers when used with an insecticide, I discovered.

By far the most effective birth control I'd employed didn't come in a pill, bottle or tube. It wasn't embarrassing to buy and it was 100 percent fool-proof. You guessed it—abstinence. Unfortunately, abstinence has one side effect.

It is useless against Stiletto.

I was glad to get out of the house. It was way too eerie with that yellow police tape and all that silence. Even with the kids coming home from school with their yelling and laughing and the base beat of Justin LaToola's souped-up jalopy *boom-bada booming* back from Liberty High School, my ears were alert to every creak and sigh inside—like my home was haunted.

Next I headed over to the Lehigh Public Library,

conveniently located next door to the police station. I had planned to cull through the *News-Times* morgue for files on Hal Weaver's life and death, but a tiny voice in the back of my brain advised me to call the paper first to make sure Lawless hadn't checked out all the clips.

He had. To spite me, I was sure.

Ah, yes, but there was no way he could steal the computer files of the Lehigh Public Library. There was no way he could fit in one of their chairs.

Braving a throng of teenagers and skateboarders by the library steps, I threw open the heavy glass doors and approached the research desk—only to find the assistants openmouthed in horror.

"You're back? So soon?" asked one alarmed woman in fashionable black-framed glasses. "I'll get the head librarian."

I rested my elbows on the wooden counter. Why is it that these librarians are so skittish whenever I want to use the microfiche or computers? I mean, they don't greet Jane that way. They wave and say, "Hi, Jane. Come on in. There's a computer free over there. Want a glass of water? Fresh paper and pencils? Latte?"

The head librarian, a gorgeous redheaded dish with a killer body too good to be locked up in the stacks, exited her office. I heard a lot of mumbling about "Bubbles" and "computer crashing" and "microfiche destroyed." Oh, give me a break. Once. Once by accident, I tore the microfiche tape with my nails. It was taped and repaired in a jiffy.

Boy, could these bookworms hold a grudge.

"I'm sorry," the librarian said, "but we don't have the staff to help you today, Bubbles." This was code, I deduced, for the fact that I was too "technologically inept," shall we say, to run a computer search.

"But . . . ?"

The librarian pointed down the hall. "Try the children's library. They're used to . . ." She hesitated, searching for the right word.

"Children?" I offered.

She smiled sweetly. "Well, yes."

Indeed, the children's library was a definite success. Sure, the chairs were miniature and kids kept sticking their candy-covered hands in my hair and asking if they "could touch it" and was "it real." My hair was blonder than Sun-Drenched Barbie with a bleach job. What did they mean by "real"? What self-respecting woman in her thirties has real hair?

I loved the place though. Bright Technicolor pictures and painted butterflies. That barfy smell of book paste. And you didn't have to keep your voice to a funereal whisper, either. It was a okay for me to holler over to the desk, "How do you work this freaking thing?"

After forty-five minutes of help from a patient sixth grader, I was able to retrieve the *News-Times* archives and bone up on Hal Weaver's life.

He had been hired straight after graduating from Lehigh University's chemical engineering program to work in what's known as the Mountaintop Lab. He soon found out he was better at explaining sheet metal finishes than making them, and his communication skills booted him over to corporate in the mid 1980s. That is where he had flakked until his death.

He was active in the Lehigh Rotary Club and, I noted, the Lehigh Historical Society.

Interesting.

I sat back and focused on a fluorescent green beanbag chair cradling a kid picking his nose and reading Calvin and Hobbes. I bet the Two Guys M.R.S. curriculum suggested marriage-minded women join clubs like historical societies in order to meet erudite future husbands. I bet that's where Susan Morse struck up her affair with Hal Weaver.

I envisioned Susan and Hal, she in a Lily Pulitzer crewneck, he in tartan pants, meeting shyly for coffee and pillow talk about cobblestone street repairs or rubbing eighteenth-century headstones.

Maybe Hal complained Carol never understood his wild spending on archaeological tools. Or that his wife tired of his ranting about the lack of federal funding for colonial and Indian artifacts along the Delaware Water Gap.

But Susan understood. That is until Hal broke the news on Valentine's Day that he was going to give his marriage another chance.

A finger poked into my shoulder. "Hey, lady," said a twelve-year-old girl nodding to the computer. "My turn. I'm next."

I got up and gave her my chair. She quickly deleted the newspaper archive on the screen and did a search for "Teen Idol True Confessions," scrolling down to heartthrob Orlando Bloom.

It gave me an idea. An idea I never would have had if I'd hung around the adults.

"Did Carol Weaver confess?" I asked Mickey Sinkler next door in the basement of the Lehigh Police Department. "It's not in the court records, but sometimes if the client pleas it doesn't have to be. That's what Angie down at the court clerk's office said."

Mickey leaned back in his chair and put his hands behind his head. "Don't tell me. You're not."

"I am." I paced in front of his drab metal desk. "And you can't stop me. This is my only chance to get a staff position, tracking down Carol Weaver's allegations."

Mickey groaned. "You're wasting your time, Bubbles. What Carol Weaver's claiming, it's a tar pit."

"A quagmire, Mr. Notch called it."

"Oh, Christ. The *News-Times* is buying her lies, too." He sat up. "Wait until my superiors hear about this."

"The paper's not involved." I didn't want the police chief ringing up Notch. Relations between us were bad enough. "I'm doing this on my own."

"Even worse. This is going to be trouble all the way around. I can smell it. Carol Weaver escapes and the department gets heat because we can't find her. Then you write a story about how she supposedly was wrongly convicted. Another glowing week of PR for the Lehigh PD."

I plunked both hands on the desk and bent over his geeky body. "No one has to know, Mickey. Not if you carefully, quietly, secretly find out from the detectives if Carol Weaver was coerced into a confession."

"Coerced?" Mickey employed his law enforcement squint, the same one he uses when examining the license and registrations of pretty girls he's pulled over. "Loaded language, that."

"All right. Cajoled."

"Cajoled. Hmmm. I'll have to look it up. Make sure you're not throwing any nuances around."

"Just like you guys threw a noose around Carol Weaver's neck?"

"I'll see what I can do," he said slowly. "But I don't like that coerced stuff. And, to be honest, I've got my doubts about cajoled."

CHAPTER 9

Dan lived in an immaculately landscaped McMansion in an immaculately land-scaped gated development where dead leaves were sucked up faster than they fell. I lined up the Donkey Sucking Mobile behind a silver Jaguar for balance and headed to the front door, fully flauting Wendy's orders.

The cocktail party Dan was throwing was in full roar. Well, as much as a cocktail party being thrown by Dan can roar. A maid in standard uniform holding a plate of water chestnuts wrapped in bacon answered the door. She was expecting me.

"Mr. Ritter wants you to wait in there." She nodded to Dan's private office. "I'll get your daughter."

Dan lived in perpetual fear that his clients would find out he was once married to a high-school-dropout hairdresser who lives for the glorious day Kansas and Peter Frampton will rise to their rightful places as top billing at the Allentown Fair. And, oh yes, that day will come, my friend. That day will come.

The office door closed behind me and a strange girl appeared looking very tightlipped. She was done up like a brunette Gidget—black A-line dress, bare waxed legs and matching patent leather slingbacks. Her brown hair was neat around her face and sprayed in place. Her eyes bore just a touch of mascara, her lips a faint pink gloss and . . . were those real pearls?

"Jane?" I asked anxiously.

She nodded. Clearly about to cry.

I ran to her and smushed her unpierced face against my fake rabbit fur coat.

"What has he done to you?"

"Wendy did it," Jane sniffed. "She said this was how I had to dress if I wanted to get into Princeton."

"That witch." I pressed Jane closer. What did Wendy, Dan's cheeseball heiress wife, know about Princeton? If Princeton was the kind of place that turned up its nose at girls in army boots, well then that was no place for my baby.

"Don't worry, hon," I said soothingly. "There's always Two Guys. Two Guys has a good physics program. Didn't we see in the brochure, something about string theory?"

"That was the theory of guitar stringing."

"Oh yeah." I shrugged. "Same difference."

Jane let out a fresh sob.

It was so disconcerting to see my teenage daughter with human hair color. No pink roots or blue tips. No black eyeshadow or onyx nose

113

stud. Without the dog collar and rubber tread eyeliner, she looked so . . .

"You look so . . . so normal," I said.

"I know. It's a nightmare," Jane agreed.

"Damn right she looks normal." Dan entered followed by Wendy, who was positively anorexic in a deep gray silk tunic and pants. Heroin-addicted vampires had more tint in their faces. Kinder personalities, too.

"Gosh, Wendy," I said, trying to bite back my anger. "A little early to be out of your coffin, isn't it?"

"A thank-you might be in order," she replied. "But I keep forgetting how you were raised."

"Drink it in, Bubbles." Dan laid his arm proudly across Jane's shoulder. "This is what good taste looks like. Jane's damn lucky she has Wendy to prepare her for society."

"Took all afternoon." Wendy slicked her super-short hair behind her ear. "I had to cancel my massage."

"Jane's finally catching on, Bubbles." Dan gave Jane's shoulder a shake. "You can do things in life the easy way or the hard way. You've always done things the hard way. Jane's the wiser."

I inhaled deeply, trying to hang on to my cool. If it hadn't been for Dan's *hard way,* I wouldn't have gotten knocked up at seventeen.

"Well, Jane," I said, composing myself, "unlike Wendy, your mother doesn't have the day to waste in a beauty parlor."

114

Hold on. *That* wasn't right.

I ignored this mix-up and continued, explaining about the BB assault and why she had to stay at Dan's. Jane was so enthralled by the story of the prison escapee, she forgot her deb redo and pried me for more information.

"Who's this murderer who showed up last night? What's her name?"

"Carol Weaver."

There was a thud. The crystal glass lay at Wendy's feet on the Persian carpet, a lime wedge dripping on her big toe.

"Carol Weaver? She's out?" Wendy whispered. I checked the floor to see if blood had pooled there, her complexion was so pasty.

"Let me get this for you, dear." Dan bent down and picked up the glass. "Perhaps you've had enough."

"It's soda water, Chip."

"You know Carol Weaver?" I was intrigued by Wendy's abrupt discomfiture. "How?"

"It's more like I know *of* her."

"Yeah? What *of* her do you know?"

"What is this, one of your crackpot interviews?" Dan handed the glass back to Wendy. "We have guests waiting. Stop bothering my wife and skedaddle, Bubbles. Jane, why don't you go upstairs and change. Isn't there homework or some computer game you can fool around with?"

Wendy, eager to be away from me, and Jane, eager to be out of her uniform, raced each other to the door. That left me alone with Dan, who turned to go before I clenched the neck of his shirt and pulled him to me.

"Speaking of Carol Weaver," I said, "why don't you fill me in on how come your old mentor Bailey sold her down the river?"

Dan shook off my grip. "Give it a rest, you ding-a-ling. This might look like a party to you, but to me it's business. I've got to get out there and schmooze with my clients."

"I'll scream," I threatened. "I'll run through your house waving a knife and spilling secrets about your pre-Viagra sex life. I'll claim embezzlement and that you have a five-hundred-dollar-a-day cocaine habit."

Dan's eyes narrowed. "You wouldn't."

I yanked open the door and opened my mouth wide. Dan shut it with his hand, closing the door simultaneously.

"Okay, okay. I left Bailey's firm long before the Weaver case, as you know, but I did hear rumors that the case wasn't quite like Bailey's others."

I pushed off his hand. "Bailey's others?"

"Yeah. The other divorces. Bailey was a family lawyer but his specialty was divorce. Successful Steel execs who were afraid to 'trade up' on their first wives for fear they'd be taken to the cleaners paid big bucks to Bailey. That way they'd have their cake and eat it, too. You know how that is."

This was a bit much coming from He Who Left

116

His Wife Broke. "Yes," I said, "I know how that is. I've been living on crumbs, remember?"

"Listen, sassafras, you want my help or don't you?"

I shrugged.

"The story I heard," Dan continued, getting into it, "was that Hal Weaver had a Steel secretary on the side who was putting the pressure on him to hurry up with the divorce. And Hal was ready to split with Carol, right?"

"If you say so."

"But at the last minute Weaver changed his mind."

"Why?"

"Don't know and never will, now that both Hal and Ken are dead." Dan stuck his pudgy fingers into his vodka tonic and pinched the lemon wedge. "I overheard at a Bar Association meeting last spring that it wasn't Weaver, but Bailey who dropped out. Told Weaver over drinks at the Union Club—hours before Weaver was poisoned—that he couldn't offer Weaver legal representation any more. Supposedly Bailey was even thinking of going to the police to report a crime."

"A crime Weaver committed?"

"Either that or a crime Weaver was covering up at Steel. Say what you want about Bailey. He was ethical."

I concentrated on Dan's oil painting of two hunters and their overbred English setters, guns and paws aimed at a pair of wild mallards. Wild,

117

brown mallards. If I didn't know better, I'd say he ripped it off the walls of the country club men's room.

"What about that lawyer/client privilege deal? Don't clients always confess crimes to their lawyers?"

Dan savored his drink, his red-rimmed eyes getting more bloodshot by the sip. "Sometimes they do. Each lawyer handles that in his own way. We are, ahem, officers of the court, you know."

Ambulance chasers, widow hunters and foreclosure fairies were other quaint terms, I was tempted to point out.

"Thanks, Dan," I said. "You've been a real help."

Dan's jaw clenched, and for once it wasn't a WASP affectation. "It's Chip, Bubbles. Chip. Chip. Chip. Chip." With that he opened the door and stepped out, stumbling slightly.

I should start calling him Chip, I thought, to return the favor. For in the first time in our eighteen-year relationship, Dan had actually proved to be more than an ass.

He had proved to be a complete asset.

This is the point where I would like to report in every sizzling detail the night of exhausting sexual escapades after I arrived at Stiletto's gorgeous stone mansion. How he carried me over the threshold to his large, romantic bedroom with its floor-to-ceiling walnut bookshelves and colorful, eclectic art he'd brought back from his international travels. Black clay Russian pots and a handmade spear from the Congo. A silk wall hanging in turquoise, red and brilliant saffron from India.

Yes, I'd like to describe how the fire blazed, how the sheets were the finest cream linen and the champagne was cold, as cold as Stiletto's kisses were hot.

I'd like to, but I can't because Stiletto is a news photographer in demand and even the hottest, the most studly news photographers have to put sex on hold when Jersey burns.

Stiletto's housekeeper, Eloise, answered his door. A surprise since Stiletto had said earlier that it was her night off. Eloise was a tiny, efficient, elfish woman with a big brown bun and even bigger forearms. You could tell she'd been used to Henry Metzger's dictatorial style because she zoomed around the house doing favors before I could ask—taking my coat, offering me soup, drawing me a bath, that kind of thing.

"He's off again," she said, running her fingers under the hot water in Stiletto's antique copper bathtub. "Chemical fire in Jersey. Who knows when he'll return. I told him I'd take tomorrow night instead, seeing as this was your first evening here and all."

So I settled for a deep bath in an antique copper tub filled with lavender-scented bubbles. Afterwards I slipped into my black Journey T-shirt and wrapped myself in Stiletto's robe before sitting sleepily by the fire, sipping Eloise's homemade mushroom soup and nibbling cheese toasts, my lids struggling to stay open.

Unable to fight unconsciousness any longer, I made my way to his bed and nestled into the deep down comforter and fresh clean sheets. This was heaven, I thought, yawning. If only Stiletto had been there. Then it would have been better than heaven. It would have been Nirvana.

CHAPTER 10

At the sound of szzt-szzt-szzt I woke with a start. The BB shots again. Where was I? I saw the fireplace and relaxed. Stiletto's. The sound I had mistaken for BBs had been the tapping of sleet against the window outside. A dull gray morning light filtered through the room's enormous windows. Somebody had started up the fire, which burned merrily.

I took a long hot shower with rough oatmeal soap I found in Stiletto's white-tiled bathroom and dressed into a pair of black leggings, a ten-percent-Spandex red turtleneck and black boots. I strapped a gold chain belt around my hips, plugged in a pair of gold hoop earrings and blew my hair dry and stiff to its rightful height. Added tasteful golden shimmer shadow to my lids, kohled my eyes to their blackest and did the basic makeup stuff. (Thank heavens I'd stopped by the house for my brow liner #6!)

Looked in my purse for the necessary reporting utensils— Reporter's Notebook, check. Two Bic pens medium point, check. Sugar free peppermint gum, check. And lip gloss. Double check. (Two shades.)

Downstairs, Stiletto—who was wearing a very alluring black chamois shirt and his usual tight jeans—was sorting through a pile of documents in the dining room. More Henry Metzger stuff.

Like every room in the house, the room was high-ceilinged and extensively windowed. Besides the cherry dining table fit for sixteen, there was a large sideboard with fresh coffee and fruit.

Potted plants—some flowering, some like trees—lined the far wall, giving what portended to be a stuffy room a tropical greenhouse aroma.

"Howdy," Stiletto said, tossing the papers aside and giving me a broad smile.

"Hi." I cocked my ears for the sound of Eloise slamming pots and pans in the kitchen. I wouldn't have put it past him to have given Eloise the morning off, too, so that we could have the house to ourselves.

He came around the table and slid his hand to the back of my neck, bending down to kiss me. I was really glad I'd brushed out the morning breath. "Sleep well?"

"I did. I needed it."

"That's what I figured. I got in around three and decided you didn't need me bothering you, so I slept in the bedroom down the hall. That is, after I kissed you good night."

"Oh, no." I envisioned me sprawled across the bed, mouth open, crusted drool at the corners. Snoring louder than a Waring blender. "Tell me I wasn't drooling and snoring."

"Not too much."

I gasped, but he winked and kissed me lightly. "Only kidding. I have to say it was very nice to find you in my bed when I came home." His voice was low and *extremely* sexy as he stroked my hair. "It's where you belong, Bubbles. It's where *we* belong."

Stiletto pressed me against the sideboard, nearly knocking off a plate of Eloise's fresh strawberries as we passionately went at it. Stiletto's lips grazed my neck and I wrapped a leg around his strong thigh, pulling him to me. This man was so hot I couldn't take it one minute more. I was ready to rip off his soft chamois shirt then and there when Stiletto said, "I have to be in New York by nine. I don't want to rush this."

He stood back and I slipped off the sideboard like the hot tart I clearly was.

"Damn," I said, perhaps too forcefully, because the crow's-feet around Stiletto's blue eyes crinkled, amused as he was by my frustration.

"Don't worry, Bubbles. We'll have our moment. I promise."

"I'm beginning to wonder," I said sourly.

"I almost forgot to ask. What's with the donkey graffiti on your Camaro?"

"Lorena." I patted down my hair, headed toward the coffee and poured myself a cup. "Her idea of a joke."

"Some joke. You want to borrow another car?"

I stopped spooning in sugar. "You have another car?"

"Two. An old BMW and one of those oversized Cadillacs Henry drove to show he was still buying American. Why don't you take the beemer? Can't beat that German engineering."

"Thanks, but no thanks." I returned to my coffee. "I don't think my insurance company would allow it. They told me in no uncertain words I'm not supposed to drive anything worth over three thousand dollars."

"I'll tell you what," Stiletto said, "I'll take the sledgehammer to the BMW and make it even."

"No. No. Don't do that!"

He laughed. "Who cares? It all ends up as rust in the wind."

Ooh. Subtle allusion to Kansas's 1978 classic "Dust in the Wind." Nice. Very nice.

"Speaking of rust." I speared a piece of fresh cantaloupe. "You might want to check out my left wheel well. At Two Guys yesterday I saw this suit in the parking lot walking around my car. Then he reached under the wheel well and did something. I felt around there after he left, but all I discovered was rust."

I didn't have to explain further. Stiletto was out the door.

Grabbing my rabbit fur coat from the closet, I met him outside. The sleet had stopped, though it had made for slippery footing on the stone steps leading down to the circular driveway. Stiletto was already under my Camaro.

It really was a spectacular estate, I thought,

breathing in the damp morning air and clutching my steaming coffee. The meticulously maintained lawns and gardens had been pruned and mulched for the onslaught of snow. The sky was gray. The trees went on forever.

Over on West Goepp a dreary November day like this would have had a dulling effect, lending the brick and aluminum-sided row homes a more seedy look, exposing bits of trash in the gutters and peeling paint on the doors.

Here in Saucon Valley the bleak weather made it all *Upstairs, Downstairs,* as though there should be hounds leaping over hedgerows. The atmosphere was accentuated by the scent of wood smoke wafting from four of the chimneys as a V of ducks migrated south over the estate's rolling lawn. Very classy.

Especially the way the day-glo pink ASK ME ABOUT DONKEY SUCKING set off the two-hundred-year-old wrought iron fencing lining Stiletto's cobblestone driveway.

"Got it," he said, scooting out from under the car and holding up his hand. He brushed himself off and showed me the tiny dirtied cylinder, about the size of a single Good & Plenty.

"What is it?"

"It's an outdated RFD." Stiletto held it up to the light. "These days there's much more advanced GPS technology that relies on satellite systems."

"English please."

"It's a tracking device. Since this has been put

on your car, some geek has been following your Camaro's every move." He placed it in my hand.

It was so small. How could it track me?

"You want to tell me what you've got cooking?" Stiletto leaned against the Camaro and shoved his hands in his pockets. "Or are you afraid again that I'll steal your story?"

A subtle reminder of our competition in coal country.

"I spent yesterday hunting down rumors that Hal Weaver was killed because he knew a secret that Steel didn't want revealed."

"Sounds like standard operating procedure to me. Under Henry Metzger's chairmanship there wasn't much that Steel did aboveboard. If you need the records on those," Stiletto removed his left hand from his pocket and pointed toward the dining room, "be my guest. I've got twenty years plus of documented dirty deeds inside."

"No way. I hate records. Maybe you could handle that end." I joined him by the Camaro. "You've been investigating Metzger. You have a kind of rap. Rap . . ."

"Rapport?"

"Yeah, that, with those Steel executives. You could snoop around for me."

Stiletto absently played with a tendril of my hair. "Men don't snoop, Bubbles."

"Okay, dig."

"Dig. Much better." He nodded. "I could do that. But what angle are *you* going to work on?"

"The feminine angle. Hal Weaver was sleeping with a secretary at Steel."

"Susan Morse?"

I trigger fingered him. "Bull's-eye. From what I learned yesterday, Hal had met with divorce lawyer Ken Bailey. Bailey either advised him not to go through with the divorce. Or, according to Dan, Ken Bailey discovered some crime Hal had committed or covered up and withdrew representation."

Stiletto let out a whistle. "Whew. Sounds hot, Bubbles. You contact Bailey? Not that a lawyer's going to tell you anything worthwhile."

"Can't. He's dead. Died the day he was supposed to file exculpatory evidence on the Carol Weaver murder charge. Slipped on his driveway and hit his head."

"That's bizarre."

I sipped the coffee. "Don't you know it."

"What happened to the evidence?"

"Disappeared. Never was filed, according to Angie down at the clerk of court's office."

Stiletto was silent for a bit, mulling over the facts, his extensive journalism experience kicking in. The questions to be asked. The people to be reached. The calls to be made. "How about Susan Morse?"

"I'm holding off on her until I get more goods. The problem I'm having is that even if she did kill Hal because he wouldn't leave his wife, where did she get cyanide?"

"You say she worked at Steel?" Stiletto cocked his head in the way I found particularly tantalizing.

"As a secretary."

"That's easy, then. Cyanide is all over steel. It's both an end product and a chemical used in sheet metal finishing up at the Mountaintop Lab. There were rumors for a while that two lab employees were poisoned at the beginning of this year, though I haven't found any documentation of that. Probably just a company myth. Kind of hard for two employees to be poisoned and for no one to know about it."

My heart thumped. "Hal Weaver used to work in the Mountaintop Lab, before he went into corporate communications."

"Let me snoop around, as you put it. See what I can find about cyanide supplies last year. They're supposed to keep strict records about that. Open your hand."

I opened my hand. The RFD was still there. Stiletto picked it up and walked toward his garage.

"Where you going?"

"To have some fun," he said, opening the door where the Jeep was parked. He knelt down and stuck the RFD under his left wheel well. "That should keep them busy."

Before we parted, Stiletto gave me a present.

"You need it," he said, handing me the package as he closed the Camaro door. I flinched.

"Oh, my God, no," I protested. "I'll end up killing somebody with this thing."

"It's for your safety," he said, reassuringly. "Everyone carries one around these days. Even high school kids. Take it."

I pincered the sleek metal object between my two acrylic red nails. "You know how I am with cell phones, Stiletto. I can't use them. All that send stuff. Why can't they just make them so you hang up like the old-fashioned ones?"

"This is easy, Bubbles. I've programmed in all the numbers you need. Mine, of course, Tony Salvo's at the *News-Times,* the House of Beauty, even Dan's, if you need to reach Jane. And look." He flipped it open to reveal a small screen. "It's a digital camera. In case you find Susan Morse in some compromising position."

"A camera?" I flipped it over, looking for the lens. "You're like Q in James Bond."

He frowned. "Q? That old man? What happened to Mel Gibson?"

My stomach clutched. "You *know* about that?"

"I know more than you think, Bubbles." Stilletto cocked an eyebrow. "I'm Q."

Now thoroughly embarrassed—how could he have heard that I described him as Mel Gibson?—I started up the Camaro and backed out, not even daring to wave goodbye. I could picture his parting glance, hands in pockets, smirk across his face.

I wondered if there could be such a thing as having too much man on your hand.

★ ★ ★

Rock Creek Lane in Saucon Valley was one of those gracious neighborhoods making a transition from 1960s families—whose children had long ago grown and left—to the young families of today. It was easy to tell where Grandma and Grandpa lived—in the stately homes with pristine slate walks and rosebushes neatly wrapped in burlap.

Skateboards and chalk drawings littered the driveways of the newcomers. Weeds were numerous—parents being too tired to pull them—as were plastic toys. Still, the houses were pretty damn big for young families to own. Who in their early thirties could haul in the kind of salary that would allow them to afford a half-a-million-dollar estate?

The Weaver home begged that question. A two-story brick Tudor structure, it was neither stately nor overrun by children. It was simply neglected. The lawn was unmowed and the browning grass was nearly knee high. Dying vines hung from the flower boxes.

These people should move to West Goepp. The babushkas there would whip them up in a jiffy. Take Mrs. Hamel for instance. Not only does she compost our garden, when I'm not looking she deadheads my begonias. And I'm talking the ones inside my house, not just the hanging baskets on my front porch.

My hopes weren't high as I knocked on the door, which is why I was surprised when a youngish man answered, clearly awakened by my intrusion.

I put him at twenty and about as responsible and upstanding as my daughter's boyfriend, G. His brown hair was mussed up and he was shirtless, his only adornment being a tattoo around his upper left bicep.

"Yeah, what?" he said through the screen, rubbing his eyes.

"I'm looking for a Kiera. . . ." I hesitated. Kiera was pregnant, but was she married? Those two don't always proceed in the order my catechism nuns said they should. "Uh, just Kiera."

He quit with the eye rubbing. "Who are you?"

"Bubbles Yablonsky. I have a message for Kiera from her mother."

This caught his attention. "No shit."

"Shit."

"Well, she's not here. She'll be back later."

Nuh-uh. Too vague. My time was precious and the clock to deadline was ticking. "You know where she is? Maybe I can track her down."

"Getting her hair colored in Allentown, at Hess's."

Whooo. Hess's, all the way in Allentown. Fancee. I've lived thirty-something years in Lehigh and not once, not even for the senior prom—well, granted, I was six months pregnant then—have I gotten my hair done at Hess's.

He squinted. "You sure you're not with the newspaper? This guy was by yesterday, warned us about a tall blonde he said would be posing as a reporter."

131

Posing as a reporter. That's rich. "Was this guy kind of fat and stupid looking? Melted cheese stains on his tie?"

Bright boy pursed his lips and tried to recall. I wanted to nag him to put on a shirt. "Maybe. I've got his card somewhere." He patted down his pants, obviously recycled from yesterday.

"Don't bother. I bet his name's Lawless and it's me who should be warning you about him."

"Get real."

"Next time he stops by, make sure you have your shirt on. He really goes for young men. Especially young men with tattoos."

Bright boy's eyes popped open and from nowhere he produced a T-shirt. "Thanks for the tip," he said, pulling it over his head. "I thought the guy was kind of skanky."

"Skanky," I said, "doesn't even begin to describe Lawless."

CHAPTER 11

I was hardly prepared for the heady world of Hess's or, for that matter, a big trip to Allentown. Allentown might be the city next door, but believe you me, there is a sea of difference between it and Lehigh.

Lehigh is famous for steel and fried dough, the Moravians and Monocacy Park. Allentown is in a different county altogether. And despite the pervasive aroma of pork roast due to the A&B meat packing plant, Allentown is much more sophisticated.

It's a metropolis where the Allentown Fair is held each August. Celebrities come here, and not just minor ones. Bands like REO Speedwagon, Journey and Def Leppard—the biggies. Billy Joel even wrote a song about the place. (Although, to be truthful, that song must be about Lehigh. There is no steel mill in Allentown.)

No. Never, ever mix up Allentown and Lehigh. That's grounds for arrest in these parts.

I clutched the wheel of my Camaro, my eyes peeled as I negotiated Allentown's confusing one-way streets, past the sewage plant and tenements toward Hess's. So many Madonna statues. So many people. It made me feel kind of queasy. (Though, again, that could have been the packed pigs.)

Hess's delivery and service entrance was off Ninth Street in Allentown's downtown. I pulled in and found what could loosely be defined as a parking space next to a white van. Whipping around, I was backing in the Camaro expertly when in my rearview appeared a stranger.

"Bring her back, bring her back." A beefy delivery man waved his arms wildly. "Whoa, stop. Little to the left."

Why do some men feel it is their duty to wave women into parking spaces like we're sixteen years old on a learner's permit?

"Hey! Watch it," he hollered as I stepped on reverse and nearly ran him over.

I leaned out the window. "Oops. Sorry. Didn't see you there. Is this better?" I shifted into forward and rocketed across the parking lot, coming to within inches of his truck.

"No, no, no." He put his hands on his hips, dreadfully disappointed in my driving inability, but determined to be patient. "What you wanna do is take it slow." Back with the flexing hands again. "Reverse her five feet and you'll be nice and pretty."

I reversed three feet and stuck my head out again. "Close enough."

"You're in the middle of the fricking lot!"

One inch more. This went on until I was where I wanted to be.

"Don't surprise me someone sprayed your damn car," he said when I got out. "They were being kind. Your driving sucks more than donkey."

Inside, I passed under Hess's famous crystal chandeliers and managed to resist the glamorous beauty department with its glittering glass cases of perfume, lipstick and eye shadow.

I nodded in respect to the Clinique saleswoman dressed in her white coat, and she nodded back. Yes, I thought, eyeing her clinical lab wear with approval, finally makeup is getting the scientific respect it has long deserved.

Bypassing the strawberry pie display and fried agave worms and chocolate-covered ants, I found the Hess's salon at the far end of the first floor.

The salon was everything I'd imagined and more. The walls were covered with a shimmering, translucent paper that glowed under the recessed lighting. There were lots of fluffy white towels stacked and folded on chrome shelves. Coffee, tea, bottled water and even chilled white wine were conveniently offered to waiting customers.

"The wine's for special occasions," I was informed by the receptionist, as I quickly put down the bottle. "Can I help you?" Her brass name plate said simply LYDIA.

I inhaled the burning aroma of permanent solution. There is a Mecca in every profession. For newspaper reporters it is the *New York Times*. For actors it is Cannes. For hairdressers it is Hess's Salon. There simply is no other.

Never would I work here. I knew that now. Of course, like all little girls growing up in the Lehigh Valley with dreams of someday curling, combing and cutting alongside the pros, Hess's had been my personal goal. But upon reaching the age of thirty, I had learned to discard some dreams, embrace others.

For me this was, therefore, a bittersweet visit. Only the best, the brightest, the most promising of my profession were invited to lay their scissors here, and sadly, I was not ever to be among them.

"Yo, yo, yo. Is that you, Mrs. Y?"

I whipped around. It couldn't be. A slouching figure with dyed orange hair peeking from under his black knit cap trucked through the doorway carrying a satchel. He was wearing a ripped black T-shirt and baggy pants hung so low on his hips that his plaid boxers billowed from the top. The nose ring was new—since the other one had been ripped out during an unfortunate air-bag incident. But the tattoo over the left eyebrow was unmistakable, as was his perfume of body odor and unfiltered cigarettes.

My daughter's loser boyfriend. What was he doing here?

"Oh, G!" squealed Lydia, jetting from her seat. "Don Carlo's waiting to see you. He's really excited about your wax project."

"G?" I peered at his satchel. "Are you robbing the place?"

136

Lydia squealed again.

"Whoa, no, Mrs. Y. I'm working here." He tapped his chest. "I'm a prod-i-gy, remember?"

How could I forget? At my cousin Roxanne's salon in Slagville, G had discovered his true talent—hairdressing. Roxanne proclaimed him a natural destined for New York or Paris. New York or Paris, sure. But Hess's? Come on. That was the major leagues.

"What's with the rapper stuff?"

G shot a guilty look at Lydia and pulled me aside. "It's for the chicks, Mrs. Y. Especially the housewives like you. They dig the Eminem persona. You know, all neglected and abused and everything. Got to have a persona."

"I am not a housewife."

"Yeah, but you are a chick. Wait . . . don't tell me *you're* working here?"

"No."

"Oh, I get it. You found out about my new gig and you're trying to get a piece of the action. Well, I'll tell ya," he said secretly, "I haven't been here long enough, but give me a couple of weeks and I'll put in a good word for you. I'll let you ride on my coattails."

I wanted to rip out his nose ring with my teeth.

"Hey, man." He placed his hand on my shoulder. "Sorry your crib got shot up. That must totally suck."

"Crib?"

"Jane says you're shacking up with your old man. Heard about that widescreen TV with a picture in a picture." He bobbed his head. "Sweet."

"G!" A tiny muscular man with a clean-shaven head and white pants trotted toward us.

"Shoot. That's Don Carlo. I gotta split." He dropped his hand and grabbed his satchel.

"Hold on, G. How'd you like to do me a favor?"

"For you, Mrs. Y, anything."

I told him about Kiera. "If she's already back there," I tilted my chin toward the salon, "ask if she'll speak to me."

"Will do." He left with Don Carlo, who threw a catty sneer over his shoulder.

As soon as I sat down, an alarm sounded. Not really an alarm, more like *The 1812 Overture.* I almost fell off the chair. Were the French attacking?

"What's that!" I exclaimed.

"Your phone," Lydia said, bored. "It's ringing."

My phone? I opened my purse and rummaged around. There was the little silver bugger. I needed to stop it before the cannons fired. Flipping open the top, I pressed the biggest button I could find. It worked. The ringing stopped.

A miniature voice screamed from the receiver.

"Are you gonna answer that?" Lydia asked. "Or just stare at it."

Gingerly I put it to my hear. "Hello?"

"Land's sake, what took you so long, Bubbles!"

Oh my God. My worst nightmare come true. My mother. Able to reach me anywhere. "Mama. How did you get my number?"

"From Steve. And guess what?"

I knew better than to guess.

"I'm on a cell phone, too. Isn't that a hoot? It's Mrs. Stottlemyer's. We're at the House of Beauty getting our hair done. Say hi to Mrs. Stottlemyer, Bubbles." There was the sound of shuffling as she passed the phone to Mrs. Stottlemyer.

"Hello?" Mrs. Stottlemyer screeched. "Is that you, Bubbles?"

"Hi, Mrs. Stottlemyer." Lydia was eying me over her Starbucks. "Uh, how are you?" What else should I say? I didn't want to be rude.

"Where are you?"

"Uh, I'm in Hess's."

"Westgate or Allentown?"

"Allentown."

"They have good reception in Allentown, say? Very clear. I think it's 'cause PP & L's there."

"Yes," I agreed. "Very clear."

Lydia rolled her eyes.

"These phones are amazing, aren't they? I like to call around and find out where the reception's good. Don't call from Clarksboro. Very weak in Clarksboro. They need more towers."

Lydia covered her ears and tried to concentrate on her magazine.

"I've got to go."

"Oh, that's all right, hon. Now that I've got your number in memory, we can call you anytime."

"Bye, Bubbles," Mama called from the distance.

I was back to staring at the phone again. How to hang up?

Lydia shook her head in pity.

"I'm new at this," I said.

"I gathered as much." She leaned over the counter and pointed with her pencil at the same button I'd used to answer it. "Press that."

I pressed it. "Pretty easy," I said.

"My eight-year-old niece has that model. She uses it to send me her dress-up pictures over the Internet."

Show off. I tucked the phone in my purse as G was coming out of the salon. His hat was off, his hair aflame. "That Kiera chick doesn't want to talk to you," he said, wiping his wet hands on his shirt. "She says some guy named Lawless warned her not to have anything to do with you."

Lawless. I could see him now in all his four hundred and fifty pounds stuffed in front of his computer, laughing to himself at my failed attempts to make hay with the story.

There had to be a way to get around his bloated frame. Somehow I had to contact Kiera.

"I gotta get back there," G said. "My wax is getting cold."

"Tell Kiera," I said, "that I have a message for her from her mother, that she's thinking of her and loves her and wants her to know she didn't kill her father."

I could see G trying to commit these three messages to memory. The "kill her father" part didn't even register.

"And G . . .?"

"Yeah?" He looked exasperated.

"Find out what you can from Kiera about her father. See if you can pry from her who he was dating. Whether or not he was sleeping with her mother. Who she thinks the murderer was. If he had any interests, that sort of stuff."

"Slow down, Mrs. Y." G put out his hands. "This is Hess's, not the House of Beauty. We actually cut hair here, you know. Gossip is so yesterday."

He slouched off, the budding professional of tomorrow yanking up his boxers as he left.

"You stylists at the House of Beauty must be pretty desperate to come all the way to Allentown for your gossip," Lydia said.

I stood and slung my purse over my shoulder. "Gossip knows no boundaries, Lydia. No mountain high enough. No valley low enough. I'd even go to King of Prussia if I had to. That," I tapped her plastic Starbucks top, "is dedication to the craft."

I had made it as far as the Allentown/Lehigh border when the phone in my purse rang again. Answering it caused me to nearly sideswipe a fire hydrant and crash headlong into a Mac semi, but I answered it.

"Moth-er," I hissed.

"I'm not your mother," my night editor, Mr. Salvo, said, insulted. "I'm your boss."

"Oh, sorry, Mr. Salvo." I tried tucking the phone against my shoulder so I could free up both hands, but this made it almost impossible to shift. "How was deer camp?"

"Ducky. The only thing I bagged was Connor Johnson's fifty bucks during a poker match." He sounded as gruff as usual. "Where are you headed?"

I was headed to the Fourth Street Diner for a doughnut and coffee, a real Pennsylvania breakfast. I was a Lehigh girl and I had the squishy thighs to prove it.

"To do some research," I covered.

"Which means breakfast. I know reporters. Listen, I want you to head over to the Northington County administration offices. There's an Open Space Subcommittee hearing being held this morning that I'd like to baby-sit, in case they pull something kooky. The beat reporter spent all night at that Jersey chemical fire—"

"Please, Mr. Salvo." I was shifting with one hand, holding the phone with the other and steering with my knees (a talent honed from years of applying mascara while rushing to work). "I'm on a tryout. I've got an exclusive I'm working on."

"Well, excuuuseee me! Must not have gotten the memo," he said. "Is there any way I can be of assistance? Send a limo perhaps?"

He was making fun of me, wasn't he?

"Last I checked, Bubbles, you were a hairdresser with minimal experience trying out for an entry-level general beat position, right?"

"Uh-huh." I stepped on the brakes to make a red light. Relief.

"And not many entry-level reporters I know get a week off to research one story. This is a daily newspaper, kiddo, not *TIME* magazine. Now get over to Eastman. The meeting starts in a half hour."

I tried to imagine how Stiletto would respond in this situation. If he were in my shoes, he'd tell Mr. Salvo to stuff himself. Then again, if he were in my shoes he'd probably be opening an antiques boutique in New Hope.

One hour later, there I was in the back row of a subcommittee hearing of the Northington County Council. The room was painted white with a chalkboard at one end. A neon light buzzed overhead. Around a wood-grained Formica table sat the three members of the Open Space Committee, who looked about as excited to be there as I was.

I tried to comprehend the agenda and two attached petitions, one from neighbors in favor and one from neighbors opposed to the zoning change. From what I could make out, the big issue was whether to let Farmer Bob Brown, or whomever, sell off fifty acres on the outskirts of Lehigh for development by a suspiciously named corporation called I.M. Ltd. I initially misread that as I Am Limited—which prompted me to laugh out loud at how true that was.

"Psst. Giggle girl." A crusty man in overalls motioned for me to join him.

"What do you want?" I whispered.

"You from the paper?"

143

"Yup."

"You read this petition?" With a shaky hand he handed me the first petition—the one in favor of the sale. "Look at the names."

I flipped through all fifty names. Largely meaningless. I shrugged. "So?"

"So that's I.M. Limited's extended family and business connections." He tapped the paper again. "They're railroading this. They got the subcommittee to hold the vote at ten a.m. on a Tuesday when everyone's at work, instead of in the evening at their usual meetings, to slip it through."

Interesting way to get around the sunshine law.

"And that bozo," he leaned over and poked at the fifth name on the petition, a Dr. Franklin Jefferson of County Road, "contributed five grand to *his* reelection campaign."

He pointed to a commissioner who seemed to be in la-la land, twirling his pencil and focusing on a spot near the door, likely thinking about whether he should purchase a new John Deere tractor with snowplow attachment.

Easy enough to verify if he'd been given five grand. Election filings were right downstairs. I once did a whole report on election filings when I was taking Mr. Salvo's Journalism 101 course at Two Guys.

"Who are you?" I asked my friendly tipster.

The tipster handed me the other petition—of those opposed—and pointed to his name. "Carlton Drake. I'm what ya call a watchdog."

144

And I was what you might call flummoxed. Because at the top of the petition was the name of Eunice. Eunice Morse, representing the Lehigh Historical Society. It couldn't be.

"Do you know her?" I asked Carlton, pointing to Eunice's name.

"Lives around the corner from me. She'd be here except she's big into the historical society and they have a rescheduled meeting today at the same time. The one they had yesterday got postponed after a couple of gals got into fisticuffs." He chuckled. "Eunice said it was a riot. Lots of hair pulling."

There wasn't *that* much hair pulling. "Is Eunice a gray-haired lady? Glasses? Smart?"

"As smart as they come." Carlton crossed a leg over a knee. "She's the one who came up with the petition idea. Said the development was nothing but suburban sprawl and it'd be the beginning of the end. Course once the other side got wind of the petition they—"

"You wouldn't happen to know if she is related to a Brian Morse." I recalled the nasty glances Eunice shot at Susan at the historical society breakfast.

"That turkey. Brian left her, ooh, boy . . .," Carlton grasped his denim knee and looked up at the ceiling, as though it held a calendar, "probably two years ago. One of those classic cases where the fella hits middle age and his eyes starts to wander . . . along with other parts." He emphasized this with an elbow nudge to my ribs.

So Eunice Morse was Brian Morse's ex-wife. Which meant that she'd been replaced by perky Susan Morse, M.R.S.

Which meant I had someone else to visit before I confronted Susan. The one person who, in the wake of pain set off by Susan's home wrecking, would have naturally aligned herself with Carol Weaver.

Eunice Morse and, I ventured, Carol Weaver's accomplice.

CHAPTER 12

It took me almost the entire day to research the I.M. Ltd. story, which wasn't bad considering I'd been assigned it cold. It was so simple, almost too simple, to collect the information.

The election records were available and clearly proved that Dr. Franklin Jefferson had indeed contributed the maximum $5,000 to the county commissioner's reelection campaign.

Dr. Franklin Jefferson, a dentist in Eastman, was one of the ten partners of I. M. Ltd., as listed in county records. When reached at his office, he cheerfully admitted on the record that he'd given to the commissioner's campaign because he thought, "It might grease the wheels when our development proposal came up."

Even the commissioner was a good sport. At first he denied knowing that Franklin Jefferson had been a contributor. Then he called me back at the newsroom to say that he would be recusing himself from the I.M. Ltd. vote, seeing as how he'd gotten money from one of the I.M. Ltd. partners. That was the lead right there.

"Airtight," Mr. Graham said after reading the edited version of my story over Mr. Salvo's shoulder.

"It all fell together," I said. "I never imagined it could be so easy."

"That's because you cut your teeth on tough ones," Mr. Salvo said, striking out a line of mine that I thought added color, but which he discarded as too dramatic. "The Laura Buchman suicide. That case in Whoopee and then the coal mine murder. A straightforward quid pro quo on a zoning issue is a cakewalk in comparison."

"Quid quo pro," I said. "That's Dutch, isn't it? For I'll scratch your back and you give me money or my fist in your face?"

Mr. Graham and Mr. Salvo looked at me blankly.

"At least that's what I heard."

"How's that other story going? The Carol Weaver one." Mr. Graham glanced across the newsroom at Lawless, who was engaged in his 5 P.M. Ho Ho fix, chocolate smeared around his rubbery lips.

"It's going okay."

"Is Lawless being any help?" he asked. "I told him to keep me apprised of all developments. You, too."

I was dying here. Dying to tell Mr. Graham how Lawless had been tossing banana peels so I'd slip up. He's a creep, I wanted to yell. He's playing dirty pool to keep a job he doesn't deserve to have.

148

"He has, um, inspired me to be more resourceful."

"I see." Mr. Graham clasped his hands behind his back. His coat was off and his blue shirtsleeves were rolled to convey the impression that he was in the thick of this mucky news business right with the rest of us schmoes. "You think there's any credence to Carol Weaver's claim that this was a Steel conspiracy?"

"I don't know. Steve Stiletto's helping me with that. He has a collection of Steel records."

"Stiletto, eh? He's no slouch. You two seeing each other still?"

"I'm staying with him until they find the shooter." What did Mr. Graham care about my love life?

"You make an interesting couple." Mr. Graham checked his watch. "Wanna meet?" he called out to his team of editors.

Mr. Salvo saved the story and took his clipboard. Billin, the copy editor in his green visor, grabbed a handful of white layout sheets and they all headed for Notch's office for the daily five o'clock edit meeting. I had turned to go back to my desk when I felt a warm hand stroke my shoulder.

"Nice work, Bubbles."

I was floored. "Thank you, Mr. Graham. Thank you so much."

"And," he stepped closer to me, so close I could see each bristly nostril hair, "you're not bad in that hot red turtleneck either."

★   ★   ★

Okay, what the heck was that all about? Had Mr. Graham just come on to me? Geesh. *Slam.* I banged the steering wheel. That geezer had to be over seventy. He was old enough to be my father. Scratch that. Old enough to be my grandfather.

It was dark and I was hungry. I hadn't eaten a bite since morning and my stomach was threatening mutiny. Perhaps if I had some food I'd be more rational.

The phone rang. I answered it like a pro.

"How's it going?" Stiletto asked.

I brought him up to date on the county commissioners story and my long-shot suspicion that Eunice Morse might have a connection to Carol Weaver.

"That's where I'm headed right now," I said. "Carlton Drake gave me directions to Eunice's house."

Stiletto said nothing.

Shoot. It had been so long since I'd lived with another grown adult of the opposite sex that I'd forgotten that whole dinner and evening together routine. What if Stiletto had gone all out in anticipation that this would be our big night?

"You had an evening planned, didn't you?"

"Caviar. Wine. A fire. Me and you in bed," he said. "Not much."

I smacked my forehead, which was really stupid because that meant I had both hands off the wheel. "I'm so sor—"

"Bubbles, don't be silly. I've been in journalism

150

for twenty years. I know how this goes. Besides, if anyone's put up with interrupted schedules, it's you. I deserve to be made to wait for once."

I didn't like to compare men (this, too, is a lie. I compare men all the time), but in a million years Dan the Man never would have been so considerate. "Thank you, Stiletto. That's very supportive."

"Well, I don't really have a choice, do I?"

"Pardon?"

"You've got me where you want me, Bubbles. I am at your service . . . whether I like it or not."

"I think you'll like it," I said, softly.

"I fully expect to more than like it," he replied, his voice low and sultry again. "And I'll do my best to make sure you feel the same."

That ache again. I hung up quickly before my legs went numb and I ran off the road.

I never would have found Eunice Morse's house—cabin, really—if Carlton Drake hadn't drawn detailed directions. "Around the corner," his phrase for where Eunice lived, meant up and down a hill and into the woods of South Mountain.

Without city lights around, it was darker in these woods than Pamela Anderson Lee's roots. I walked up the unlit wooden front steps and knocked on Eunice's door. Through the window I could see her inside, humming and stirring a pot over a gas stove. Like a little gray-haired, historical society witch.

She took a moment to place me, and when she did, her eyes grew wide and she said, "Uh-oh. If this is about the fight—"

"No," I said, smiling in an "I'm-really-a-nice-person" way. "It's about Carol Weaver. I'm doing a story on her for the paper. May I come in?"

I noticed that she locked the door with a deadbolt and pulled down the window quilts after letting me inside. Not usual procedure, I would imagine. Not deep in the serene woods of South Mountain.

The house was lit by kerosene lamps and warmed by a woodstove fire. It reminded me of my week in Amish Country when I bravely faced the world without an electric blow-dryer. Boy, that was tough.

I sat down on a wicker couch before the flickering fire. Eunice sat across from me, her wrinkled face slightly anguished. She was wearing a hand-knit blue sweater, a gray wool skirt, rag socks and clogs. I tried not to be visibly horrified by the presence of so many natural fibers.

"I don't know Carol very well," she said. "Her husband, Hal, was more of a friend. From the historical society. Though he was part of the faction that wants to fund the Underground Railroad expedition from the Monocacy Creek. A total waste of taxpayer dollars, as I told the group when you were there Monday."

Immediately I was disappointed. Eunice didn't seem like the kind of person who could lie about her hair color, let alone whether she was harboring a fugitive from prison. She came across as a trust-worthy soul. Nevertheless, I told her the whole story about Carol Weaver's visit, hoping some detail would trigger a response.

"So if you don't mind," I concluded, "I'd like to ask you a few questions about you and Carol."

Eunice got up and went to the stove, turning it down and stirring the pot. "First let me ask you a few questions, if you don't mind, Bubbles. A bit of quid pro quo."

I wasn't even going to go near that one. "Shoot."

Eunice put the lid on the pot and turned to me. "Do you have any idea what you are doing to yourself?"

"Excuse me?"

"I mean, for God's sake, look at you." She raised her hand and then slapped her skirted thigh. "You're killing yourself."

"I am?" Well, I was working pretty hard. Then again, I'd always worked hard.

"Start with your hair. How long have you been bleaching it?"

My hair. What had my hair to do with hard work? "I can't remember."

"Haven't you ever worried about apes?"

"Apes? In Lehigh? We don't even have a zoo."

"Not those apes. Alkylphenol ethoxylates," she exclaimed as though I were a complete idiot. "APEs. Found in so many hair dyeing products. Why, they can drastically alter a woman's hormonal functioning, Bubbles."

Yes, but they gave me blond hair. You had to weigh the pros with the cons, you know. Sunshine #8 versus cancer. Not easy. There were valid arguments to be made on both sides.

"And your nails."

I splayed my fingers and their pretty red acrylic nails. "Bad for me, too?"

"Read the side of a nail polish bottle sometime. I'd do it right now, but I wouldn't keep the stuff in my house."

I zipped open my purse and thumbed through my polish collection, finally pulling out a bottle of Precious Metal nail enamel #356. Gold. "Ethyl acetate, Butyl Acetate, Isopropyl Alcohol." I paused. "I think that's what they put in the fruit punch at Lehigh fraternity parties."

"Probably." Eunice was back to stirring the pot. "Go on."

"Nitrocellulose, Adipic Acid/Neopentyl Glycol/ Trimellitic Anhydride Copolymer, Trimethyl Pentanyl Diisobbutyrate, Triphenyl Phosphate, Styrene/Acrylates Copolymer, Stearalkonium Bentonite, Stearalkonium Hectorite, Benzophenone-1. Whew."

"At least that one doesn't have any dibutyl phthalates," she said. "Causes infertility in women of reproductive age."

That would solve my birth control dilemma.

"Many ingredients in nail polish and cosmetics actually suffocate your natural membranes, Bubbles. And let's not skip those boots of yours."

154

Eunice clogged over and lifted my left foot. "That heel must be at least two inches."

"Is that all?" I turned my ankle for a better view. "The Payless saleslady said they were at least three."

"You'll have osteoarthritis by the time you're forty if you keep wearing these. And don't tell me you're too young." She dropped my boot, which landed with a clunk on the wooden floor. "Women in their twenties are crippled from this kind of footwear. It should be abolished."

I pointed my toe. Damn if these puppies didn't make my legs look hot.

"Sorry," she said. "I get so aggravated when I think of the male-ordered conspiracy to confine women, Bubbles. Would you like some of my vegetable soup? My own canned garden vegetables are in it."

"I'd love some." Caviar and wine were not enough to satisfy my Polish/Lithuanian appetite. Not unless you smeared the caviar on a plate of puffy fried dough with powdered sugar and whipped cream. Yum yum.

Eunice pulled down two bowls from a green-painted cabinet. "If you're interested, I can give you some literature to read about the danger of cosmetics. Once your awareness is raised, you won't be able to go about killing yourself."

No, thanks. Ignorance is bliss. "About conspiracy, Eunice." I got up from the couch. "Do you think there's any truth to Carol Weaver's claim that Steel was behind her husband's murder?"

Eunice sighed and ladled out the soup. My stomach growled in anticipation. "When Brian and I were together, I heard stories about the shenanigans at Steel. Especially during the days when Henry Metzger ruled the roost. But were Steel's executives ruthless enough to murder one of their own? That's unlikely." She opened the tiny oven and pulled out a loaf of homemade bread. I practically swooned with desire.

Sawing it in thick, steamy slices she said, "Though, in a way, Steel killed Brian. At least the old Brian." She handed me the bowl of soup and bread. I thanked her and we sat at the kitchen table. "By the time we divorced he was a completely changed man."

"Did he leave you for Susan?" I asked bluntly.

"Everyone thinks that. Everyone who doesn't know me. Actually, it was the opposite." She dipped her spoon in the soup. "I left him."

"You did? Why?" My understanding was that Steel wives clung to their husbands. That they lived in fear of their men hitting their career high point and trolling the waters for more supple fare.

"Because he wasn't the man I married." Eunice lay down her spoon and opened a jar of canned beans. "Brian and I met in college during the sixties. He was an Environmental Sciences major and I was a teacher in training. Both of us had a vision of living a simple life off the grid."

"The grid?"

"No electricity. No sewer." The jar popped open. "Want some to go with the bread?"

My mother used to do that, beans on bread. Icky. "Not right now, thanks."

"Suit yourself." She dumped beans onto her plate. "We moved to South Mountain when Brian got a job at Steel, which was then under pressure to reduce its toxic emissions. On paper he was hired as a consultant, but in reality he was no more than a mannequin on display. Steel's attitude was here, look at this hippie we hired. See how progressive we're becoming?"

She bit into the bread and I sucked down some soup. Tomatoes. Carrots. Onions. It wasn't bad, though it lacked oomph. Salt, maybe, or a healthy dose of MSG. Pepperoni might be nice.

"Brian built this house by hand. Dug the well. Set up the solar panels. We intentionally chose not to have children. We didn't feel it was right considering how dangerously overcrowded the world is." Eunice played with the corner of the placemat. "All those sacrifices," she added sadly.

Surely she couldn't be talking about the same Brian Morse, the one who gave Stiletto a hard time in his pursuit of Henry Metzger's evil deeds. The one who married preppy princess Susan Morse, M.R.S.

"What happened?" I asked.

"Like I said, Steel got to him. Twenty years at the place and he wanted to move to Saucon Valley.

157

He wanted to get NFL on cable and eat steak. He wanted," she said slowly, "an SUV."

"So you kicked him out?"

"Not at first. But then the red meat and the boardroom really got to him. It's as though he became poisoned. He became mean."

"Mean?"

"That's when we split. Two years ago." She dabbed the napkin to her uncolored lips. "Frankly, I think his bosses at Steel were glad to see me go. The day the divorce went through, Brian got promoted to vice president. And when Hal Weaver died, Brian got his job, along with a car and driver and a country club membership."

Got Hal's pretty and stylish girlfriend, too, I thought.

Eunice chuckled to herself. "Brian got everything he secretly wanted. Almost overnight."

"At least Steel didn't try to kill him or you," I said. "Carol Weaver believes that as top flak, her husband knew a secret that got him killed and that Steel framed her for his murder. Now Steel's trying to poison her with cyanide, just like they poisoned Hal."

"Brian never had any secrets about Steel. At least, none that he told me about." Eunice chewed her bread thoughtfully, asking with surprise, "Has your reporting shown Steel was behind Hal's murder?"

"Not exactly, though I've learned that there's lots of cyanide floating around Steel. It's key to the sheet metal process and it's also an end product."

"Cyanide is a natural substance, Bubbles. It's found in the earth and in vegetables. Lima beans. Almonds. Mustard. It could have come from anyplace."

"Vegetables?" I glared at my killer soup just swimming with natural cyanide. "Come on. Generations of parents can't be wrong."

"Oh really? Do you know that the root used to make tapioca is filled with cyanide?"

I pushed back my chair indignantly. "Mrs. Morse, I will ask you to rescind that statement. Tapioca has been a staple in the Yablonsky house for years. It was our Tuesday night dessert. Are you accusing my mother of attempting to poison me?" A concept not beyond the realm of possibilities.

"I'm not accusing your mother of any such thing." Eunice placed a pale white hand over mine. "Tapioca has had the cyanide removed. It's the root that is dangerous to eat raw, before preparation. Cassava."

"Cassava?" Where had I just read about Cassava? In a flash I saw Mrs. Cathobianco's computer screen and Susan Pendergast's Two Guys transcripts from the Domestic Studies M.R.S. program.

"What's wrong, Bubbles?" Eunice's hand gripped mine tightly. "Is the soup making you sick? Are you choking?"

"No," I said, gathering my thoughts together. "I'm fine. I just remembered. Susan Pendergast, I mean, Susan Morse."

"Yes?" Eunice smiled encouragingly. "It doesn't bother me to talk about her. Go on."

"At Two Guys Community College, where Susan did her M.R.S. She did her thesis on the cassava, something like, 'A Hundred Uses for Nature's Most Versatile Root.'"

Eunice frowned at me. "You can't seriously think . . ."

"That Susan Morse feigned an affair with Hal Weaver and then poisoned him to further her future husband's career? Yes, I can seriously think that."

"For a woman who douses on carcinogens like perfume, you're not so much of a dim bulb, are you, Bubbles?"

"No," I said, "not so much."

CHAPTER 13

My jubilation at being able to connect the dots between Susan Morse, her husband Brian and Hal Weaver quickly turned to confusion as I left Eunice's cabin. Shuffling through the dead leaves, I inhaled the brisk November night air, the spicy smell of smoke, opened my Camaro, got in and found a flaw in my theory.

If Susan Morse dated Hal Weaver on the sly with the sole purpose of getting him out of the way so that Brian Morse could get his job and perks, then why would Carol Weaver have pleaded to a reduced charge of manslaughter and willingly served time in prison?

I jotted down a mental note to call the district attorney tomorrow and ask him for insight on why Carol copped to the plea—or why Susan Morse was never investigated as a murder suspect.

It was now after eight. As soon as I got out of the woods and in range, I punched the green glowing numbers on the cell phone and dialed Stiletto at home. No answer. When I tried to call his cell, I got one of those bizarre recordings that sounded as if I had tried to reach the mother ship.

"Message RU 867. The caller you are trying to reach is unavailable or out of the zone."

Out of the zone, that's how I felt. Lost and disoriented. I dialed Dan's with the hope of talking to Jane for grounding. She was at the Lehigh University library, Dan said. G had just called looking for her, too.

"And Bubbles," Dan said, "I don't want the numb nut stopping by tomorrow morning. Not for one minute."

"What numb nut?"

"G. What other numb nut is there? Bo Wimble is going to be by at seven a.m. sharp for his breakfast interview with Jane. I've got it all arranged, more perfect than a Swedish clock. *Capisce?*"

"Okay." I groaned at the thought of getting up at five-thirty to do my hair and get over to Dan's. "I won't bring him."

"Bring him? What? You think you're coming, too?"

"I am her mother, Dan, and—"

"I'm her father. I'm clearing out tomorrow morning and you should as well. Keep this between Jane and Wimble. She's almost an adult. This is Princeton, for Christ sakes. She doesn't need her parents poking into every aspect of her life. Give her privacy, Bubbles. Let go."

Wow. I was stunned by Dan's sudden burst of maturity. I've always maintained that Dan wasn't a bad father, just a bad husband. Maybe he was right. "That's impressive, Dan. Okay. I'll stay away."

"Thatta girl. Oh, and Bubbles?"

"Yes, Dan?"

"It's Chip."

Since Stiletto appeared to be "out of the zone," I decided there was no harm in dropping by Susan and Brian Morse's. I was in the area, after all, and now I was burning with curiosity. Just who was this domestic goddess who could have affairs with two men at the same time? Who could kill one and boost the other's career, all the while keeping her floors?

I pictured Susan Morse at home, the former executive secretary efficiently organizing her husband's neckties by importance. Planning parties down to the last stuffed mushroom while writing grants for the historical society and boning up on her natural herbal methods of homicide.

What irked me about Susan was how incredibly bland a first impression she had made. Her body was certainly nothing to have a heart attack about. A straight B cup, if that. Legs that were passable, but not worthy of worship, kind of round at the top and short. Her hair, while shiny (I'm still betting on a beer rinse) was a nondescript brown and her personality was about as appealing as a root canal. She panicked when Lorena and I raised our voices, and then she went ballistic for no reason.

Then again maybe I was biased. She did have

me bounced from the historical society. Ruined a ten-week bounce-free record. (The last event was at Uncle Manny's, when I jumped on top of his pool table at a bachelorette party to play air guitar to Lynyrd Skynyrd's classic "Free Bird.")

The lights were on at the Morse's home, a better-than-average Saucon Valley mansard-roof deal. The road in front of their house was gently lit by tasteful gaslights. I counted chimneys, the common currency of home status in these parts. Two—two less than Stiletto's, but why be snotty?

The front lawn could have easily held the first fifty yards of the Liberty High football field and was too long for me to sit in my comfortable warm car and spy into their comfortable warm home to make sure Brian wasn't around. I wanted to meet Susan one on one. I couldn't risk the husband getting involved.

I got out and minced across the thick, cut grass, wet with dew. Good thing my boots were imitation suede. Every reporter ought to be obliged to shop at Payless.

Big bushes obstructed the front windows, so I had to go around the side, where I could peek into what appeared to be a den. The walls were painted a dark green, which flickered with the reflection of a large television.

I thought I heard a man's voice. Brian's? Or was it the ESPN sports channel? He was mad. Argumentative. Dictatorial. Bossy. In other words, an average male on an average night in the typical

164

home of a suburban, married couple. She, for I was almost positive I had heard a she, was meek. Crying?

And out of nowhere *The 1812 Overture* blared from my purse.

I must have accidentally punched up the volume because lights went on at the neighbors two doors down. Finding the phone was not easy in the dark as I fumbled through nail polish bottles, pens, lipsticks, numerous ATM receipts (saved with good intent, but never actually recorded in a check register) and my Reporter's Notebook. Aha! Found it.

"Hello?" I whispered, bending down and covering the phone with my hand.

"Hi, Bubbles. It's me, Rachel."

"Rachel? Rachel who?"

"Rachel Stottlemyer."

Just my luck. Me on a stakeout and Rachel Stottlemyer, the cell phone madwoman, gives me a ringy dingy. Why couldn't my mother have normal friends besides a hulking conspiracy nut and a ditzy dialer?

"Why are you whispering?" she hollered. "I've got the volume on loud and I still can't hear you. Is the reception bad where you are?"

"Mrs. Stottlemyer, this is not a good time. I'm still at work." Did I just hear a door open?

"Still at work! It's almost nine o'clock. Go home, Bubbles. You've been working too long, dear."

"I've really got to go, Mrs. Stottlemyer." I didn't

want to be rude and hang up. If Mama ever found out I'd done that . . .

"You must be on the late shift. That's so unfair, you a single mother on the late shift. Can't you complain to your supervisor? Can't they give you a nice nine-to-five?"

"It's not like that, Mrs. Stottlemyer, I—"

"You're going in and out now. Where are you? I'm coming back from bingo, on the Hellertown road, and I think there's a tower nearby so the signal will be clear. Oh, there it is. Is it clear now?"

"Yes, it's very clear, Mrs. Stottlemyer." My legs were aching from crouching on heels. Maybe there was some validity to Eunice's ostoe-whatever claims. Nahhh.

"Are you leaving work yet?"

"*What* are you doing?" an angry voice demanded.

I lifted my head and simultaneously hung up on Mrs. Stottlemyer, Mama be damned. A man in a dark sweatshirt and a pair of chinos stood over me. He was wearing glasses. I thought he might be Brian Morse.

"Why are you hiding in my bushes?" he demanded. "I should call the police."

No, he shouldn't. That would be a stupid thing to do. "Uhm, I uhm," I searched for a rational explanation. I was checking for termites? Admiring your hostas? Had to pee and this was the nearest bush? "I didn't know if it was too late to knock. I didn't want to bother you."

166

I stood, and he examined my face in the light pouring from his den window.

"Who are you?"

"Bubbles Yablonsky. I'm a reporter at the *News-Times*. And who," I said jauntily, "may I ask, are you?"

"Brian Morse. I live here. I'll be the one filing the complaint with the police."

"Take a number." Remembering how Brian Morse had benefited from Hal Weaver's untimely death filled me with new confidence. "Because I'm filing a complaint about your wife. On account of her fighting at the historical society I broke a nail."

He stabbed a finger into my chest. "You. You're the one who assaulted my wife."

"No. That was Lorena Ludwig. Our photographer. Photographers have better footwork than reporters."

"I don't care. It was outrageous! I complained to Notch and Graham about it this afternoon. They said you were going to apologize. I never expected you'd show up at my house at nine o'clock at night."

Forget that Susan had more reason to apologize than either Lorena or I. I felt like I had cashed out at the lottery. Like God had handed me a golden hall pass.

"Well, here I am. Apologizing." I got up on my tippy toes and looked in the window. "Is Susan around?"

"As though I'd let you come near her." Morse clutched my elbow and brought me to the light of the front porch. "You can write a letter to her like you should. And—"

"What a wonderful idea." I opened my purse and pulled out my trusty Reporter's Notebook and pen. In big letters I wrote. "Susan: I'm sorry that you body-slammed Lorena. Bubbles Yablonsky. P.S. I'd like to interview you about the Hal Weaver murder." I concluded with Stiletto's number.

Folding it up, I handed the note to Brian. "Here. She'll understand when she reads it."

Brian took it, opened it and read it. So much for domestic privacy.

"What's this about the Hal Weaver murder?" he said. "She knows nothing about that."

I closed the Reporter's Notebook and deposited it in my purse. "I think she does. But that's not important."

"Why not?"

"Because even if she claims she doesn't know about the murder, I do," I said, backing down the driveway to my car. "Right down to its cassava roots."

It was around nine-thirty when I finally made it to Stiletto's, shaken and stirred by the close encounter with Brian Morse. As I locked the Camaro and slowly tread the stone steps, I thought of how nice it would be to be greeted at the door

168

by a friendly face. Someone on my side for once. To be hugged and asked how was my day. Here. Have a glass of something. Put your feet up and tell me all about it.

You didn't get that kind of treatment being a single mother at home with a teenager.

And, as I discovered, you didn't get that kind of treatment living with a guy, either.

Stiletto was in the TV room, the one with the cardinals on the drapes, feet up, watching a football game on the wide-screen TV with the lights out. I dumped my coat in the hallway closet and my purse on the end table below the large gilt mirror. I resolved to ignore my exhaustion and perk up.

No one likes a whiner, as Mama was always reminding me.

Fluffing my hair in the hall mirror, I applied a new coating of Hot Red lipstick and another of eyeliner. I was presentable, even somewhat sexy, for a Tuesday night. Slinking into the darkened TV room, I approached Stiletto from behind, sliding my hands over his chest and kissing him upside down.

It was like kissing an ashtray.

"Oh, Mrs. Robinson," he said.

I shrieked the shriek of the tortured. G! I had kissed G! I had kissed my daughter's grungy loser of a boyfriend. I actually felt the metal ball of his pierced lip against my teeth.

I ran around the room searching for the switch

plate, which I finally found on the wall. "What!" I screamed. "What are you doing . . . here?"

G blinked in the light and smeared the back of his hand against his now Hot Red imprinted lips. "Ugh," he said. "Give me some warning or something next time."

"Next time?" I was still shouting with all the power my lungs could muster. "There won't be a next time. I didn't mean to kiss you. I meant to kiss Stiletto."

"Whatever, Mrs. Robinson." G aimed the remote at the TV and muted the sound. "I've heard how you middle-aged ladies are. Hitting your sexual peak while guys your age, old farts like Stiletto, are on the decline."

I yanked my hair with both hands. This wasn't happening. "What do *you* know? You're a teenager who failed shop class. And I'm *not* middle aged. Stiletto is *not* an old fart."

"Geesh." He put up his hands. "Is this like a blazing hot flash or what?"

"Aggh!" I had to leave the room. In Stiletto's expansive gourmet kitchen with the cathedral ceilings and smooth granite counters, I paced. I opened the refrigerator, the stove, ran the water. What if Jane found out? Wait, what was I thinking? There was no if. Of course Jane would find out. As soon as the football went into halftime, G would be on the phone.

"You'll never believe what your whacked mother did." I could hear it crystal clear.

Returning to the TV room, I said, "You cannot tell Jane."

"Okay, Mrs. Robinson." G's eyes were firmly glued on the Steelers. "But I'm going to see Elaine, Mrs. Robinson. You can't stop me."

Great. G couldn't quite comprehend that N meant north on a road map, but every word of dialogue from *The Graduate* was committed to his memory thanks to twenty-four-hour cable.

"Do you know that Anne Bancroft was about your age, only thirty-six, when she played Mrs. Robinson, Mrs. Robinson?"

Cyanide. Where are these so-called natural sources of cyanide when you need them? I returned to the oversized stainless steel refrigerator and pulled open the vegetable drawers. How come Stiletto didn't keep cassava?

Back to the TV room. G now had the split-screen thing going. The Steelers bashing each other on one side; on the other a stripperlike diva gyrating to MTV. "What happened to your hair? It was orange this morning. How come it's black?"

"Reminds you of Benjamin Braddock, is that it, Mrs. Robinson?"

I sat down on the leather hassock and snatched the remote out of his hand.

"Hey!" G sat up in protest.

"You'll get this back after you start talking."

He slumped and folded his arms, which were encased in a black fleece jacket. "I thought that was supposed to be my line. You know how we never talk before we . . ."

"What are you doing here?" I had no patience with this boy.

G let out a long sigh. "I called here about an hour ago to tell you what went down with that Kiera chick. You weren't home so I talked to Stiletto."

"Uh-huh." I rolled my arm. "Keep going."

"That was the part where you were supposed to say, 'Thank you, G. Thank you for risking your job at Hess's, of which I am so very, very jealous, to grill a client.'"

I pointed to the TV. "Stiletto hates this thing. I can have it removed tomorrow."

"He can move it to my dad's house."

"Where it'd be stolen in an hour? Don't think so. What did Stiletto say?"

"Your old man said he had to go on assignment or whatever. He said to tell you he found out something about cyanide at Steel."

Dang. I hate waiting, a side effect from having grown up in the instant generation of cereal and TV. "Okay, but what are *you* doing here?"

"*I* am your protection." G fingered his nose ring. "Stiletto didn't want you coming back to an empty house so he invited me to crash here, including full use of his entertainment system and domesticables."

"Domesticables?"

"Soda, food and junk, though there's no potato chips in this house so I had to settle on the fish eggs. Actually, they're not too bad if you put ketchup on them. You know where there's any more? The jars are so tiny."

Two hundred dollars of beluga drowned in ketchup and downed in one gulp. Stiletto would kill him if I didn't beat him to the punch. First I had to squeeze all the information I could out of the delinquent.

"What did Kiera say about . . . everything?"

"Let's see." G focused on a replay. "She said she doesn't care if her mom is thinking about her. She hates her mom."

Spoiled kid.

"She said her dad was a great guy, but he had these dark moments where he would go off for days."

"Days? She say where?"

"No." G picked at his nails. "Said her pop was really into some tunnel. That's where he went the night he died. She knows because she talked to him when he came home."

Not according to the police report. According to the police report I read at the Northington County Court, she never heard her father come in.

"A tunnel?" I asked, trying to figure out exactly where Hal Weaver had been that night.

"More like a subway."

I thought about the possibilities and how they might be translated in G's feeble brain. "You don't mean the Underground Railroad?"

"That's it. The Underground Railroad. He used to take her to the cave by Monocacy Park. You know it?"

Absolutely I knew it. Every kid who skipped school at Liberty knew it. It's where you went to smoke cigarettes and pot and any other illegal substance you could at ten in the morning.

"No," I lied. "Where is it?"

G gave me a telltale look. "Oh, you can't kid me, Mrs. Robinson. Don't tell me you were squeaky clean in high school, 'cause I'm not buying that."

"I think we'll donate the TV to the Salvation Army."

The phone rang.

"Phone's ringing," G said. "You might want to get that."

I tossed him the remote and went into the hall to answer it. Maybe it was Stiletto coming to rescue me.

"Bubbles. What are you doing to me?"

Susan Morse, if I had to guess. And she sounded close to hysteria.

"What's the meaning of this note you gave to Brian? He's absolutely livid. He's thinking of suing you."

"Oh, you wouldn't like that, Susan. Then you'd have to testify about where you were on the night of February 14, the night Hal Weaver was poisoned with cyanide."

Susan was silent. G had turned the TV to full

volume. Nice to have a big house where I didn't have to shout at him to turn it down.

"This can be cleared up," she said calmly. "When can we meet?"

"Now is fine by me. At your house?"

"God no. We need a neutral spot."

Where to meet. Where to meet. The library was closed. Diners and bars were too public. Not Stiletto's. Not with G here. That left one choice.

"The House of Beauty," I said. "It's on Fourth Street next to Uncle Manny's Bar and Grille."

"I know it. My mother's housekeeper used to get her hair done there. Meet you in an hour, or later. I have to wait until Brian goes to sleep."

I hung up and thought about our conversation. Why did she want to meet in a neutral spot? What was she hiding? Why after her husband went to sleep?

Ding. Dong.

"Doorbell," G announced from the TV room. "Anybody going to get that?"

What would I do without him?

All these people. It is not a healthy sign when your home is more stressful than work. I opened the door an inch in case it was the BB shooter with more normal working hours, stopping by for a second try.

It wasn't a BB shooter. It was a hulking rectangle in tweed with a floral head scarf. At her black rubbered feet was a wriggling thing.

175

"For St. Pete's sake, Sally, it's chillier than a bucket of penguin spit out here. Let me in."

"Genevieve?" I opened the door. Genevieve trundled in, a white plastic baby carrier in one hand and a diaper bag in the other.

"On baby-sitting duty." She unwrapped the scarf and handed it to me. "Meet Waldo."

I stared down at Waldo in the carrier, perhaps the ugliest baby God had had the cruel misfortune to create. Nearly purple in color, with a mug that could strip wallpaper, he appeared to be about a year old. I pegged him as a howler.

"My first husband's great grandson," she said, pulling off her gloves. "I got called in on emergency. Waldo's mother collapsed tonight. Nervous exhaustion. Had to get Waldo out of the house."

"Why are you bringing him here?"

Waldo looked around, surveying the room for acoustics.

"Won't allow babies in the senior citizens apartment and it wasn't like I could sneak him in." Genevieve struggled out of her coat. "You can't take this tyke anywhere without him putting up a caterwaul that would empty a kennel."

White spit-up bubbled from Waldo's pink mouth. "He's cute," I fibbed.

"No, he's not. He's possessed. Now, where's that wide-screen TV I've heard tell?"

I pointed to the TV room. Genevieve hauled Waldo and the baby carrier in there, her rubbers squeaking on Stiletto's walnut floors.

176

"Change the channel, Butch. I'm here for the duration." She dumped the carrier next to G on the couch. G flinched like Waldo was a box of snakes.

"What's that?" he said.

"That, boy, is the product of sex. Keep that in mind the next time you get a hankering to walk your willy."

Genevieve, who had managed to steal the remote, switched to the Home Shopping Network. A two-piece lounge suit in rose or green terry cloth was on sale for $69, without monogramming. Monogramming was $10 extra.

"Now, that's what I call style," she said.

G and Waldo studied each other. Waldo scowled at G with what I took to be a particularly vengeful stare.

"Looks like he's about to let one loose," Genevieve said, reaching into the diaper bag and pulling out an insulated bottle. "Here. You ain't doing nothing, Butch. You feed him. I gotta make a phone call about that lounge suit. I've been looking for one in green."

"A bottle?" G held up his hands. "No way, man. I don't do bottles. Not bottles for babies."

As though Waldo had understood this, he scrunched up his face, balled his tiny fists and opened his mouth. At first there wasn't a sound. It was strangely silent, silent like it is before a hurricane hits shore with 100 mph gale force. And then Waldo made landfall.

"Waaaaaa! Waaaaa!"

"What the . . ." G slapped his hands over his ears as Waldo's bellowing cries became louder and louder. The TV, still at full volume, was muted in comparison. The mirrors on the walls shook. An antique vase rocked precariously.

Genevieve, meanwhile, merely pulled a pair of headphones from her pocket, snapped them over her gray head and plugged them into the phone. Then Grandma Bell dialed the Home Shopping Network number from memory and calmly ordered the green lounge suit. At least, I think that's what she was doing. I couldn't tell because Waldo's cries had drowned out all sound.

"Do something!" G yelled. *"I can't take this."*

Genevieve tossed the bottle into his lap.

G stared at me with pleading eyes.

"Here." I uncapped the bottle and stuck it in Waldo's gaping pie hole. It took him a few seconds to realize he had received what he had demanded, so we were forced to suffer more hearing loss. At last he settled down to sucking, his fat little cheeks working industriously as he replenished energy that would later be used for more caterwauling.

I handed G the bottle. Stunned and reeling slightly, he held it dutifully.

"And when you're done feeding him, you can change his diaper," Genevieve commanded. "Peee-uuu. What a stinker that tyke is."

Last sight before I left to meet up with Susan

was of one terrified G gingerly holding Waldo, who continued to feed contentedly, stopping now and then to smile upward and give G's nose ring a lusty tug.

CHAPTER 14

During the day the South Side is a fairly safe place. The frowning babushkas do a competent job canvassing the streets, pinpointing suspicious cars and strange men who shouldn't be loitering about. Not much escapes their radar. That is before 7 p.m.—the Wheel of Fortune hour.

From 7 P.M. on, the battleaxes, as Dan used to call them, are inefficient zombies, their eyes having turned from the sidewalk to the TV screen. Once *Wheel of Fortune*'s done, it's on to *Jeopardy*, a little QVC and then bed, where not even a nuclear bomb could rouse them.

That is unless the nuclear bomb comes in the form of a stray cat looking for a litterbox in one of their gardens. Then just one scratch in the tomato patch and the babushkas are out of their beds and outside, pumping vinegar spray faster than Rambo with an AK-47 and a convoy of Vietcong.

Realizing this, I should have thought to meow instead of scream. As it turned out, my screams had no effect.

This is what happened. I arrived at the House of Beauty on the dot. I wore tight-fitting spandex black leggings, a black turtleneck top and my favorite black boots. I was sleeker than Catwoman (Julie Newmar, not Lee Meriwether or Eartha Kitt). To be honest, I looked terrific. Too bad Stiletto wasn't with me. His loss.

I used my spare key to enter the back door, which was locked and secure. Flicked on the lights in the office and then the salon and sat on the couch to wait for Susan. A half hour passed.

In that time I ate two of the lemon yellow lollypops we give to kids who don't hurt us (much) while they get their hair cut. Washed those down with a Diet A-Treat cola. Read a *Newsweek* article about how potato chips will kill us all. (Excuse me, but I'd be in the grave already, thank you very much.) And started a *Cosmo* survey about "How Well Do You Know Your Man?"

Turns out I knew my man pretty darn well. That is if the man we were talking about comes weekly to haul my garbage. (Likes it in the morning, not at night. Is reliable.) If by man we were referring to Stiletto, then I knew squat.

Do you know where your man is right now? No.

Has he ever dated someone without your knowledge? What?

How well do you get along with his parents? Hmmm. Well, his stepfather tried to kill me—twice.

I was adding up my depressing score when

there was a terrific squeal outside the window. Peeking through the venetian blinds, I spied a car stopped in the middle of the block. Its white reverse lights went on and then it backed up doing about 45 mph.

Didn't seem like Susan's upper crust style, especially since the vehicle in question was a muscle car with an elevated rear end and a purple neon-framed license plate that said "8ME."

Punk trouble. Teenagers around here were well aware that no men ran the House of Beauty, that if a light was on late at night it meant either Sandy or I was working late, catching up on accounting or inventory.

Me alone in the House of Beauty, loaded register just waiting to be emptied, was not an ideal situation. The situation didn't improve when the car door slammed and footsteps started marching up the walk. Fast footsteps. Not the kind I'd attribute to size six Etienne Aigner pumps as were worn by Susan that morning at the historical society.

There wasn't enough time to lock the rear door, so I flicked off the salon light and dashed to the front desk, crouching in the kneehole. That way I could grab the creep's legs if he went for the cash register.

I held my breath, waiting. The footsteps stopped then resumed, along with my heartbeat. For a nanosecond I considered calling the cops. But what would I report? Car parked in front of salon? 8ME alert?

The back door slammed and the footsteps proceeded through the office. Step. Step. Step. Step. Slowly and methodically. The light under the office door to the salon went off. We were in the dark. He wanted to be in the dark.

I adjusted my assessment. What if this wasn't a punk? What if this was the BB shooter?

I reached over my head and felt around on the cash register for a weapon. All I came up with was a Bic pen, and it was attached to a string. When I yanked the string, the pen came off in a snap—right as the door opened.

Step. Step. Step. The steps stopped. I crouched down further.

"Bubbles?"

"Susan?"

The streetlights through the venetian blinds illuminated a woman with her hair pulled back.

"Did you say Susan?" she asked.

"Susan Morse?" I slid out from the desk, fumbling for the light.

"Susan Morse! That's it. . . ."

Suddenly, fingers went around my throat and I felt the sharp stab of a knee in my groin. I reached for hair, tugging a handful so hard that she fell backwards, sending us both to the House of Beauty floor with a painful thud.

We growled and screamed, tearing at whatever we could grasp. Earrings went flying. Hair clips and ponytail holders. Her shoes rocketed into the air while the slim heels of my boots slid along the floor. We rolled into the hard metal salon chairs and my wet lips picked up stray hair. (Sandy needed to clean more often.) Where there wasn't hair there was blood.

"Stop it!" I cried, after we bumped into a vanity and knocked over the glass jar of sterilized combs.

"I . . . will . . . not."

We wrestled some more. My spandex leggings had ripped straight up the seam and my turtleneck was stretched to a wobble. I could feel scratches on my cheeks and swelling bruises on my arm.

"Why?" I gasped.

"Why?" Another yank of hair. "Because I owe you from the other day, you donkey-sucking . . ."

With one quick turn, I flipped her over and seized both wrists, expertly wrapping them with a ponytail holder from the floor. Then I got up, staggered a bit and turned on the light.

"Lorena!"

Peanut Butter Legs lay face down. Her brown hair was a snaggled clump and several of my red artificial nail tips were mixed in it. Lorena's nail tips, red also, were scattered about, too. It was a nail tip massacre.

"That manicure cost me forty-five bucks at the mall." She squinted at her bound hands. "You owe me . . . again."

"Look." I held out my fingers. "Look what you did to me."

"Yeah?" She rolled over. "But you work at a salon. You can get them done for free."

Common laywoman misperception. I always reimbursed Sandy for materials, and then it took my professional time to do the manicure. Part of my job. I tried writing off manicures as continuing education once, but the tax folks at H&R Block in Sears would have none of it.

"Aren't you going to undo me?" Lorena's mascara and liner had smudged all over her face.

I knelt down. "First tell me what in the hell got into you that you had to attack me."

"I didn't mean to attack *you*. I got confused. I thought you were saying you were Susan Morse." She spit out something. Another nail tip. "When I saw the lights on in the House of Beauty and your car parked out front, I decided to stop by and let you know that I got a lead on that story about Carol Weaver you're working on."

I maintained my lips in a rigid grimace. "You scared me half to death and beat me up to tell me that?"

"What can I say. I'm slightly reactionary. It's genetic." She held up her wrists. "If you don't untie me, my hands are gonna fall off from lack of blood circulation."

I slid my fingers under the yellow and blue hair bands and sprung her. "You should know that Susan Morse is supposed to stop by." I got off Lorena and checked my watch. Nearly two hours since Susan had called. "Though she's a little late."

"She's not going to stop by. Women like her don't come to the South Side at this time of night."

Lorena sat up, massaging her wrists. "And if she does, I still got enough energy to take her down."

"Please, Lorena. Not every moment has to be spent throwing fists." I helped her over to my old stylist's chair. "So what's the lead?"

"First you have to promise that if something comes of this, you have to use me as a photographer."

I nodded, my ear cocked for sounds of Susan. I was going to humor Lorena and then shove her out the door. The last thing I wanted was for Susan to walk in and find me with Lorena.

"Okay, here's the scoop." Lorena crossed her legs and reached into her leather pants for a pack of cigarettes. "I've been working for this caterer while I get my photography career started." She lit a butt and flicked the ash. "Miss Delilah's Delectables."

"You have a boss named Miss Delilah? Sounds like she wears petticoats."

"Underneath her blue gingham dress, she does." Lorena exhaled. "Believe me, I live it down every day. The only perk about the job is the uniform. White. Don't have to worry about what to wear."

I thought back to Lorena smoking, per usual, outside the historical society in her white chef's coat on Monday morning.

"Anyway, on Thursday night Miss Delilah's doing this highbrow catering job in Saucon and I volunteered to work, even though that's not my night, because I figured I could get me a piece of Susan."

"Susan Morse?" The smoke was hazing up the place.

"She's hosting the event. Guess where."

I shrugged. "The historical society?"

"The historical society?" Lorena made a face. "They're too cheap to hire caterers. No. It's a baby shower for Kiera Weaver at her house, the same one where Hal Weaver was murdered. How cake is that?"

"Pretty cake." And pretty coincidental. Carol Weaver breaks out of prison because she's concerned about her pregnant daughter, the same week a big shower is being held by the rival for her late husband's affections. Hmmm.

Did another murder loom on the horizon? I could see it now, the baby shower underway, pink, green and yellow balloons everywhere. Susan cooing over the brand-new baby quilts and booties, strollers and bottle warmers. Bibs galore.

And then Carol Weaver in her orange prison jumpsuit, a hand-embroidered layette under one arm, a shotgun under the other, arrives for good-will and justice. Fires a BB right at Susan's . . .

Snap. Snap. Lorena snapped her fingers by my ears. "Hey, Bubblehead. Anyone home?"

"Sorry. Daydreaming."

"It's night. Wake up."

"How do you know so much about Hal Weaver's murder, anyway?" I asked.

"After you called I went over to Candy's Room." Candy's Room was the newsroom euphemism for

187

the *News-Times* morgue, which was guarded by a sallow-skinned spinster named, yup, Candy. "The file on Hal Weaver wasn't there so I stole it off Lawless's desk."

"You're a ballsier woman than I."

"And you're thinking." Lorena leaned over and rubbed my furrowed brow. "Don't do that. Makes you look ugly. Blondes like you shouldn't think. Like Laura on *GH*."

"Laura's history," I said.

"No, she's not. She's in a mental hospital in England after those flashbacks of murdering her mother's lover David Hamilton when she was fifteen. It all came back to her after the rape and the underground crystal city being run by the evil Cassadine family."

We took time out for a moment of silence, recalling with awe and respect the Glory Days of *General Hospital,* when Luke raped Laura on the floor of the Campus Disco and Mikkos Cassadine tried to freeze the world starting with the obvious target of Port Charles, New York. Sigh.

The office door to the salon shut. Lorena and I froze, as if Mikkos Cassadine himself had bewitched us.

But it wasn't Mikkos Cassadine or even Susan Morse who had arrived.

CHAPTER 15

What I noticed about Carol Weaver right off—after I got past the ladylike .22-caliber Ruger in her hand—was the pearls. What was with the pearls? There she is, on the lam, the cops want her, the Corrections Department has the dogs out and maybe even the dark side of Steel is trying to bump her off, and she's wearing pearls.

"Who's this?" asked Lorena, her gaze squarely on the Ruger.

"This is Carol Weaver," I said. "Carol. Meet Lorena."

Carol ignored Lorena, choosing instead to direct all comments toward me. She was dressed in a black sweater set, those pearls of course, gray slacks and a black trench coat. What all the best dressed walkaways were wearing. Her hair, by the way, was perfect.

"You've gone too far, Bubbles." Carol assumed the isosceles position. Both arms parallel to the floor, gun aimed straight at me. "I asked you to investigate my case, to ferret out the weasels at Steel. I did not ask you to pry into my personal life."

Give me a break. I was a reporter. Not a lackey for inmate no. 42369 at the Jakeville.

"Excuse me," Lorena declared. "I'm here, too. Common courtesy to say hello, nice to meet you, Lorena."

Carol remained mum, her Clinique Autumn Russet lips set in a firm line.

"Lookit, Carol." I leaned my elbow on the vanity to convey a false impression of relaxation. "I go where my investigation leads." All the while I was thinking, Stall her. Get the gun from her. This woman's a killer and a really annoying dresser.

"Did you have to go to my daughter?"

"You said you were worried about your daughter being pregnant and—"

"So?" Carol lowered the gun slightly. "My daughter is my business. What does she have to do with Steel trying to frame me?"

"I'm not so sure Steel did try to frame you." I was sliding out of the chair a half an inch at a time. "Because if Steel did, why would you suddenly change your plea from not guilty to manslaughter?" I was now standing. "Why would you essentially send yourself to jail?"

"I didn't send myself to jail. That wasn't in our game plan."

"Game plan?" I took a step forward. "What game plan was this?"

"The one my lawyer drafted. And it would have gotten me out of jail if he hadn't died." Carol took a step back. "That's what you should be concen-

190

trating on, Bubbles. What secret Steel is so afraid of being leaked that its top executives are willing to kill my husband, our lawyer and me to keep it hidden."

"There's a secret?" Lorena slapped the vanity so hard all three of us jumped. "Since when? I didn't know about no so-called secret. You didn't tell me, Bubbles."

"I *did* tell you about it, Lorena," I said low, out of the side of my mouth, "when I called from the courthouse on Monday. You were too preoccupied with Viki Buchanan to listen."

Lorena scratched her head. "I remember Viki Buchanan, but I don't remember anything about a big secret. So why are you spending so much time on Susan Morse?"

Yikes. Shut your big fat trap, Lorena, I wanted to scream.

Carol gaped at Lorena, then at me. "You think Susan Morse killed Hal? Is that what you've been investigating?" The tone of her voice was indignant, as though she were personally insulted that I was not working solely on her tip about Steel.

"Makes sense, Carol." I tried to assess her reaction. Was she startled? Alarmed? Disbelieving? "Your husband was poisoned with cyanide. Susan Morse wrote her thesis on a cyanide producing plant when she was at Two Guys." I took a deep breath. "And your husband was having an affair with her. A hot and heavy one, from what I gather."

Carol's eyes narrowed as she walked toward me,

191

menacingly. "My husband was *not* having an affair with her and we *were* working on our marriage. You're a menace. I want you off this case, Bubbles. I want you to stay away from my daughter, get it? You're fired. And if you so much as knock on Kiera's door again, I will make sure that—"

A hand reached out and hooked the gun from her. "Park it, Betty Crocker." Lorena twirled the gun around her finger, one of the ones with a ripped red nail. "Lorena Ludwig does not put up with being dissed by some bitch who cannot so much as properly introduce herself. What am I, invisible to you people?"

Carol didn't bother to reply. Seeing that the gun was lost, that she had made her point about me staying away, she speared me with a meaningful last glance and ran out of the office. Outside on the corner a car started up, and Lorena and I dashed to the window to see whose it was, but it headed the wrong direction up Fourth.

"Oh, she's on my shit list now," Lorena said, waving the revolver like it was a paper fan. "I don't put up with women who think they're better than other women. You know what I mean? I can't stand that."

"She can't fire me," I said, stunned by the last ten minutes. "I wasn't even hired."

"See, that's the thing with these society chicks." Lorena pointed the gun for emphasis. "Automatically assume the whole world is there to serve them. Take it from me. I'm a caterer. I've got to be nice to them every freaking minute of my freaking working day. All sugar and cream."

I nearly had a heart attack when the barrel appeared inches from my nose. "Mind putting down the Ruger, shortcake?"

"Like it's loaded." Lorena aimed the gun at a Styrofoam wig mannequin and pulled the trigger.

Pow! The redheaded wig zoomed across the room and landed in the sink.

"Whoops." She gingerly placed the gun by Sandy's cash register. "My bad."

It was three hours before I got back to Stiletto's place. To play it safe, Lorena and I called the cops to report that there'd been a Carol Weaver sighting. Two uniformed officers arrived, dropped the gun in a Baggie and interviewed each of us separately.

"How did Carol Weaver know you'd be here, in this salon, at ten-thirty at night?" asked a young cop, Lieutenant Heller, a knockout woman with a cute hair bun who clearly was destined for higher duties than the Lehigh PD.

"Good question. I don't know how she knew." I tapped a broken nail against my teeth. Susan Morse had never showed, but Carol Weaver had. How did that work?

Not being a man, Lieutenant Heller zeroed in on my manicure. "Looks nasty." She pointed her pen at my nail.

"Ripped it."

"All of them?" Her gaze dropped to the floor

and she pushed aside a couple of nail tips with the toe of her boot. "You have some sort of ruckus here?"

"Lorena and I. We kind of got into it. A bit of a misunderstanding."

Lieutenant Heller glanced at Lorena, who was vociferously arguing with Lieutenant Heller's partner. "Old Peanut Butter Legs, eh?"

"Know her?"

"The Muscles of Macungie? Sure."

"Anger management problem?"

"She's got issues with being ignored."

Like this was a news flash.

After the cops left, Lorena and I cleaned up so Sandy wouldn't be too ticked. Lorena tried to patch the bullet hole in the Styrofoam wig head with some chewed Dentyne gum and the filter from one of her Parliaments. The final effect was a big white head that smelled minty fresh and had a wad between the eyes.

Lorena was kind enough to escort me to the *News-Times,* where I wrote a succinct ten-inch story about Carol Weaver's appearance for the midnight late edition deadline. Mr. Salvo read it and sent it upstairs.

"Two stories in one day, that's the way to get a job," he said, rolling back his chair while he waited for the first proofs to come down from composing.

I finished a bag of stale peanuts from the hall vending machines. "Carol Weaver has a mental disorder. I'm coming around to Notch's way of thinking, that following her tip is like falling into a quagmire."

Salvo placed his hands behind his head, his trademark sweat stains glowing yellow on his white shirt. Mr. Salvo should never wear white, not with his complexion. Being a night editor, the guy never saw the light of day because he never had the chance. And when he did have the chance, like being at deer camp, for example, he hid in his darkened tent playing poker and drinking beer.

"Doesn't matter now what Notch thinks," he said. "Graham said at tonight's edit meeting that he wants us to hold space on Sunday for your Weaver exposé. He's hot on this story."

Or for me, I thought, feeling slightly nauseous at the thought.

"Something you want to tell me, Bubbles?"

Mr. Salvo had his reporter face on. The bland what-me-investigating? mask that he had taught us at Two Guys every reporter should employ when asking a particularly probing or personal question.

"Nuh-uh." I crumpled my empty peanut bag.

"Is that cad Stiletto treating you okay?"

He bent down and picked up a piece of scrap paper as a distraction. There was scrap paper scattered all over the newsroom floor, and neither he nor any editor gave a damn because editors as a species are slobs.

Mr. Salvo was just embarrassed about what Stiletto and I might be up to, now that we were

195

living together. For months my boss had been warning me to stay away from his childhood buddy, whom he believed was a chronic womanizer, for fear that I'd be dumped and broken-hearted. Doesn't do much to boost a girl's confidence.

"Stiletto is treating me okay."

"He better. He'll have to answer to me if he doesn't."

The stars were out, twinkling, when I got back to Stiletto's house. It was a brisk November night and the moon was high in the sky. Nice to see a moon and stars so clearly. Back on West Goepp they were usually shrouded in the orange haze of the steel plant.

Nice guy that he is, Stiletto had left the hall light on for me. I quietly dumped my stuff and was about to make my way upstairs when I heard the oddest sound coming from the formal living room. Was it singing?

Peeking in, I found Stiletto half-asleep in an antique oak rocking chair, rocking back and forth, humming Bruce Springsteen's "Dancing in the Dark." The monster Waldo was peacefully zonked on his shoulder.

"I wish I had your camera," I whispered.

Stiletto startled. "Jesus. I didn't hear you come in."

I sat on a chair next to him and patted Waldo's curly head, which still bore traces of dried milk and oatmeal. Waldo sucked on his thumb contentedly. He had the longest lashes.

"He likes The Boss," Stiletto said. "I started with the 'E Street Shuffle' and I didn't get him quiet until 'Born in the USA.'"

"Kid's got commercial taste." It was touching seeing this side of Stiletto: Stiletto the famous, daring international photojournalist comforting an infant like a pro. "Since when are you so good with babies?"

"Since Genevieve threatened to drop-kick him off the second-floor balcony. It was a rescue mission on my part."

"Where's Genevieve now?"

As if to answer, a house-rattling snore emanated from the TV room. "Passed out in front of Jay Leno," he said. "I wouldn't go in there. Not a pretty sight."

I imagined Genevieve's cement-post legs spread wide, revealing her knee-high's curled down, her black rubbers toes up.

We continued to whisper in the dark, like new parents. Stiletto rocked and hummed "Atlantic City," trying not to laugh out loud when I described Lorena's hair-pulling moves on the floor of the House of Beauty. By the time he finished with "Streets of Philadelphia," I had told him every detail about Carol Weaver's visit, how I now believed she was insane and capable of doing violence to stop me from reporting the story.

"Are you?" Stiletto asked. "Going to stop your investigation?"

"Hell no," I said too loudly, causing Waldo to momentarily open one angry eye. "She fired me. She ordered me to stop. You know how that is."

Stiletto nodded. "I wish you had a gun."

"No, thanks. Genetically I can't handle one. All my ancestors who had guns ended up shooting themselves in the foot or the ass."

"The ass?" Stiletto got up slowly. Waldo stirred but did not wake. "How can you shoot yourself in the ass?"

"It's possible," I said, following them up the stairs. "With Yablonskys and guns anything is possible."

We settled Waldo in his baby carrier and stared at him. "Where should we put him?" I whispered. "We can't leave him with Genevieve. Her snores will wake him like that."

"How about at the end of our bed?"

I nearly melted when Stiletto said "our bed." *Our bed.* What a delicious concept.

When I emerged from the bathroom in nothing but my Journey T-shirt, I found Stiletto kneeling, stoking the fire. As he stood, those unbelievable six-pack abs under his unbuttoned shirt caught the reflection of the fire, reawaking that familiar ache in my legs and arms.

My hands wanted to slide over those abs. They wanted to slide under his jeans and over those strong thighs, too. Instead, they gripped the mantel, which was a good thing because my knees seemed to have lost all support, what with Stiletto so near . . . and so near naked.

"Oh, um," he said, taking in the sight of me. "Uh, wow."

We approached each other cautiously and silently, so as not to wake the sleeping infant. It felt incredibly awkward to be making out in front of Waldo, even if he was passed out in baby la-la land. Stiletto neatly hung the poker, took me in his bare arms and kissed me prudishly on the lips, like I was his sister. It wasn't right.

This was not the usual Stiletto. The usual Stiletto would have flung the iron poker aside and taken me right then in front of the fireplace. Up would have gone the Journey shirt; down would have gone the jeans. And God help the beams and rafters if the earth shook under our writhing bodies.

Then again, this was not what you'd call a usual circumstance.

We both eyed Waldo, who let out a yawn. "I hope he sleeps through the night," I said. "What if he cries? What if Genevieve comes up and finds us . . ." I searched for the Italian phrase from that Led Zeppelin song I'd heard once. "In flan grand dictation, or whatever?"

Stiletto smiled, amused. "You mean, in flagrante delicto."

"Yeah," I said, blushing to think Stiletto and I were imaging the same lustful thoughts. "That."

199

He let go of me and nodded. "You're right. We shouldn't risk it."

And with that he slid off his shirt and unzipped his jeans. I tried not to gape, but I couldn't help it. Stiletto was wearing red plaid flannel boxers. They were so adorable, so easy to slide off that I immediately regretted mentioning Waldo.

Maybe we could put him out in the hall.

"Got a preference on which side of the bed?" Stiletto motioned to the large four-poster. "Or maybe I should sleep in the guest bedroom again," he said, getting control of himself. "You know, spending the night next to you . . . I'm not sure I could, you know," he coughed, "hold back."

I took his hand and kissed him lightly on the cheek. "Tomorrow night, Stiletto, really. No Genevieve. No G. And I swear, no Waldo."

His chest heaved a sigh. "It had better be, Bubbles. I'm using every ounce of restraint I have. I don't know how much restraint is left."

"I understand," I said, walking over to the side of the bed nearest the door. "Me, too."

We slid between the sheets. Stiletto held out his arm and I lay my head on his smooth chest. It was nice, awfully nice, the two of us there, side by side. The fire crackling. Waldo whistling tiny baby snores. The November wind blowing outside our window.

Still, the scent of Stiletto's warm body was almost too much to bear. I tried to focus on mundane activities. Registering my car. Follow-up phone calls on the Carol Weaver story. Making sure Jane saw the dentist about her wisdom teeth.

At the thought of Jane, I was transported back to those sleepless first days of my daughter's life when the concept of sex and sexuality seemed as distant as the moon.

"How come it seems like we just skipped five years?" I said, looking up at Stiletto.

But Stiletto, knowing sex was not an option, like most men in his situation had conked out. As for me, I couldn't sleep. Being here with him in the cozy bed was heaven and heaven is something you don't take for granted.

Not when it feels like Stiletto.

CHAPTER 16

I slept in, or at least I thought I slept in, because Waldo and Genevieve were gone when I arrived downstairs at seven dressed fetchingly in a faux brown suede miniskirt and a leopard print top and matching heels. (Eunice had had no influence on me whatsoever.)

My nails were gone, removed by a searing soak in nail polish remover. Underneath, my natural nails were weak and flimsy, hardly deserving of being called nails at all.

Stiletto, in a white oxford shirt and jeans, had his feet up on the gorgeous dining room table, sorting through the boxes of records and taking notes. I saw him and reddened to think how close we'd been the night before.

However, whatever had passed between us hadn't fazed him one bit.

"I forgot to tell you what I found out yesterday," he said, as though we'd just been talking.

I took a plate with a bagel with cream cheese and strawberries Eloise had left for me, along with a cup of coffee, plenty of milk, one sugar. "What's that?"

"Five grams of potassium cyanide went missing from the Mountaintop Lab on February 5 this year." He put down his coffee cup and leaned forward. "And you'll never guess who was in the lab that day."

"Henry Metzger?" I bit into the strawberry. For an out-of-season fruit it was spectacularly juicy.

"No." Stiletto grinned. "Hal Weaver."

"Hal Weaver?" I nearly choked. "How did you find that out?"

"Culled the labs safety logs for February. When I saw the missing potassium cyanide, I matched the dates against the sign-in sheets. Considering that Weaver must have known the protocol, it's as though he wanted to get caught."

Wanted to get caught? I sipped my coffee and thought about this. "What do you think?"

Stiletto leaned back. "How about suicide?"

"He scratched himself to death?"

"Maybe the scratches are unrelated."

Amazing. "Where were the cops on this case? How come they didn't dig up Steel's safety logs?"

"It's the Lehigh PD, Bubbles. Their knees shake when they get to the gates of Steel." Stiletto shrugged. "Besides, overworked prosecutors and cops don't look gift horses in the mouth. If they've got a wife confessing to a murder, especially where there are rumors of divorce and affairs swirling about, they'll take it if they don't see any other obvious suspects."

But there *were* plenty of other suspects,

including an odd one who hadn't attracted my attention so far, but whom I definitely wanted to check out.

"I'm going to try to catch the DA this morning," I said, finishing the last strawberry. "Ask him why Carol Weaver caved."

"Reggie Reinhold's the DA. He's a putz." Stiletto started organizing the papers into a pile. "He gives reporters a hard time, but he might be easy on you. He has a thing for blondes."

"A-ha." And who doesn't? "By the way, sorry about G eating all the caviar. I'll try to repay you."

Stiletto wrapped a rubber band around the papers. "Forget it. He and I discussed it this morning and we worked it out."

"This morning?" I checked my watch. It was seven-fifteen. G is never up before nine. "Where is he?"

"Dan's. Wanted to meet Jane before her big interview."

"Shit." I licked cream cheese off my fingers. "I've got to get over there, fast, before Dan finds out. G's not supposed to be there."

"You'll have to drive fast. He left a half hour ago."

I had turned to go when Stiletto somehow managed to intercept me at the French doors, closing them quietly.

"First I have to ask you something." He leaned close to me. His blue eyes were mesmerizing.

"Uh-oh."

"It's not like that." He cocked his head in that endearing way I so love. "Can I take you out on a date tonight?"

I sucked in a deep breath. "Tonight?"

"If that's okay. I mean," he dropped his arms and shoved his hands into his pockets, "I know you have this big story you're working on and . . ."

"I'd love to." Joy was leaping into my heart. "Where are we going?"

"Let me surprise you. I have only one request."

"What's that?" Anything. Anything to help make it perfect.

"No Waldo."

I turned into Dan's gated development. He was dressed for work in a suit and tie, directing Wendy as she positioned her brand-new yellow Hummer in their driveway so Mr. Wimble wouldn't miss it. I pulled in next to her and parked.

"No, no, no," Dan yelled. "Not your clunker in front of my house. Hold on. What's that crap?"

He read the side of my car, his lips moving like a kindergartner. "Donkey sucking?"

I got out and pointed to the trunk. "Read the back."

Wendy joined him. "Ask me about donkey sucking," she read.

"How's the donkey sucking?" I asked.

Wendy gave me a withering look and then moved her bony body back inside. Ten more minutes in

205

this freezing weather and her fat-free frame would have cracked.

"This is outrageous." Dan kicked my tire. "You can't park that heap here. What if Wimble sees it?"

"Maybe he knows all about donkey sucking, so he won't have to ask, like Wendy." I dropped my keys in my purse. "Maybe he studied it at Princeton."

Dan narrowed his beady, slip-and-fall shyster lawyer eyes at me. "You look like hell. Bar fight?"

"Salon fight. Much dirtier. Harder on the hair."

I headed inside the garage, toward Wendy's kitchen.

"You're not staying, are you?" Dan said, following me.

"I'm here to get G." I opened the door and sniffed. Hmm. No smell of cigarettes *or* dirty socks. Where could the boy be? "G!" I yelled. "Come out from under your rock, G!"

Dan slapped a hand over my mouth. "Shhh. Jane's in my office with Wimble. What the hell do you think you're doing?"

I bit his hand. Hard.

"Owww!" His hand flew off and he muffled a cry of pain into his coat sleeve.

"Stop doing that," I said. "You're always putting your hand over my mouth. I hate it. And how come your hand smells like FDS?"

"Wendy's moisturizer." Dan shook his hand. "G's not here. What makes you think he's coming?"

"That's what he told Stiletto this morning."

"Goddammit! I thought I told you—"

Wendy came around, holding a blue enamel coffeepot. "Would you two keep it down? I can hear everything you're saying." She headed to the office, putting her lips to her fingers as she knocked and entered to refill Wimble's cup.

I could barely see Jane, who appeared tense and artificial in her black dress and pumps. She flashed me a look of "help me!" before Wendy closed the door.

"It's going swimmingly," Wendy reported. "Right before I came in I heard Bo ask Jane what eating clubs she was interested in."

Eating clubs? This Princeton sounded more like a school for Mama. Let's see. There'd be the Meatloaf Club and the Anything-Fried-Please Club. Too Much Vinegary German Food Club, not to mention the Gooey Desserts with Sauces Club and . . .

"Yoo, hoo. Ding dong." Dan was waving his red hand in front of my face. "I have to go to work. You gotta leave."

"No, I'm staying until . . ." I wanted to say, "Until Jane is through with her interview because she looked as scared as hell in there." But instead I said, "Until G comes. I'll need to get him out of here fast, for Jane's sake."

"I'll stay with her," Wendy said, checking her thin, gold Omni watch. "At least until my tennis lesson." Tennis lesson? How many lessons did this

207

woman need? She'd been taking them since age three.

This appeased Dan, who grumbled something about making sure G didn't disrupt the interview. I watched him head out to the garage and mentally flipped him the bird.

"Want some coffee, Bubbles?" Wendy in her white tennis skirt and navy sweater held out the pot in a perky pose that reminded me of June Cleaver. Something was up and it wasn't just her starched collar.

"Thanks," I said, sitting down at the table in her kitchen nook.

Dan and Wendy's house miraculously changed with the seasons. Her kitchen nook windows, white-trimmed and lined with flowers during the summer, were now cozily nestled in sprigged green curtains. An earthenware pot of purple mums graced the table, which was laid out with place-mats and matching napkins in the autumnal colors of orange, brown, red and dark green.

"So, tell me more about this Carol Weaver story you're working on," she said cheerfully, pouring me a half cup of Starbucks French Roast. "Sounds juicy."

Aha, so that was it. Wendy wanted the dirt on Carol, a member of her own social club gone awry.

"That's right. I forgot you knew Carol. Is that why you dropped your drink the other night when I said she was free?"

"I was just shocked that she was out so soon.

She's the only murderer I've ever known personally. Though," Wendy wrinkled her rhinoplastered nose, "as I said, I only know *of* her . . . through Susan."

I tried employing that bland face Mr. Salvo is always encouraging me to use during exciting journalist moments. "Susan Morse?"

"Yup." Wendy sipped her coffee. Was she screwing with me?

"Susan's in my tennis league. And, of course, Chip plays golf with Brian."

I kicked myself under the table for asking Dan so many questions about Carol Weaver and her lawyer. Should have considered that he was part of—correction—*trying to be* part of that high-brow crowd.

"What's Susan like?" Besides good at delivering right hooks.

"Awfully nice. She and Brian make a perfect couple. I'm so glad she found a man she can settle down with."

"You mean after Hal."

Wendy blinked. Barbie doll confusion.

"Hal Weaver," I explained.

"I don't get it." Wendy lowered her cup. "Is there something I'm missing?"

Maybe Wendy was better at this journalistic poker face than I. Nevertheless, I bit. "Susan Morse and Hal Weaver were having an affair."

Wendy pulled all the facial moments appropriate to learning such stunning news about a friend.

Jaw dropped. Brows furrowed. Eyes popped. "That's impossible."

"Impossible? Why?"

Wendy composed herself. "Wait. When did she and Hal have this supposed affair?"

"From what I understand, right up until his death."

"No." Wendy shook her head, her silky short hair not moving an inch. "No. And I'll tell you why. . . ."

The front door opened. "Yo. Jane!"

It wasn't Tarzan, but close. Tarzan was a better dresser. It was G. G with a cigarette between his lips and mud on his boots.

"Chip's going to hit the roof," Wendy whispered. "G is here. He looks white trash."

"Don't tell him. He'll be flattered."

I got up and confronted G at the door before the smoke alarms blew. G was dressed in the exact same clothes as yesterday—black baggy pants, sweatshirt, knitted cap.

"Take your Basic cigarettes outside, G. Wendy's having a hissy fit."

There was a *spzzttt* followed by the smell of artificial spring rain—Wendy already out with the aerosol air freshener.

"No problemo, Mrs. Robinson."

I had to buy me a brain eraser for that boy.

G opened the door, stubbed out the cigarette in yet another pot of mums and proceeded to thoughtfully take off his boots until the foyer filled with the scent of what I can best describe as a load of dead fish from Sea World.

"Keep them on," I said. "We'd all like to breathe."

"Personally I kind of enjoy the smell. Reminds me of a Mickey D's fish sandwich. Man, am I starved."

My stomach retched. "Jane's in Dan's office with Mr. Wimble, so keep your voice down." I nodded to the kitchen. "Come on. There's coffee."

Wendy was back at the table, an autumnal cloth napkin pressed against her nose.

"Hey, Mrs. R." He waved one hand and made a beeline for the Sub Zero. "Got any Coke?"

"What?" Wendy's eyes went like saucers.

"Not that kind of Coke, Wendy," I said, sitting down. "The usual."

"In the bottom drawers." Her voice was so shaky she could have played a bank teller at a stickup.

"Ignore him," I said as G rummaged around the fridge, searching past the roasted red peppers and sun-dried tomatoes, natural pollen, organic miso and vitamins for good old-fashioned Coke. "Why was it impossible for Hal to be having an affair with Susan?"

"Because Susan was dating Brian for a full year before they got married this summer."

"So? Plenty of women fool around before they get married."

"And because she and Carol were, I mean *are*, best friends. They gardened together. The summer before last they took a kayaking cruise around Hawaii." She lowered her voice. "With the Indigo Girls." As though that were meaningful.

I stared blankly.

"There were . . . rumors."

"Rumors?" Call me thick here, but I just wasn't following.

"*Lesbian* rumors."

While I tried to comprehend how a lesbian rumor was different from, say, a heterosexual rumor, Wendy jumped up like a jack-in-the-box and carried her cup to the dishwasher.

"Wow. Olives. Can I eat these?" G held up a jar. "I love olives, man. Hey, you know who loves the Indigo Girls, Mrs. Y? Your daughter. First time I met Jane she was on her way to an Indigo Girl concert at Musikfest and I thought, wow, that chick is hot. Too bad she doesn't go for guys."

He sucked the pimento out of an olive. "Later Jane explained that just because the Indigo Girls were gay, doesn't mean their fans are. Or, at least some of their fans aren't."

Now I understood. Carol Weaver and Susan Morse were . . . Oh my God!

Ladies and gentlemen of the jury, may I present one stunned and very, very dense Bubbles Yablonsky. How had I been so stupid? Of course, it all made sense. More sense, in fact, than Hal having an affair.

Susan wasn't at the court hearings because of Hal; she was there to support Carol. Angie the court clerk had just assumed that Susan, besotted with love, was there for a man, and assumed wrong. Susan was so close to Carol that she was even acting as a surrogate grandmother-to-be and throwing a baby shower for Kiera.

Pieces were clicking together like pink foam snap-on curlers. That's why Carol and Hal had separate bedrooms. And why Hal was seeking a divorce. And why Kiera hated her mother.

Because Hal wasn't having the affair, Carol was.

And *that's* why Carol showed up at the House of Beauty the night before. Because Susan Morse was Carol Weaver's accomplice.

Whoa. I sat back and stared absently as Wendy got ready for her tennis lesson. Whoa, did I miss the boat.

Unless, I thought, my mind scheming, unless Susan's romance with Carol was a fraud.

Don't forget, the nagging voice in the back of my brain said, that Brian Morse ended up with everything Hal Weaver had. Including his woman.

Isn't that what Eunice said? Or had *I* planted the notion in Eunice's mind that Susan was Hal Weaver's mistress. Wait. We talked about Susan, but only in the context of her being Brian Morse's second wife. Or had we discussed more? Damn, why didn't I take notes?

I needed to call Eunice. Needed to call her right away.

"I'm going," Wendy said, coating her lips with

fresh clear gloss. "I assume you'll take care of you . . . know . . . who."

"Who?" asked G, an olive on each stubby finger.

"You," I said.

Wendy gave him a disgusted look and left, her Hummer zipping down the road in a blur.

"Hand me that phone book, G." I pointed to the big yellow thing on the table.

"Where?" G scanned the room.

"There. Right in front of you."

"Oh." G picked it up and carried it over to me with his olive-free fingers. "I never use phone books. Just information."

At one dollar fifty a pop on my bill, I bet. I found a Eunice Morse on South Mountain and opened up my cell phone. I dialed and waited for Eunice to pick up.

"You know what I don't understand?" G bit into a green olive and examined the middle. "Is who came up with the sucky idea of putting these red things in the middle of olives."

"Pimentos?"

G peered at the pimento. "Pimentos? Are those a kind of fruit or something?"

"Pimentos are peppers."

Eunice's phone rang and rang. I checked my watch, eight-fifteen on a Wednesday morning. She had no job that I knew of. Wouldn't she be home at this hour?

G went over to the sink and spit it out. "I don't do vegetables."

214

Eunice must have been out for a walk or some equally earth-mother activity. I hung up, wrote down the number in pen on the palm of my hand and returned the book.

"Well, looky here." G pointed an olive-adorned finger toward a metal box hidden in the middle of Wendy's healthful cookbooks. It was no bigger than a powder compact. "I haven't seen one of these in years."

A strange feeling came over me, a sense honed after years of living with a man whom I put through law school only to have him dump me when he reached success.

"What is it?" I stooped to inspect it.

"It's a spy-cam. They had them all over juvy hall when I was there."

"A Minicam? Why did they . . ." Hold on. I punched him on the shoulder. "Jane never told me you were in juvy hall."

G swallowed an olive. "That's because Jane doesn't know."

One of those old-fashioned trusting relationships. G pushed a button and a tiny screen lit up. Jane and Bo Wimble appeared in miniature. Jane was pale, stricken. Bo was taking notes in a leather binder. Whoever dressed him in a blinding green pullover and plaid pants should be arrested for abuse.

"Sweet." G sucked off an olive from his pinky. "LCD. Looks like your old, old man is doing some pretty expensive surveillance."

Dan that rat. He promised he was going to let Jane be an adult on her own. This wasn't fair. Especially since I couldn't hear what was going on.

"Where's the volume?"

G turned a tiny dial. Bo Wimble's lock-jawed voice came out whiny and high-pitched.

"To explain further," Bo was saying, closing the binder, "getting into an Ivy League university has never been more competitive. As you may have read, Princeton was recently rated the most desired school in the country, even over Harvard."

Jane nodded stiffly. Why did she look like she was about to cry?

G turned it down. "Isn't this unethical or something?"

"I admire the good intentions. Now crank it." G cranked it.

"You can't blame yourself that we at Princeton feel you would be more comfortable at another institution. Perhaps a state school. Princeton is, after all, the cream of the cream."

A bubble of heat rose inside me. He was rejecting her. My straight-A, nearly perfect SATs, takes-courses-at-Lehigh-University genius of a daughter. This was the big blow-off and it was only November. Applications weren't due for another two weeks.

"Comfortable?" Jane said, straightening. "What do you mean, comfortable?"

Thatta girl. Make him squirm.

Bo let out good ol' boy chuckle. "It's not a state-ment I would like repeated, but we are alone."

"That's what he thinks," G said.

"I'll give it to you straight."

G scoffed. "That wanker couldn't get his dick straight."

"In the upcoming Princeton class we will have students entering from Andover and Exeter, Choate, Taft, Milton and Hotchkiss."

Was that supposed to mean something?

"Their education has been of the highest caliber," Wimble continued. "Of course we take many students from public schools, schools almost as excellent as the preps. Bronx Science. Berkley. Newton."

"But not Liberty," Jane said dryly.

"Not Liberty." Bo shook his head. "Not without being a prodigy."

"Hey." G raised his hand. "I'm a prodigy."

"And while your SAT scores are excellent, your extracurricular studies certainly a plus, your course work counts for zero. It's Liberty High School in Lehigh, Pennsylvania, the grades are inflated, the teachers are poorly trained and the class sizes are too big. I can't even compare your grades to other applicants."

I was too angered to answer. Liberty had been the best education I had been able to offer her and Jane had grabbed every opportunity and then some. There is no greater failure a parent feels than knowing she has let her child down.

And no greater pain than watching her get hurt.

"I'm going in there," I said.

G clutched my arm. "Mrs. Y, no. You go in there and you'll blow it for Jane. Let the wanker shoot his wad and Jane can do another interview."

"There is no other interview." I shook off his hand. "This is it."

Marching toward Dan's office, I threw open the door. Jane and Bo were shaking hands and startled to see me. Jane looked more tired than sad.

"Just who the hell do you think you are, you plaid-panted windbag?" I said to Bo. He was a hair shorter than I (though that might have been because my hair was higher than his) and puffy white. He was only in his late forties, but half glasses sat on his nose.

"And you are?" There was a distinctly patronizing air to his question.

"I'm Bubbles Yablonsky. Jane's mother."

"Ah, yes." He patted his leather binder. "The hairdresser. As I told Jane, that could work in her favor. Princeton likes to gather students from different backgrounds."

"Work in her favor?" I looked from Jane to Bo and back to Jane, who was sending red hot rays of "What the heck are you doing?" from her tragically unmade-up eyes. "What works in her favor when you've already told her she's not good enough for your fancy dancy college?"

Bo lowered his glasses. "Pardon?"

"Don't pardon me." I got close enough to see

the gin blossoms that crisscrossed his nose. "I heard every word you said about how Liberty wasn't as good as Choate and Kiss-off."

"Hotchkiss."

"Whatever. The point is you have no business rejecting her because she couldn't help going to Liberty. She had no other choice and she made the best of it. You are a mean, mean," I poked his green-sweatered chest, "mean man."

"Mommm!" Jane collapsed in Dan's leather wing chair and covered her face.

"How did you hear this?" Bo looked over my shoulder as G came in. "Did you have your ear to the door?"

"Jane's dad's got a spy cam!" G announced proudly.

"Ohhh," Jane moaned.

"I see." Bo Wimble pushed up his glasses. "For your information, Miss Yablonsky, I was recounting for Jane a particularly painful Princeton interview in which the student was initially rejected simply because he attended Liberty High School." He paused. "Mine."

"Yours?" I felt all eyes on me. "Yours?"

"Oh, shit." G doubled over in a belly laugh. "Excellent, Mrs. Robinson. Beeeautiful."

Complete embarrassment swept over me. What a fool I'd been. What a snooping, impulsive idiot. I looked over to Jane. All that hard work for four years to get into her dream school and I had blown it with my big, big mouth.

"I am so sorry." I bowed my head. "Please forgive me."

Bo put his hand on my shoulder. "I'm a parent, too. I understand your frustration. Though may I recommend you save your surveillance for that guy." He jerked his chin toward G. "He looks like he'd walk out with the family silver."

He smiled warmly, patted me again, and left the room.

"There's silver here?" G said. "Sweet."

CHAPTER 17

Mama once told me that all parents should sit their children down when they turn twenty-one and apologize for everything. It doesn't matter if you were a drug addict while they were growing up or you simply forgot to attend a school play. As parents, we will eventually fail our kids. It's human nature.

And, as Mama says, if we didn't fail them, consider the horrific alternative: they'd never leave home.

Jane forgave me, or so she claimed, after I apologized all the way from Dan's house to the steps of Liberty. G, who left for his job at Hess's, helped by erasing part of the tape so Dan wouldn't see my embarrassing entrance. Another trick he had learned at "juvy hall."

After dropping off Jane, I headed straight for the Court of Common Pleas to find the D.A. Reggie Reinhold, aka The Putz. Reinhold, the security guard told me, was probably already in court on a DUI injury resulting trial—another ongoing news story of which I would have been thoroughly familiar if I bothered to read the paper.

Peeking through a window in the padded court-room doors, I saw a curly haired man in glasses using a large pointer and a diagram of a traffic intersection to illustrate how the defendant's car zoomed through a stop sign and plowed into a crossing car. The judge yawned, two jurors looked like they could really use the bathroom, and it was a little past ten.

A break was imminent.

In the meantime I called Mickey Sinkler from a pay phone in the hall. It didn't reek too much of lawyer cologne, more like guilty defendant sweat. Yuck.

"Another rumble I hear," the wiseass Sinkler said, "this time down at the House of Beauty. What's gotten into you?"

"Lorena 'Peanut Butter Legs' Ludwig."

"Ah, yes. The Muscles from Macungie."

"The Muscles from Macungie. That's what Lieutenant Heller called her. Say, there's a babe. How come you don't date her?"

I heard Mickey close his door. "Because I never date coworkers, that's why."

"And that's why you never date."

"Is there a point to this call, or are you bored because you can't find anyone to take out?"

"I'm calling to find out if Carol Weaver confessed."

"Indeed she did. You were right. Carol claimed she killed her husband in a fit of passion, that she was out of her mind due to stress over her failing marriage and wasn't in her senses. That's why they let her cop to the manslaughter." Mickey's delivery was short, to the point.

There was a rumbling from inside the courtroom and a faint "All rise." Break time had arrived.

"Listen, Mickey, I know this isn't your case or anything, but I have a suspicion that a woman named Susan Morse may be Carol Weaver's accomplice."

"Damn, Bubbles. If you know that, you should have called me right away. I could pick up Weaver and get a huge job promotion. She's been out of the Jakeville for four days. She's made a fool out of the entire department."

"Not so fast."

The doors opened and spectators were coming out, retrieving packs of cigarettes and heading toward the pay phones to check their messages.

I lowered my voice. "Susan Morse is Brian Morse's wife. Brian Morse is the head flak at Steel."

Mickey's grunt of disappointment spoke volumes. Steel executives and their wives got kid-glove treatment in Lehigh. It was a fact of life. Which meant that before Mickey rushed in and searched the spotless home of Susan Morse, M.R.S., he would have to be assured beyond a speck of doubt that Carol was there.

"I will promise to turn over to you any evidence I find if you can sniff around the department and dig up proof that Susan Morse and Carol Weaver were lesbian lovers."

"Lesbian lovers!" Mickey shouted. "Oh, no. You've been watching *All My Children* again, haven't you? Bubbles, I've told you to stay away from the soaps. With a sponge brain like yours they're toxic."

Reinhold appeared, straightening his tie and talking earnestly to what I took to be an assistant D.A. He carefully avoided the defendant's family, a ragtag bunch who sucked on cigarettes in the smoking area as they sneered at him with uniform loathing.

"Gotta go, Mickey. Trust me." And I hung up.

"About time," said a woman behind me. "There are only three phones, you know."

I dashed after Reinhold, who was bending over the water fountain, holding his tie to keep it from getting wet. Pulling out my Reporter's Notebook, I introduced myself as Bubbles Yablonsky, Lehigh *News-Times* reporter, doing a story on Carol Weaver's escape.

Reinhold stood and took me in. I could see that he was making a snap judgment about whether to take me seriously. And if this was my natural hair color.

"Isn't Lawless doing that story? He's been calling my office all week. I've been so swamped with this trial I haven't had a chance to return his messages."

"That's the difference between Lawless and me," I said. "I get my ass over here."

Reinhold didn't blink, but his assistant smiled.

"I've only a few minutes, so give me your best shot," he said.

I bit my lip. If I had one question to ask, what would it be? "Why did you let Carol Weaver cop to a manslaughter plea?"

Reinhold observed that I was ready to take notes and chose his words carefully. "As was stated during her sentencing, Carol Weaver confessed to poisoning her husband in a fit of rage, which may have been partly fueled by alcohol. Manslaughter was clearly merited by the case law." He gave me a look that said, Well, *that* was a stupid question.

Of course it was. Mickey had just told me all that. I must have gotten up on the moron side of the bed this morning.

The bailiff poked his head out. "Two minutes."

"I really have to go," said Reinhold, like a celebrity tired from signing autographs. He started moving toward the padded doors.

"Let me clarify that last question." I hurried to keep up with him. "Why did you let Carol cop to the plea when you"—I took a risk here—"*knew* that there were other suspects?"

Reinhold stopped. "Miss whatever your name is, perhaps you didn't understand my previous answer. Carol Weaver confessed—"

"To protect her lesbian lover," I interrupted.

The assistant raised an eyebrow.

Reinhold shot his cuffs. "Make an appointment. This trial should be over by next week. Then we can talk. I'm too busy to explain the case to you now." And he went into the courtroom, leaving me alone with the assistant D.A.

Now the assistant D.A. was by far better looking than Reinhold. He was taller, which never hurts in a man, blond and had the trustworthy demeanor of a lifeguard accustomed to rescuing babies from pools and old ladies from nipping dogs. He was the kind of guy a jury would believe.

The kind of guy voters would elect to be the next D.A.

The kind of guy who knew that, too. Including the nasty truth that bad press for his boss might help him down the road.

"You're Chip Ritter's wife, aren't you?" he said.

"Ex-wife," I corrected. Still, I was impressed. Since when had Dan been talking about me to the boys in the Bar?

"Can you keep this on the QT?"

I closed my notebook to show that I could.

He checked the doors and then pulled me aside. "The office screwed up on this one. The evidence against Weaver was flimsy and Reinhold figured for sure he'd lose the trial. He was worried that the papers would say he's easy on the white-collar crowd, hard on the working class."

Made sense to me.

"So he panicked and took Weaver's plea even though our own investigator had doubts. Thought she was covering for someone else."

"Susan?" I suggested.

226

"That's a new one on me, but it's worth a try."
He stuck out his hand. "Hope that helps. Nice to
meet you."

"Nice to meet you . . .?"

"George Thomas." He winked a wink that said
we'd meet again—most likely on next November's
ballot.

It was a glorious day. The sun was out. The sky
was blue and the air was refreshingly cold. I zipped
up the fake rabbit fur and made my way to the
Donkey Sucking Mobile. I was close to cracking
this case . . . and not just any case.

The case that would get me a job where every
day I could stroll around Common Pleas, where
Reinhold would have to talk to me because I was
the official cops-and-courts reporter. Police would
know me by name and, for once, in a legitimate
way.

Oh, the stories I'd write, I thought as I opened
the Camaro. Art thefts and jewelry heists, murders
of passion and tragic tales of child abuse. I
wouldn't just write the bare, dull basics, like
Lawless does, I'd get to the meat of the matter.
I'd write about the stories behind the stories. I'd
write about the people.

Why the victim didn't run. Why the beaten wife
stayed. Why parents neglected their children and
husbands ran out on their families.

Courthouses were brimming with dramas played
out in glaring, black-and-white reality. I'll never

forget the reckless driving trial I attended when I was a student in Mr. Salvo's Two Guys course and saw the defendant, who had just been pronounced guilty, being led off to jail.

He's going there and he has no choice, I remembered thinking as the defendant caught one last glimpse of his sobbing wife at the back of the courtroom. No windows. Metal bars. Cement floors and eight-foot cells. Screaming inmates and hard cots. That's where he'd be for six months.

I shivered. Reality TV had nothing on the Court of Common Pleas.

Before I confronted Susan, however, I needed to check one last time with Eunice. Eunice could provide important details about Susan's relationship with Carol. I read the number off my hand and dialed, all the while taking the hairpin turns on Route 22.

Eunice's phone rang and rang. Not even an answering machine. I was blithely letting it ring when a loud beep sounded in my ear, nearly causing me to jump the Jersey barrier.

"Incoming call" the message said on the screen.

Incoming. Incoming. I didn't know what to do, so I hung up. *The 1812 Overture* blared.

"Hello?"

"Where are you, Bubbles?" Mr. Salvo again.

"I'm coming back from the Court of Common Pleas. You'll never believe what I found out. Carol Weaver and Susan Morse are lesbian lovers. I think

Carol is covering for Susan and that she came to me with this bogus Lehigh Steel conspiracy claim so she could deflect suspicion onto Steel and get the heat off both her and her lover."

Mr. Salvo didn't say anything. "You done?"

"Isn't that wild?" I slammed on the brakes to avoid rear-ending a Wise Potato Chip truck. "I'm going to visit Brian Morse's ex-wife now and run this past her, see if she knows anything about Susan and Carol. Then I'm going to go over to Susan's house, snoop around if I can, to find if Carol's there."

"No, you're not."

I slumped. "You're not going to squeal to Notch about my trespassing, are you? I promise I won't trespass much. Just a little."

"First of all, it sounds to me like you're going on nothing but your sob-sister mind. So what if Susan and Carol were lovers? Why do you think Susan killed Hal Weaver? What evidence do you have?"

I turned off onto Center Street and took a left under the highway, pulling into the empty parking lot of a restaurant by the Monocacy. Mr. Salvo was right. What evidence did I have?

"Well," I said slowly, "the assistant D.A. told me off the record that the investigator in the office thought Carol was covering for someone else. He said Reinhold rushed to accept Carol's plea bargain so that he wouldn't lose the case."

"This was Thomas who told you that?"

229

"Uh-huh."

"Ambitious twit. It was off the record, right?"

My heart was sinking from its ebullient state just minutes before. "Yes."

"And he didn't say *who* Carol was covering for."

"No."

"In fact, you don't even know for sure that Carol and Susan are lovers."

"But they went on a cruise," I whined, "with the Indigo Girls."

"I don't care if they hiked the hills of San Francisco with the Village People. A week on the water does not a lesbian murder pact make. Put aside this Carol Weaver case, Bubbles. I want you to get over to the Evergreen Senior Center in Whitehall."

No way, I thought, not the Evergreen. The last story I did at the Evergreen had been about abused racing greyhounds being adopted as pets for the elderly. Before those dogs, I had never encountered a more flatulent animal in my life. Besides Dan.

"Irene Stucklyn is celebrating her one hundred and eighth birthday." It sounded like Mr. Salvo was reading from a press release. "She is Lehigh's oldest living resident. They're having a birthday party for her at noon and I'd like you to cover it. Nice, easy human interest piece about ten inches or so. A photographer's already taken her photo, so . . ."

"Uh, Mr. Salvo?"

"Don't give me a hard time with this, Bubbles. You're still a rookie, kind of."

"It's not about that." I couldn't take my eyes off the rearview mirror. "I'm being followed."

I fumbled for a lipstick I keep in a case by the stick shift, cradled the phone against my shoulder and tried to pretend like I was chatting and making up my lips.

"You sure you're being followed?" Mr. Salvo and I had been through this routine before. He knew to take me seriously.

"I didn't take any notice of him when I was on 22. It's kind of a nondescript car. He pulled in behind me at the Appletree. There's no other car here. Now that I think of it, he's been on my tail since the courthouse."

There was the sound of paper on Mr. Salvo's end. "Give me the description."

"A navy blue sedan. License plate." Geesh, this was going to be tough, reading letters and numbers inside out in the rearview. "LSC 387 hyphen 6."

"That's a Lehigh Steel corporate car. They all begin LSC. For Lehigh Steel Corporation."

"There's a man sitting in it. A blockhead type. Might be the same dude I saw at Two Guys."

"Two Guys?"

I told him about finding the suit fooling around with my Camaro. "Stiletto found a tracking device in my right wheel well, no bigger than an earring. A BFD I think it was."

"RFD, Bubbles."

"Whatever. Stiletto's having it checked out, to see if it belongs to Steel."

"What do you want to do?"

Before I could answer, the blue sedan started up with a loud roar and peeled out past me, kicking up dust and gravel. It was a Crown Victoria, the same model I'd seen at Two Guys.

As he turned left onto Center and then up the exit to 22, the driver gave me one quick look. He wore sunglasses and his hair was short. Federal agent, I was thinking.

"That him?" Mr. Salvo asked.

"That's him. He's gone. East on 22."

"I'm going to call the cops, see if they can check him out. In the meantime," he said, not giving me so much as an inch, "get your tracked butt over to the Evergreen. You wait a minute more and Irene Stucklyn might be unavailable for comment. Permanently."

CHAPTER 18

The Evergreen was a much improved institution from my last visit, especially with the flatulent greyhounds gone. Like most nursing homes it gleamed with white linoleum and reeked of that odd half urine/half Sanibac odor.

And, like most other nursing homes, everyone yelled.

"How are you feeling, Mrs. Stucklyn?" a nurse hollered in Mrs. Stucklyn's ear.

"This is quite a day," a volunteer screamed. *"The mayor's coming!"*

Mrs. Stucklyn, dehydrated and withered like a dried apple, smiled her toothless smile as she was wheeled into the linoleum reception room. The orchid corsage was bigger than her chest and some goof had had the bright idea to put a purple paper crown on her head.

The nursing home director, a Miss Anne, hovered about me anxiously, fearing, I suppose, that as a reporter I might sneak down the hall and search for state violations. (Aha! Not enough Depends. I thought as much.) However, it occurred to me later that Miss Anne had concerns that a bleached-blond tryout might need help with a difficult story like a birthday party.

"Mrs. Stucklyn remembers the first movie theater coming to Lehigh," Miss Anne coached. *"Isn't that right, Mrs. Stucklyn?"*

Mrs. Stucklyn smiled and snapped her gums, her eyes fixated on the three-tier, pink-frosted birthday cake.

"No, no, no," said Miss Anne sadly. "That's for the staff and guests. You get pudding. You love pudding, don't you? Vanilla. It's your favorite."

Mrs. Stucklyn frowned.

"Pudding!" Miss Anne said louder, clapping. *"We love pudding!"*

"Pink cake," said the birthday girl, her first words of the party. "I want pink cake."

Miss Anne rubbed her middle. *"It's bad for our tummy. Remember?"*

"I don't give a flying fig about your tummy." Mrs. Stucklyn pointed to the cake. "I want that."

The staff and Miss Anne forced laughs to show what a crazy old dame Mrs. Stucklyn was that she would want cake on the last birthday of her life. I knelt beside her and said, "Maybe I can get you cake."

"You can?" Her faded blue eyes peered into mine, not really seeing.

"I'm Bubbles Yablonsky, a reporter from the paper. I'm here to do a story."

"A reporter?" She cupped her hand to her ear. "Did you say reporter?"

"Yes. Reporter." I refused to yell.

"I thought you said hooker."

I was tempted to give Mrs. Stucklyn a little birthday pinch for being such a card. "How did you live to be so old?"

"Everyone asks me that and I haven't a clue." She glanced around the room. "I know. Cake."

I wrote this down. I needed a lead and I wasn't sure cake would do it.

"Clean living?" I suggested. "Didn't drink. Didn't smoke. Lots of veggies and exercise. Was that it?"

Mrs. Stucklyn moved one shoulder in a half shrug. "Took long walks, that was it. Me and Joe."

Finally we were getting somewhere.

"*Who's Joe?*" Miss Anne demanded like an army sergeant.

Tears sprung to Mrs. Stucklyn's eyes. "My husband. He died . . ." She bit a nail and looked down. "He died. . . ."

"*1958!*" bellowed a nurse, the captain of the wheelchair. "*We visited his grave yesterday, remember?*"

"Joe," said Mrs. Stucklyn, wringing the bib in her lap. "Joe and I went for long walks."

I patted her hand, which was as soft as Waldo's. Aging sucked and losing people you loved was even suckier. As God would have it, the two went together. The older you got, the more loved ones you collected and then lost. Who came up with that brilliant scheme?

"Where would you go for walks?"

"That park. The park Joe built." She looked up at her nurse. "What's that park?"

"*Illick's Mill,*" the nurse replied full volume. "*Joe was in the WPA. You told me that yesterday.*"

Illick's Mill was one of those overbuilt parks ordered by President Roosevelt to give out-of-work laborers jobs during the Depression. Stiletto and I had found a dead body there once. Good times. Good times.

Which made me think of our date tonight and his promise to walk me through sex. My pulse raced. I blinked back to reality. Mrs. Stucklyn was staring at me.

"Where's my cake?" she said.

"It's coming." I wrote down Illick's Mill. "Was the Depression hard?"

"Awful. We were so poor. Joe and I had four kids to raise." She gripped my hand. "Do you know that they're all passed on. Two died from polio and Joe Junior, he drowned in the quarry. On the day he graduated from high school."

I felt my heart twist like the bib in Mrs. Stucklyn's lap. "And your other child?"

Miss Anne whispered in my ear. "You're upsetting her."

"No, she's not," protested Mrs. Stucklyn who, contrary to common knowledge, possessed radar-like hearing. "She was my only daughter. Bettina. Died in childbirth in 1955. It's what killed her father. He loved her so."

How had this woman survived to be 108? I would have checked out after the first polio case.

"How did you . . . overcome those tragedies?"

Miss Anne let out a long, irritated sigh. This was not birthday fun. Mrs. Stucklyn would definitely not agree to pudding after this.

"Joe and I would walk," she said, repeating herself. "We walked in that park and up the creek."

"Up the creek." I made a note. "Up the Monocacy?"

She smiled. "We took long walks."

Up the Monocacy. The other side of my brain, the side that was usually up all night culling over the Carol Weaver files and thinking about alternative angles, messaged over a question to the side of my brain interviewing Mrs. Stucklyn.

"Did you ever hear about a tunnel leading from the cave off the Monocacy?"

Mrs. Stucklyn might not have been able to immediately recall the date her husband died, but she didn't take a half second to answer about the cave. "I wouldn't go in it. Too scared."

"No?"

"Oh!" Miss Anne started clapping again. "It's birthday cake time!"

"Birthday cake?" Mrs. Stucklyn brightened.

"Pudding," Miss Anne checked herself.

"Do you know where the tunnel leads?" I asked quickly, now treating the fragile old lady with the same brusque interrogation I'd used with the district attorney.

237

"Went downtown someplace. They blew it up. In the twenties, because kids were getting lost in it. I was too scared." Mrs. Stucklyn rubbed her arms, her blue eyes widening with fright. "Too scared to go in."

"That's quite enough." Miss Anne took over the chair. "Thank you, Bubbles, I look forward to reading your story tomorrow." And with a nod to a nurse, I was helped up and escorted to the door.

Only to wonder if Mrs. Stucklyn would ever have her cake and eat it, too.

No nondescript navy Crown Victoria followed me from the Evergreen, down the spur route to the South Side of Lehigh. I parked in the *News-Times* lot, and aside from the curious bystanders who were drawn to read the Donkey Sucking graffiti, no one else bothered my car. I was getting used to the gaping onlookers. It wasn't so bad having a Donkey Sucking Mobile after all. There could be worse vehicles. Like a hearse.

It was around one-thirty. I was starving but determined to write the story before Mr. Graham got back from lunch. Mr. Graham took long lunches, often with local businessmen, to drum up advertising.

At the Henny Penny on Second Street, I grabbed a tuna salad, a bag of chips, a Diet Pepsi and a slice of angel food cake for Mrs. Stucklyn. Walked past the lot and glanced at my car, which sat worry free in its same old spot.

Maybe I had jumped to conclusions. Weren't there Lehigh Steel corporate cars all over town? Absolutely. Wasn't it reasonable that a businessman on a cell phone had pulled off the highway to the nearest lot as I had to take a phone call? You bet.

So what was I so skittish about?

Dying. That was what I was skittish about.

It took me no more than an hour to write up the bittersweet celebration of Mrs. Stucklyn's 108th. I made a personal promise to deliver the cake to her as soon as I was out of there and before I visited Eunice.

I had sent the story over to Mr. Salvo and was dialing Stiletto's cell phone when I suddenly felt woozy from the intoxicating scents of lime and vodka.

"Hello, Bubbles." Mr. Graham stood over me. He was in a Hugo Boss charcoal pin-striped suit and his gray-striped tie was slightly askew. His gray hair looked white against his flushed face.

I hung up. "Yes, Mr. Graham?"

"See me in my office. I want to discuss the Carol Weaver story. Tony Salvo told me what happened this morning and," he sniffed, "it needs to be dealt with."

I got up to follow him, taking my purse and Reporter's Notebook with me.

"Hey, Yablonsky." Mr. Salvo was eating coleslaw out of a plastic cup and motioned for me to come over to his desk.

His desk, for the record, was a cluttered mess facing the copy editors' U in the middle of the newsroom. It was piled with newspapers, white layout sheets, assorted paper coffee cups and rubber bands. We could use it as a bonfire on a cold day.

I pointed at Mr. Graham. "I've got to . . ."

"Come here." Mr. Salvo waved more insistently.

When I got there, he said, "What does Graham want?"

"To talk about the Carol Weaver case."

He dropped his glance to my legs. "Lower your skirt."

Looking around to see no one was checking, I tugged on the hem. "What's wrong?"

"Three vodka gimlets at the Union Club, that's what's wrong." Mr. Salvo forked out another helping of coleslaw and went back to reading the *Morning Call*. "Sit two chairs away from him and don't make eye contact."

Ay, yi, yi. So it hadn't been my imagination that Mr. Graham had been coming on to me.

Lois, Mr. Graham's secretary, was still on lunch break, her gray plastic cover neatly over her IBM Selectric, a dinosaur she and perhaps two other people on Earth still used.

The air seemed purer up here on the wood-paneled fourth floor, home to the publisher and vice presidents in charge of sales and marketing. There were fresh cut flowers in vases, the aroma of freshly brewed coffee, thick cream carpeting on the floor and butt ugly oil paintings of past publishers and vice presidents trying to look impressive for generations who didn't know them and who wouldn't care, either.

Downstairs in the newsroom we reporters got flickering neon lights, vending machine cardboard-flavored food and cracked linoleum. No wonder reporters taped dimes to their computers. The message from on high was clear: reporters were a dime a dozen.

Mr. Graham's door was slightly ajar. I knocked.

"Come in, Bubbles."

He was at his desk and working. Heeding Mr. Salvo's advice, I chose a hard wooden chair next to a far table and sat down.

"Why are you sitting all the way over there?" He put down his pen and smiled at me broadly.

I swallowed and tried to think of the most reasonable answer. "This chair suits my back. My back is killing me."

"With those heels, I don't doubt it. I can take care of that."

Oh, no. Massage!

But all Mr. Graham did was move my chair near a big leather one in which he conveniently settled himself. My chair was higher than his, putting my thighs at his eye level. I was glad I'd taken Mama's advice and decided to wear underpants for once. (That's a joke. I always wear underpants. Of course!)

"What's this I hear about you being followed?"

I blathered about the navy blue Lehigh Steel car

and how I wasn't sure if the driver had actually been following-me following me. Or if he happened, as I had, to get off at the exit and make a call on his cell phone.

"Aha." Mr. Graham kept his rheumy eyes squarely at non-sexual-harassment level. "And have you uncovered any more evidence that Carol Weaver was right about there being a Steel conspiracy?"

He really wasn't being gross at all. Just politely and professionally concerned about my well-being. I scolded myself for not being more grateful to be receiving special attention from the publisher.

"Uhm, lately I've changed gears. I'm thinking maybe Carol Weaver had an affair with Susan Morse, who used to be a secretary at Steel and who's now married to Brian Morse, a steel vice president."

"I know Brian," he said. "He plays golf down at the country club."

I was beginning to wonder if Brian did anything else.

"I never heard about Susan being a lesbian, though. Are you sure you're not focusing on her personal life because of the fight at the historical society?"

"The historical society fight had nothing to do with it."

Mr. Graham brushed lint off his knee. "A lesbian affair seems rather tabloid, don't you think?"

I could understand why Mr. Graham might be

reluctant to run a kinky story about homicidal soccer moms in love on page one of the Sunday *News-Times*. But, like they taught us at Two Guys, facts was facts.

"Susan did study the cassava root at Two Guys," I pointed out. "The cassava is filled with cyanide. Cyanide is what killed Hal Weaver."

"Yes, I know." You ditz brain, he might as well have added. "I'm much more interested, though, in Carol Weaver's original assertion, the assertion that started this investigation. My question for you is, is there any indication that Steel had Hal Weaver eliminated simply to hide some wrongdoing? And, if so, what was this so-called wrongdoing?"

A drowning sensation came over me. In the three days I'd worked on this story, the closest I'd come to implicating Steel was a far-fetched fantasy that I was being followed by a corporate car. Other than that, I'd turned up nothing to even hint that Steel had engaged in any mischief, or that Hal Weaver himself had discovered a secret.

What I had found out was that Carol Weaver's daughter, Kiera, thought the world of her dad and that, from the looks of the unkempt lawn and flower boxes, Kiera and her slackjawed boyfriend would probably run the family home into the ground. I knew that Susan Morse liked to throw a punch and that she and Carol went on a cruise with the Indigo Girls.

Geesh. I had nothing. Absolutely nothing to show for all my work.

"Why don't you write the story as far as you've got it," Mr. Graham said impatiently. "Print it out and I'll take it home with me to review tonight."

A surge of anxiety ripped right through me. "Write the story? But I'm not done. Not even close."

"Not even close?" Mr. Graham furrowed his brows. "Bubbles. You've had three full days to work on this. That's more than most of the veterans on the staff get to do a Sunday takeout.

"But . . ."

He held up a finger. "I would expect from them, and from you, a first draft by noon on Thursday. Final draft by six p.m., giving Salvo most of Friday to edit it and you time to make follow-up phone calls and implement any changes he suggests."

Impossible. It was impossible to have a first draft done by Thursday.

"Want me to ask Lawless to give you a hand?" he asked cruelly.

The hairs on my arm—at least the ones I hadn't had waxed—rose in fury. Lawless? I wasn't about to work with a fat, lazy slouch who had screwed me every step of the way.

"Lawless could run the Steel angle for you," Mr. Graham continued. "It sounds sexist, but from my experience Steel executives respond better to men than women, and from what I've heard from you so far, you haven't even scratched the surface over there."

I scanned my research to produce any evidence that might show I had scratched.

"There was cyanide missing from Steel," I said quickly. "Right before Weaver was murdered. On February 5. And the day it disappeared from the Mountaintop Lab Hal Weaver had signed himself in and out."

Graham sat back and rested his chin against his two fingertips. "Why would Hal Weaver have been in the Mountaintop Lab?"

"I don't know. Maybe because he used to work there. That's where he got his start at Steel or. . . ." Suddenly I remembered a startling piece of information Stiletto had mentioned offhand. "Or maybe he was preparing to handle flak about those two deaths."

"What two deaths?"

"Two employees were poisoned by cyanide at the beginning of the year."

"They were . . .?"

"Dead."

"No." Mr. Graham sighed. "I mean who were they, their names? How were they poisoned? How soon before Weaver's murder? What happened to their cases? Did their families sue?"

"I don't know." I didn't have the guts to tell Mr. Graham those deaths were barely a rumor.

"Did OSHA get involved?"

"OSHA?"

"Occupational Safety and Health Association, Bubbles. I can't imagine that two people could die in the lab from cyanide poisoning and OSHA wouldn't have immediately started an investigation."

OSHA. I hadn't even thought about OSHA.

Then Mr. Graham leaned forward and touched my bare knee. "How, exactly, did you find out about those deaths, anyway? I don't remember reading about them. That would have been front-page news."

I was now fully alarmed, half of me because I didn't know if it was kosher for Stiletto, a photographer with the Associated Press's national bureau, to be helping me out with this story. Reporters aren't supposed to discuss their investigations with the competition, even the AP.

The other half of me was alarmed by the way Mr. Graham's finger was circling my knee . . . and it wasn't budging.

"Inside source," I said, thanks to sudden inspiration. "I have an inside source at Steel."

"I see." There was still that finger. Still on the kneecap. He pressed harder. "And this inside source, can he—or she—provide more details?"

"Perhaps." Please take your hand off my knee, I prayed. Because I really, really don't want to have to bitch slap you, buddy, especially since you sign my checks.

"I'll be interested in seeing what your inside source can provide." He finally removed his hand. "In the meantime, why don't you type up what you have and show it to me. If you'd like," his voice softened from its previous testiness, "I can give you feedback over dinner."

Ding! That was it! The big hit.

"That's awfully nice of you, Mr. Graham." I started edging to the door. "But I already have plans for dinner."

"With your inside source?"

"Kind of."

"You're a girl after my own heart, Bubbles. Reel 'em in any way you can." He winked. "But you're not getting off *my* hook that easy. Consider that invite a rain check, which I definitely plan to cash."

Fine. Just as long as it wasn't layaway.

All afternoon I tried to reach Stiletto, with no luck. He wasn't at home and his cell phone repeated that spaceship computerized message. Eloise said she hadn't seen him since he left in the morning to go to Steel.

A spokeswoman for OSHA, a Judy Herman, said she could not discuss the Mountaintop Lab case without first getting the names of the two Steel employees who had died. From what she knew, however, there was no record of any cyanide-related injuries ever at Steel. She had done a word search through OSHA's press releases and turned up zilch.

I also tried to reach Eunice because, while Mr. Graham may have been lukewarm to a story about lesbian love gone wrong, I was not. The way I saw it, a woman is more likely to murder her husband, or her girlfriend's husband, if he is standing in the way of her sexual and spiritual fulfillment than because Steel has a problem keeping a cork on the cyanide bottle.

Men have never cottoned on that love and sex are more powerful forces in our lives than money or war or all the other boring news that clouds the *New York Times*. Forget budget deficits and Congressional votes. *Cosmo* is right. Sex should be the lead story every day.

Eunice didn't answer her phone again, either. I called the historical society and was lucky to find someone in the office, a very nice lady named Betty Jo Potrushnka. Betty Jo Potrushnka hadn't seen hide nor undyed hair of Eunice, though why would she have? Eunice volunteered on Thursdays, the only day of the week the historical society ran field trips at the Moon Inn. Maybe Eunice was visiting her sister in Philly, Betty Jo suggested. She did that a lot.

I would, too, if I had to live off the grid.

While I was sitting there typing up my flimsy story for Mr. Graham and trying not to be nauseous watching Lawless digest—make that, inhale—his 5 P.M. Ho Ho, the phone rang. Stiletto.

"I'm so glad you called," I said. "I need any information you can find about the two people who were poisoned in the Mountaintop Lab."

"It's just a rumor, you know, Bubbles."

"I know. But my career depends on it."

"Okay," he said. "I'll see what I can do, Yablinko."

"Also any further information you have about Hal Weaver visiting the lab. Like, what hour of February 5, when he signed in, signed out."

"That I can get for you tonight. I've got a copy of the sign-out sheet right here. I'll bring it when I show you my other surprise," he said.

Sex! I thought. He's talking about sex!

"You have a surprise for me, big boy?" I tried to say this in a sultry way, but instead ended up sounding like a bad Mae West.

"I found some more information about Hal Weaver's mistress."

Was that all? What a disappointment. I thought for sure it was going to be about sex.

"I know about his mistress. She's a lesbian." I crooked the phone against my ear.

That caught him off guard. "She is?"

"And she was having an affair with Carol Weaver. They went on a cruise," I paused for effect as Wendy had, "with the Indigo Girls."

"Who the hell are the Indigo Girls?"

There was no hope for Stiletto. If it wasn't The Boss or Yo-Yo Ma, he was clueless. "G says they're lesbian folk singers. Apparently, Jane saw them at Musikfest last year. Granted, they haven't produced the musical mega-wonders like Journey's 'Any Way You Want It,' but talent like Journey's comes along, what, once in a lifetime?"

"Thank God," Stiletto said under his voice.

"Excuse me?"

He got back to work. "Are you sure we're talking about the same mistress?"

"Susan Morse. I mean, Pendergast." Eavesdropping bugger that he was, Lawless swiveled slightly from his desk to hear better. He sucked chocolate off his pudgy fingers.

"That's where you're wrong. Hal Weaver was not having an affair with Susan Morse. Susan Morse was dating her future husband last year."

Keeping up appearances, I thought. Men are *so* naive.

"Her name is Debbie North. She was Hal Weaver's secretary for fifteen years. Word has it that he bought and paid the mortgage on her town house in Fountain Hill. Here's what I'm thinking . . ."

Sex? (That voice of his, it was so . . . so masculine. Such a turn-on.)

"What do you say we pay Debbie a visit before we go out tonight? I've told her I might be stopping by and she seemed fine with that."

Sure. She didn't know I'd be tagging along with my handy-dandy, trusty-wusty notebook.

"Why don't we meet in front of her house in an hour?" he said.

Cripes. Was it that late? Lawless's five o'clock Ho Ho should have been the warning bell. I needed to get dressed and ready.

I reflected on my leopard print top and skirt. Maybe those would do, if we were going someplace respectable, like Applebee's or Chili's.

Anything fancier and I might want to run home and grab my zebra minidress. I loved my zebra minidress because one side had a long sleeve and the other side didn't have any sleeve at all. How cool and sexy was that?

"Where are we going for dinner?"

"The Black Bass Inn. I hope you'll like it. It's in a two-hundred-year-old inn overlooking the Delaware Canal down in Bucks County. It's very romantic."

I did not have the guts to ask if he had made a reservation for after dinner, too. All I knew was that the leopard print definitely would not work.

The Black Bass sounded even nicer than Applebee's—if that were possible.

CHAPTER 19

I was not as afraid as I'd expected to return to my quiet house alone, at dusk after being away so long and with the BB shooter still on the loose. I wasn't afraid because I wasn't alone. Not only had Mrs. Hamel taken in all my mail, deadheaded my begonias and turned on and off my lights, she had practically moved in.

"Vat are you doing here?" she asked, waddling up from the couch where she had been knitting a peach and white afghan.

As was required by municipal ordinance (I think, though I'm not positive) Mrs. Hamel, like most postmenopausal women of European descent in Lehigh, PA, was a good fifty pounds overweight. She had hip problems and swollen legs, both of which caused her to amble in a teeter-totter motion. Like a big, muumuu-covered Weeble.

"They catch the shooter?" she asked, weebling and wobbling to where I was standing, which happened to be by the door in awe.

The house had been thoroughly sanitized and germanized. That may sound like a contradiction until you understand that the germ in germanized comes from the root word—German. That's right, every single speck of dust had been sucked, wiped and washed away. Or, as Mrs. Hamel like to put it, exterminated.

The windows gleamed, the venetian blinds were actually white for once and the kitchen floor sparkled. I didn't have to open the drawers to know that the forks would be in the fork tray, the spoons in the spoon tray, etc. It vas purrfect!

"You like?" she asked, patting the braids on her head. "I tot as surprise for you I vould do it."

"It's wonderful. I've never seen the house so clean. How long did it take?"

She shrugged. "Two days, max." She held out her thick, calloused hands. "That kitchen floor vas a bitch, say? Look at my fingers, so much wax off I scrub."

I sniffed. There was a peculiar odor in the air, something akin to ammonia, onion, Mr. Clean and ginger snaps. "Is that sauerbraten I smell?"

"In Crock-Pot. You should use it sometime."

I didn't even know I owned a crock pot. "No BB shooter?"

"Nah." She curled her lip. "No BB shooter come near me." She reached into her muumuu and pulled out her rosaries. "Nothing betveen me and my beads comes."

Take note, Calvin Klein.

Mrs. Hamel didn't appear the least bit disappointed that I wouldn't be staying to enjoy her slow-cooked, beer-and-vinegar-marinated hunk of tough, dead cow, or her spotless—uh, *my* spotless—house. She settled back in the couch and resumed her knitting, glad, I supposed, to be away from Mr. Hamel, who hadn't for nothing been nicknamed by Jane as "The Little Kaiser."

When I came down the stairs forty minutes later in my kick-ass, black-and-white zebra dress with the one sleeve, my hair down and blown dry so that it hung about my shoulders, my eyes glittering, my feet in high heels (screw it, Eunice) and a groovy black-and-white woven leather belt with turquoise trim tied around my hips, all Mrs. Hamel said was "Call if you get in trouble."

As if.

After stopping by the Evergreen to deliver Mrs. Stucklyn's birthday cake (Mrs. Stucklyn was asleep, but the dress was a big hit with the mahjong table), I headed down the spur route to Fountain Hill.

Fountain Hill was a quaint, tree-lined section near Lehigh's South Side. I had been born at St. Luke's Hospital in Fountain Hill and so had Jane. Lehigh University professors lived there in old Victorian houses, which made it all the more remarkable that Hal Weaver had been able to get his mistress a chunk of this exclusive real estate.

I followed Stiletto's directions and found 34 Loomis Street, home to Debbie North. And what a home it was. A three-story Victorian with a wrap-around porch, looming elm trees and flower boxes.

It was the Mary Tyler Moore home come to life.

"Ready?" Stiletto leaned in the window and, let me tell you girls, he was gorgeous.

I've seen Stiletto cleaned up before, but this was different. As I stepped out of the car and joined him on the sidewalk, I could barely take my eyes off him. It wasn't that the five o'clock shadow was gone and that he smelled great, all showered up with fresh soap, it was that he had done all this for me. The man whom women would empty their piggy banks to date had done this for *me*.

I'd never seen him in a tweed jacket, just the leather one, which was nothing to sneer at. He looked academic and, at the same time, masculine. Underneath the tweed was his usual white oxford. The jeans were still there, but they weren't as faded as his others. And, since I am a hairdresser, I was fascinated by his hair. It was still longish, but groomed so that it curled slightly at the nape of the neck. Totally New York. I mean, the guy could have been on the cover of *GQ*, if he didn't happen to be straight.

I was focusing so much on checking him out, that I didn't realize he was doing the same.

"Bubbles, my God." He took my hands. "You look. . . ."

"Wild, right?"

He grinned. "I think you look great. Very Bubbles."

I assumed that was meant to be a compliment. If I had any doubt, he pulled me to him and kissed me. Right away, I knew. The energy between us was different. This was definitely going to be the night. Our night.

We'd always had a passion for each other, a passion that had been squelched by chastity vows and gun injuries, buttinsky family members and assorted criminals, not to mention kids. Now, though, we were like thoroughbreds at the gates. Ready to race.

If I could only get over my Bon Jovi fear.

"Let's go," he said, giving my hand a little shake. "Let's get this over with as fast as possible."

Gulp.

He led me up the brick walk to the front door. There were three names. The top one was merely "NORTH." How fitting.

Debbie buzzed us right in after she heard Stiletto's voice. I had a bad feeling climbing the two flights of stairs. I knew what it was like as a woman to misread a man, to assume he might be interested in romance when, well in this case, when he was interested in helping his girlfriend write a story.

Yup. I'd been right. Soft jazz floated from the apartment as Debbie opened the door. The lights had been dimmed and poor Debbie was dressed in nothing but a rose silk robe. God bless her.

"Hi, Steve," she cooed before catching sight of me in my zebra dress.

"Debbie," he said, as we both stepped into her plush and, may I say cattily, very single-woman's apartment. "This is Bubbles. Bubbles Yablonsky. Maybe you've seen her byline in the *News-Times*. She's a reporter."

Debbie's moisturized hands shook mine limply. She was a hot dame, or had been, once. Her blond hair was twisted in the back and her makeup was expensive and reserved. But she had crossed a line, a line drawn by her fortieth birthday, or, more likely, drawn by Hal Weaver's death. Slight traces of age marred her face, around her eyes and mouth. Her neck was slightly wrinkled, as was her forehead.

She'd be an ideal candidate for plastic surgery, if such a thing were allowed in the Lehigh Valley. (What? Suck out my fat? But winter's coming.)

Debbie gradually put us together. "You're with . . . with Steve?"

"Hmmm," I replied neutrally. I didn't want to blow my chances of getting a decent interview. Reading Debbie's expression, however, I could tell I'd never have had a shot at questioning her, much less entering her apartment, if Stiletto hadn't been involved.

Stiletto stepped up to the plate. "It was my idea to have Bubbles join us, Debbie. I took a chance that if you were willing to discuss Hal Weaver's death, maybe Bubbles could take notes. She's doing a story on his murder."

Debbie halfheartedly motioned for us to sit on one of her absurdly white couches. No children had been here, that was for sure. White couches, white carpets. I wouldn't dare drink a cup of coffee in this place.

"I thought Hal's murder was over. That Carol confessed." Debbie perched herself on a stuffed ottoman and crossed her long, bare legs, glancing at Stiletto as she did so.

Stiletto kept his gaze level. That's my man.

"I guess new information's surfaced that . . .," Stiletto pointed to me, "well, I'll let Bubbles tell you."

I told Debbie the basics of my investigation. She could barely make eye contact with me, and not because we were discussing the murdered man with whom she had supposedly had an affair and who had paid for this love nest.

Her problem was she couldn't stop stealing glimpses of Stiletto who, I'll say it again, looked really, really hot. The way he casually rested his forearms on his knees and then leaned and stretched his arm along the back of the couch.

I wasn't doing any better. Here I was with the woman I'd been searching for all week, Hal Weaver's mistress, the femme fatale who may have scratched him to death with her claws dipped in poison, and what was I thinking?

Contraception. Where can I get some? Did Stiletto bring any? I hope I didn't miss a patch on my legs when I was shaving in the shower. I do that sometimes. Did I wear enough deodorant? What did I read in *Cosmo* about driving your man crazy? Am I supposed to lick first, then suck? Or vice versa. Geesh. Why does such a natural act have to be so complicated?

Finally Stiletto cleared his throat and I realized I'd stopped talking. Debbie and I were sitting there, staring vacantly like imbeciles.

"I didn't kill him, if that's what this is leading up to," Debbie said, coming to her senses. "The police interviewed me twice. I didn't even see Hal that night. I was at my sister's house and, and look . . ."

Like Mrs. Hamel had done, Debbie showed me her fingers, though these looked human. Her nails were neat and freshly painted a deep pink—for Stiletto no doubt—but those fingernails were short. Plus my expert eye could detect that they bore none of the telltale traces of acrylic abuse. No dents or spots of weakness.

"Nails aren't my thing," she said, curling her fingers self-consciously. "I do so much typing that I can't stand to have acrylic tips in the way."

That statement amounted to blasphemy in most secretarial circles, but I believed her. Debbie was innocent. You don't bite the hand that feeds you and Hal had fed her very well, if the pricey address, cushy furniture and nice silk robe were any indication.

"Do you have any idea who might have killed Weaver?" Stiletto asked.

Debbie stopped frowning at her nails and beamed. He'd spoken. The god had talked. "I thought, that is until a few minutes ago, that Carol had."

"Carol claims she didn't, and I, for one, think she's telling the truth," I said, trying to draw her attention back to me. "She had acrylic nails, but they weren't sharp enough to leave those scratches."

Debbie nodded in womanly agreement.

"What Carol thinks is that Steel ordered a hit on Hal because he was hiding a secret, a secret that she says could have brought down the entire company. What do you think?"

I'd hit a nerve. Debbie uncrossed her legs and went to the kitchen. "Where are my manners?" she said, pulling a chilled bottle from the refrigerator. "Can I get you some wine?"

In this situation the *you* was for Stiletto. It wasn't a *you two* you.

"That'd be great," Stiletto said.

"No, uhm, that's okay," I said, giving him a look of *You're going to have wine?*

He shrugged a *what the hell.*

Debbie returned, handing Stiletto a glass and leaning over a peek-a-boo too much. As I expected, there was nothing under that robe but more moisturized Debbie.

"Thanks," Stiletto said, unperturbed. Seen it all, done it all.

"So how's your research going into Henry Metzger's legacy?" Debbie sat back on the hassock and recrossed her legs, of which she obviously was very proud.

I wanted to interrupt and point out that she still

hadn't answered my question, but Stiletto responded that his research was almost through and had been very enlightening. He'd disbursed a chunk of Metzger's money to people who'd been injured, that kind of stuff.

Debbie gazed at him in awe and kept asking him more questions, oohing and ahhing over every single detail Stiletto described.

Stiletto would say something like, "The family of Walter Donavick never knew that he was in charge of plate metal, which would have entitled him to a larger pension."

"No!" Debbie would gasp in horror.

When Stiletto was done explaining Metzger's evil deeds, he drank some more wine and said, "What about it, Debbie? Did Hal Weaver have a secret?"

Smooth. So smooth it took Debbie a second to realize what he had slipped by her.

"Yes." She closed her eyes and breathed in and out, chest heaving dramatically. "Yes, Hal was working on something. Had been for about six weeks before he died. He told me it was his ticket out of Steel."

"Do you know what it was?" I was hesitant to break the spell Stiletto had cast over her.

"No," she snapped. "I don't know *what* it was. He wouldn't tell me."

Hmmm. Kept both of his little ladies in the dark, did he?

"Then how do you know he was working on

something?" Stiletto asked gently. "Something that could bring down Steel."

Actually, Debbie hadn't said it was something that could bring down Steel. Carol had. But Stiletto was so good that Debbie fell for it.

"Because it was supposed to be our ticket out, too. In order for us to leave Lehigh together, Hal needed enough money for me and him and Carol and that," she closed her eyes again, "that spoiled kid of his, Kiera."

"Kiera was spoiled, eh?" I tried Stiletto's technique and let the question hang.

"Oh, was she ever. As soon as she hit adolescence, bang!" Debbie clicked her tongue. "It was a temper tantrum every night. She fought with him over everything—what to wear to school, whether to get her navel pierced—and then there was the money. Always more money. Money. Money. Money. He shelled her with cash and still it wasn't enough."

Sweet, G would say if he were here. Which, thankfully, he wasn't.

"Looking back, I think sometimes that's why Hal came to me. To get away from her as well as that sow."

"Carol?"

"Steel Ordered Wife. SOWs, the secretaries at Steel call them. You know, their only job is to look perfect, keep the house decorated and throw parties. Well, I could do that, too, if I didn't have to show up at work every day."

She took another sip of wine. A big sip. "Hal

had to carry the whole load. He even paid the bills, wrote the checks because sensitive Carol found that too stressful. I'll tell you, if Hal had married me, I would have made his life heaven. He was a saint. An absolute saint. He was too great a man to be with her."

She caught herself and eyed Stiletto and me guiltily. Had she said too much?

"You know," I said, scooching forward on the couch, "Hal did talk to his lawyer about divorce."

"I know." She finished her wine. "His lawyer also advised him to give his marriage another try. Do you know why?"

Stiletto and I said nothing. We knew enough to keep our mouths shut.

"Because of that kid." Debbie got up. The glass was shaking slightly in her hand. "Hal told me on Valentine's Day, on Valentine's Day no less, that it was over. That Kiera needed all of his attention. She needed a family because . . .," she was about to cry, "because Kiera was pregnant."

Kiera pregnant in February? I tried secretly counting on my fingers. Did that work?

While I was tackling the heavy math, Stiletto said casually, "I thought you didn't see Hal the day he died."

Busted!

Debbie gripped the glass and sat down, her face ashen. "I didn't see him that night, I said. I mean I wasn't with him that night." She was fumbling. "We met, but not here. We talked."

"Where?" Stiletto leaned forward.

Debbie wiped away a tear. Stiletto took her hand. "It's okay, Debbie. We're not the cops. We're just trying to put a story together."

She sniffed and nodded. "We drove to the park. It was our meeting point."

"Illick's Mill?" Stiletto coached.

"Hmm, hmm." Carol sniffed again. "He said we were over. It was snowing and dark and an awful night. I'll never forget it." She wiped away another tear.

"Would you say it was sevenish, eightish?" Stiletto was so mesmerizing that, had I been in Debbie's place, I would have given him any information he wanted—social security number, bank account, mother's maiden name, real weight not fake weight on the driver's license. Uh, maybe not *that*.

"Eightish, I think." Debbie took another breath. "We'd been together a long time, ten years, you know. So I thought, he'll get over it. He'll be back after Kiera decides to have an abortion. Hal was still in shock, trying to do the right thing. She had just found out that day."

So maybe it did work. Back to the counting.

"And then what happened?" Stiletto said.

"He left. I left. We drove off in separate cars."

Stiletto squeezed her hand. "Come on, Debbie."

Hey. What was this? The woman left. Hal left. That's it. End of discussion. And we're out of here. Off to dinner and then to . . .

"Well," Debbie bent her head more, "well, I did kind of follow him."

"Because," Stiletto said, "you wanted to know if he'd found another woman."

Debbie gave a tiny shrug. "Kind of."

"And had he?"

She shook her head. "I waited for him by the park entrance, but he never came out. So . . . so I turned around and went back into the park. His car wasn't there and there was only one direction it could have gone."

"Up the park road."

"Right. Past the broken gate toward all those private, fancy homes. I drove up a bit and I saw his car. It was parked in front of that cave off the Monocacy. I'll tell you . . ." She looked up. Black streaks ran down her cheeks. Women like Debbie and soap opera stars in general really should invest in waterproof mascara. "I thought the worst. I thought he'd gone to commit suicide."

"What happened then?" Stiletto pressed.

"I went in a few feet and called for him, but I didn't hear anything. It was pitch black and freezing. There was ice all around and I didn't have the right boots. I didn't even have a flashlight. I called for him about a hundred times, but he was gone."

"Where?"

"I don't know. I drove to my sister's. We had a pity party, drank a lot of wine and I slept over. When I woke up, a friend of mine from work had called and she told me the news. Hal was dead. Dead in his own bed."

"You think it was Steel who ordered the hit?" I asked yet again.

Debbie's eyes were glazed, depressed. "No. No, I do not. That's not how Steel operates, at least not with its executives."

"Who was it, do you think?" Stiletto said.

Debbie didn't pause to consider the implication of her words.

"Kiera. I'm convinced of it. She killed him and she's letting her mother take the rap."

CHAPTER 20

"Makes sense to me," I told Stiletto as we descended the steps from Debbie's apartment.

"It makes sense that Kiera killed her father? Could you imagine Jane ever doing that . . . or letting you go to jail for it?"

A burst of fresh air hit us as we stepped outside into the dark. "No, but Jane is Jane. However," I held up a finger, "I'm a mother and I can easily imagine going to jail for Jane. You should have seen how I humiliated myself for her at her Princeton interview."

"What happened to the suburban lesbian lovers angle?" He put his arm around my shoulder and escorted me down the walk.

"A girl's got a right to change her mind, Stiletto. I'll probably switch between spoiled teenage brat and jealous lesbian lover for days. All I need is one hard piece of evidence to cinch it."

We arrived at my Donkey Sucking Mobile and Stiletto rubbed my arm. "Cold?"

"Freezing."

"Then you better get your coat."

"Don't tell me you're still driving around with the Jeep top down." I retrieved my fake rabbit fur from the backseat.

"No, it's not that. It's because where we're going you'll need a coat. Also," he looked down, "better shoes."

I scrutinized my pumps with the two-inch heels. "What's wrong with these?"

"You can't hike in a cave with those."

"I . . . Oh, no."

"Oh, yes. Come on, Bubbles." He took my hand and led me over to his Jeep.

"But why?"

"Because, unlike you, I don't buy that either the daughter, the mother or the mother's friend, lesbian or not, killed Hal Weaver. Not until we find out what secret about Steel he was hiding. I have the feeling that a squirrelly flak like Weaver would not hide his supposed secret at home or at work."

"You think he hid it in the cave?" I climbed in the Jeep.

Stiletto got in on his side. "There's something in that cave, something that would make a man go there at night during a February snowstorm."

"And on Valentine's Day, don't forget."

"Uh, yeah, right." He started up the Jeep.

I studied him as we drove off. "There's another reason you're not giving up on the Steel angle. What is it?"

"Remember that RFD I found on your Camaro?

The one that had been put there at Two Guys?"

"Yup."

"It's an outdated mechanism Steel liked to use. Management used to stick them on the cars of workers whom they suspected were stealing products from the plant. My guess is that Steel management put the RFD on your car to track you."

I didn't speak after he said this. I did not like to think that Steel had been tailing me, that the power-hungry executives over there assumed it was in their rights to know where I went and who with.

"What about our date tonight? And . . . afterward?" I said, changing the subject.

Stiletto grinned as we zoomed across the Hill to Hill Bridge, the frigid November air blowing back my hair. "We've held off for four months, Bubbles. Forty minutes more won't make that much of a difference."

As we drove to Illick's Mill Park, our old stomping ground, I remembered other clues that lent more and more credence to Debbie's theory. The way Carol had at first vehemently protested her innocence and then copped to the plea of manslaughter. Clearly what had happened was that she had discovered her daughter's culpability and decided there was no other option. Carol couldn't let her pregnant daughter serve time in prison, so she sacrificed herself.

That was the exculpatory evidence Ken Bailey,

Carol's lawyer, must have uncovered and what he planned to tell the prosecutor when he slipped on his driveway, hit his head and died. Accident? Murder? Who knew?

Maybe Kiera.

And weren't those poisoned molasses spice cookies, the ones meant for Carol, weren't they sent from Saucon Valley where Kiera lived? Didn't Norma Lubrecht, the Weavers' former maid, say that Kiera stood to inherit the whole kit and caboodle if Carol corked? Maybe Kiera and her loser boyfriend were running out of money and needed an ASAP on the inheritance. Work? Heavens no. Murder? Hey, she'd done it before.

Which finally explained why Carol instead of Susan showed up at the House of Beauty, pointed a gun at me and told me to back off the story. I was getting too close to uncovering the truth. That truth being that her daughter had murdered her husband.

However, Debbie's theory still had holes as well. The biggest being, where did Kiera get the cyanide?

It must have been kismet because Stiletto said right at that moment, "I forgot to show you something. In my glove compartment is a copy of the Mountaintop Lab sign-out sheet."

We turned into Illick's Mill Park. It was after eight and therefore the park was closed.

"I know what to do." I slid out of the Jeep. As Stiletto had on our first unofficial date together,

270

back one steamy August night, I yanked the pin out of the cement post and let the chain fall. Stiletto drove over it and I put it back.

"Seems like yesterday." He leaned over and gave me a kiss. "Our first date. You, me alone in the park. You'd just hung off a bridge to get a story and I thought you were the most beautiful, the craziest, sexiest reporter/hairdresser I'd ever met."

And I thought he was the most gorgeous man with the biggest ego I'd ever met. Couldn't get my name straight—kept calling me Yablinko—and left me in the park to fend for myself. Ahh, how far we'd come.

I kissed him back and said, "Let's not get too sentimental, Stiletto. Remember the dead body."

"Right." He shifted gear and we headed into the park. In contrast to that steamy August night, the park was now dead and wintry. There was the sound of bare tree branches clicking in the wind, and a white mist was rising from the creek. It smelled like an old grave.

"Spooky," I said, shivering.

"Just dark."

We got to the end of the park and the broken gate, which appeared to have been repaired. Stiletto idled the Jeep and fooled around with the lock. Finally he stepped back and kicked it with all his might.

It flung open.

"There," he said, getting back in the Jeep.

I couldn't believe he had simply kicked it open. That was a heavy iron gate. That was a *padlock*.

"How did you do that?" I said, breathlessly.

"Come on, Bubbles." He navigated the Jeep past the gate and up the stone road. "What do you expect? I'm a man."

As though there was any doubt.

Stiletto parked and opened the glove compartment. A sheet of paper fell out, as did a flashlight.

Stiletto grabbed the flashlight, leaped out of the Jeep and opened his tattered camera bag. He took out a lens, batteries and film.

I read the sign-out sheet by the glove compartment light. Hal Weaver had signed in and out of the Mountaintop Lab at 6:30 on the morning of February 5, before staff arrived. His name was neatly printed and his signature signed like a professional, all flourish. I went back to that printing. The printing . . . the printing was off. The "n" was rounded and the "e" and "a" were joined.

Girlish writing.

"There's a pair of boots in the back, Bubbles. I'm sure they're too big for you, but they'll have to do."

I reached into the back and felt around, finally hooking a pair of heavy, black rubber Wellingtons, standard photographer issue. "I'm not wearing these. They'll make my legs look like tree trunks."

"Jesus, Bubbles, I don't care." The handsome tweed was gone. Stiletto had his photo vest on and white shirtsleeves rolled up. He was already at the mouth of the cave.

Yuck. I slipped off my pretty pumps and slid into the cold boots. They were huge. What size was Stiletto, anyway?

Big hands, big feet, big. . . . My naughty brain singsonged. *Stop it!* I scolded back.

I zipped up my rabbit fur and flip-flopped to the cave, slipping on the gravel as I climbed into the mouth. My hands scraped against the rock face. As soon as I got inside, water dripped on my head. Some date this was turning out to be.

"Don't pout, Bubbles." Stiletto shone the flashlight all around the cavern. "Think of it as an adventure."

The light illuminated wet rocks and black clumps. It took me a few seconds to realize the black clumps were bats in hibernation. There was a *drip, drip, drip* that echoed against the walls, as did our voices.

"This reminds me of our fun in Slagville, in the Number Nine mine," he said, rubbing my back. "Remember that?"

"You mean where we found the dead body and were nearly killed by the explosion?"

"Fond memories to share with the grandkids."

He took my hand. It was, yes, big. "You want to try there." He pointed with the light to where the cave narrowed.

"I interviewed a one-hundred-and-eight-year-old woman today who said she remembered when this was the opening to a natural tunnel. They blew it up in the twenties." I followed Stiletto, who negotiated the rocks confidently. "It was part of the Underground Railroad, you know."

"Where was it supposed to go again?"

"Someplace downtown, though I don't know where."

"I'd estimate that downtown is about a mile from here."

A mile? I didn't want to hike a mile underground. What about dinner? What about the Black Bass Inn and views of the Delaware?

We inched our way through the narrow part of the cave. I was curious about the children who had gotten lost here back in the twenties and what happened to them that the town would decide to blow up a part of the Underground Railroad.

"People have been hanging out in here," Stiletto said.

"How do you know?"

He picked up a rusted can of Yuengling, sure sign of Lehigh civilization. Archaeologists discover some cultures by excavating their artwork or arrowheads. Centuries from now they'll identify Lehigh, buried under a mountain of steel dust, by its beer cans.

"And cigarettes." Stiletto showed me a pack of Basics.

"Kids," I said. "That's G's brand. Liberty must have held the prom here." Now I felt like a fool for having been so scared to go in. What had happened to the tough steel girl in me?

"Kids and hillbillies," Stiletto said. "They always find the coolest spots to congregate."

Yes, but what was Hal Weaver doing here? Socializing with delinquents like G? Smoking Basics and drinking Miller? Or was he—my imagination raced—was he looking for Kiera? I pictured a concerned father inquiring after his troubled daughter, awkwardly asking questions of her whereabouts. The surly responses he'd get. The snickers and jeers.

My heart went out to him as a fellow parent. We parents, we're all caught in the same web spun by us and our children. The fly moves, the spider reacts. Though, the more I thought about that image, the more I decided what a repulsive metaphor that was. I'm not a blood-sucking. . . .

"That's it. Can't go on," Stiletto said.

We had arrived at a seemingly impassable wall of boulders. The result of the 1920s explosion, I expected.

"Should have brought Genevieve." I kicked the rocks with my oversized boots. "She's got a load of dynamite to take care of this."

"Knowing Genevieve, she'd end up exploding all of Lehigh." Stiletto was inspecting the pile. "Anyway, I don't think we'll need dynamite."

He handed me the flashlight and moved several rocks—rocks that had been moved before. By golly, there was space to get around.

Since I had the flashlight, I slid through the crevice first. Beyond, the tunnel was about six feet wide and fairly navigable.

"Incredible," Stiletto said. Somehow he'd managed to get the flashlight and move in front of me, leading the way down the rocky, gravelly path.

"What's incredible?"

"If it's true, if local myth is not just that, then to think of slaves coming up the Monocacy at night and being led into this cramped, wet space, not knowing if they were being marched to their deaths or captivity—it's mind blowing. What the hell do you suppose they were thinking?"

"They were probably thinking that they were alive and, for the moment, free. Or that they were tired and hungry. Cold." Complaints I could have made about now. This zebra dress was not what to wear in a cave in November. The cool air shot right up my whazooey.

Stiletto climbed over a rock. I did the same. "I guess it was as simple as that. When you're on the run, it comes down to the basics, doesn't it?"

"Yes, but not cigarettes."

Stiletto stopped suddenly, causing me to nearly bash into him. "There's stairs here."

"A metal stairs? Like the one in the mine?"

"No." Stiletto moved around a bit, shining the light up and down. "How do you like that? They're crude, stone stairs. Like the ones you find in old, colonial root cellars."

Had we gone a mile already? "This would put us under the historic section," I said, as Stiletto ventured up. "The Moravian buildings."

"Have to admit. It's an efficient way to get supplies to a boat."

"Or people." I stayed at the bottom of the stairs and watched as he got to the top.

"I bet it floods in high rains," he said, banging on something. "It's wood. A trapdoor."

He took a few steps down. Dirt and tiny rocks followed. Then he pushed hard and the door opened. "Locked but not very well."

"Where does it go?"

"Let's find out."

We climbed into what the flashlight revealed to be exactly as Stiletto predicted. An old-fashioned cellar built with native stone and chinked with mud. It was empty except for a few benches covered with dust and spiderwebs, rusted pots, empty mason jars, garden tools and lots of empty barrels.

I did not entertain the possibility of centipedes— my most feared creature.

"Store food here in the winter and take it into the tunnel, down to the boats." Stiletto nodded. "Wouldn't be surprised if the Indians showed the Moravians that tunnel and they built on top of it intentionally. Or," he grinned, "if the Moravians weren't engaged in a bit of smuggling."

"What kind of smuggling? Liquor?"

"Don't think so. The Moravians didn't drink.

Didn't fight in wars, either. Spies, maybe. Supplies for soldiers. Have no idea." His light illuminated hooks on the ceiling. "When you think about it, this is a perfect setup for ferrying slaves."

"What were those hooks for?"

"Hanging meat, I expect." Stiletto started searching for a way out. "Seems to me this trapdoor has been opened recently, though not lately."

He exited through a door in the wall and I followed. It led to a room about the size of a closet, no bigger, and another set of stairs. These stairs, however, were musty and wooden. We trod them slowly. They were so steep that I was afraid of falling over, especially with these boots.

After what seemed like several flights we came to a tight wooden landing. There was no door at all.

"It leads to nowhere," I said. "What's the point?"

"This is the point. Stand back, Bubbles." I took a few steps down and watched as Stiletto pushed on a wall. It creaked open.

"Revolving bookcase," he said.

"A revolving bookcase?" I whispered. "What are we going to do? Enter some poor person's living room and say howdy do?"

Stiletto shrugged nonchalantly. "Yeah. Why not?"

He pushed the wall open and I squeezed in after him. We were in a tiny bedroom with plaster walls, wide wooden floors and an eaved ceiling. In the middle there was a four-poster bed covered with an antique wedding ring quilt. The only window was small and paned. Below it was a cushioned seat.

"Where are we?" I asked, fingering the hand-made quilt.

Stiletto didn't answer, lost as he was in assessing the situation. "That makes a lot of sense."

"What makes sense?" I was still stunned to know there really were revolving bookcases. It was so . . . Scooby-Doo.

"Looks to me like we've made it to the Moon Inn." He shined the flashlight down the hall. "Perfect. What a perfect place to shepherd people in secret."

"Is the inn closed?"

"No one's around that I can see." He stepped back into the room. "How do you like that?"

"So this was where Hal Weaver went." I slipped out of the blasted boots.

"What I'm thinking is that his so-called secret, or whatever evidence he was collecting, is stored here," Stiletto said. "Didn't you say he was big into the historical society?"

"Eunice Morse said so and it's where he and Susan Morse got together, though I guess they didn't really get together, because she's a homicidal lesbian in love with his wife." I studied the bookshelf with the flashlight.

Stiletto rubbed his forehead. "I don't know about you, Bubbles. All this lesbian intrigue. It's kind of kinky for Lehigh, don't you think?"

Nothing of interest in the bookshelf. "It is what it is, Stiletto. Ten percent of the populations is gay. Get over it. Why don't we search the other rooms?"

We started with the three other bedrooms on the second floor. They were similarly furnished in colonial style. A plaque on the wall said that the inn had stopped housing guests in the early 1900s. No kidding. Four rooms. It was barely a bed and breakfast.

Downstairs Stiletto and I split up. He took the living room. With the flashlight I searched the kitchen—holding off from sneaking into the refrigerator even though I was starving—and the dining room. I kept the light low so we wouldn't attract attention. Fortunately the Moon Inn was set back from Main Street, tucked in an alley. Otherwise the cops would have been called much sooner.

We searched every drawer, cabinet and desk. We looked through bookshelves and in cubbyholes and even in the dumbwaiter.

After an hour we were out of ideas. I was positive a silent alarm had been set off and that a security guard, if not the Lehigh Historical Society en masse, was on the way to bust us. It was frustrating that we had turned up bupkis.

Just what had Hal Weaver been doing here, anyway? And on Valentine's Day no less. Valentine's Day may not have been significant to Stiletto, but it was meaningful to me. A man does not sneak down a tunnel to play with his records on a frigid Valentine's night when he has just split with his mistress and resolved to work on his marriage.

Like I've said, love and sex are more powerful forces in our lives than we care to realize. Love and sex. I sighed heavily. Love and sex.

The wide floorboards creaked in the dining room as I carefully shut and locked a pair of sideboard doors. Heavy footsteps approached and a yellow glow cast a large shadow as Stiletto, holding a lit candle, entered from the main hall.

"You had the flashlight. I had to improvise," he said. "I didn't find anything. Ready to go?"

I couldn't answer, though I wanted to, badly. I wanted to tell him all the thoughts, all the feelings that had suddenly rushed over me as he entered in that beautiful light. A light that flickered warmly against the golden plastered walls and off the glass china cabinets.

Stiletto stood there so tall and manly, his forearms exposed and his face smudged with dirt, black boots up to his knees. He might have been a Revolutionary soldier seeking a bed for the night. My heart ached. I loved him. I wanted him.

Wind howled outside, rattling the shutters. It whistled through the inn's ancient cracks and nearly blew out the flame. It was a sign. A sign that the time was now.

"Yes," I whispered. "Let's go."

He smiled and held out his hand. I took it, but as he was about to blow out the candle, I put my finger to his lips.

"No."

"No?" He looked down at me and I felt my stomach tighten into a knot. Oh, God, I was scared.

"Follow me," I said. Still holding his hand, I turned and led him back up the narrow winding stairs to the second floor, to the bedroom we had entered through the revolving bookshelf.

"You want to go back out through the tunnel?"

I said nothing until we closed the door of the tiny bedroom with its uneven floors, its cozy eaves and leaded paned windows. And its four-poster bed.

"I don't want to go back through the tunnel." I removed the candle from his hand and placed it on the oak table by the bed. I reached up and kissed him, pulling him to me. He still seemed confused until I said, "I want to stay. Here."

Stiletto looked around the room, and then, the implication of what I was suggesting dawning on him, he cocked his head in that way I so love and said, "Are you sure?"

I nodded. I could feel my heart beating and my breath tightening. "It's right. This place is right for us. Don't you think?"

His hand caressed my hair and he smiled at me. "I know you're scared."

"I am. I don't know why. It's not like I haven't had sex before. Before the chastity vow, I was, rather, well, free with my affections."

"Come here," he said softly. The bed was right

next to us, but Stiletto led me over to the window seat under the eaves. He sat me down. Shadows moved about the room as the wind through the chinks played with the flame.

He took my hands and studied me with his blue eyes, which looked black in the dim light. I tried to remember that this was my ally as well as my lover. The man who had rescued me from death on a Pocono dock and in an Amish field. A man who loved me for me.

"I've thought about this night a lot, Bubbles. I've thought about why you've been scared lately and, the thing is, I'm not sure if it will work with us if you're scared."

Oh, shit, I thought. Don't think that. It'll work. I smiled bravely. "I'm not that scared. Really. It's just a Bon Jovi thing."

"You've said that before. What are you talking about?"

"If you knew Jon Bon Jovi, you'd know what I'm talking about." I averted my eyes because I couldn't bear it if Stiletto made fun of me while I explained my most humiliating moment in life, ever. "You see, Bon Jovi, like you, is a total stud. A hunk every woman wants to meet. I had a major crush on Bon Jovi from his first hit, 'Runaway.' hung his poster in the House of Beauty office and tried to never miss a concert, especially the ones in Jersey. I swore that I could die a satisfied woman if I met him, just once.

"And then I was at the Allentown Fair a couple

of summers ago and I ran into this hairdresser I knew from beauty school, Denise. She was so excited because she'd been called in to sub for a stylist who'd gotten sick and did I want to come to the trailer and meet Jon Bon Jovi."

I put my hand to my chest, remembering how my heart had beaten back then, too. "I was so floored I was shaking all over. Denise led me into this trailer and like, there he was, sitting with his sunglasses on top of his head and his sandy hair kind of mussed up, goofing with a couple of band members, and Denise said, 'Hi, Jon, I'd like you to meet Bubbles.'

"It was my dream come true. I couldn't believe I was actually meeting Jon Bon Jovi in the flesh. Then he swiveled around and looked at me and smiled and I. . . ."

I stopped. I couldn't go on. It was too embarrassing.

Stiletto lifted my chin. He wasn't laughing or even his usual amused. He was actually interested. "And what happened? The suspense is killing me."

"I froze," I said bluntly. "I choked. I couldn't say hello or wow or even holy shit. I couldn't move or shake his hand or even blink. It was awful. I was petrified. Like a kid meeting Santa Claus. For five long minutes I was physically petrified. One of his buddies started laughing and then his bodyguards had to carry me out."

"Petrified?" Stiletto laid his arms on my shoulders and bent his head to mine. "Is that what you're afraid of? That you'll freeze?"

"I know it sounds weird, but kind of." Boy, he smelled good.

"Why? I'm not a rock star. Even a bad one like Bon Jovi."

"Hey, hey, hey." I threw off his arms. "Watch that kind of talk. Bon Jovi is a god."

"That's my point. I'm not."

"You have to understand it from my point of view." I traced my finger along the worn knees of his jeans. "You've been with a lot of women, Stiletto. Sophisticated women. Women who live in Paris and London, who drive sports cars and shop high couture, who. . . ."

". . . are not you, Bubbles." He made me look at him again. "Listen to me, I'm going to explain something."

His shoulders were so broad in that white shirt, all that weight lifting after his gunshot wound, that it was hard for me to concentrate on what he was saying. "Okay."

"Your fear has nothing to do with me. It has to do with you."

Wham! Same old, same old. Just what Dan used to tell me—that it was my fault, not his, that I was a dud in bed. "I know. Dan used to say that all the time."

"Fuck Dan." Stiletto frowned. "He's exactly the problem I'm talking about."

"He is?"

"Bubbles, I know this is an intimate question, but, then again, we're about to embark on a very intimate night."

There was hope, I thought. Stiletto went back to playing with my hair.

"Men have had sex with you, but has any man ever made love to you?"

I considered this. "Aren't they the same thing?"

He shook his head slowly. "No. That's what I mean. Making love is on a completely different level. It's even more intimate and frightening, for me as well as you. And," he pushed my hair behind my bare shoulder, which he leaned over and kissed, "it's what I intend to do with you tonight."

Oh my God, I thought. He's kissing my shoulder.

"Part of the problem with sex," he continued, moving his lips up to my neck and sending shivers all over my body, "especially for two people who've never had sex with each other, is that they can feel so apart."

"Yes!" I exclaimed.

"You understand?"

Actually I'd shouted "Yes!" because I could feel every inch of me springing to life, but I suppose I agreed with him. "Hmm, hmm."

"So what I'm going to do, Bubbles," I felt his hand on mine, pulling me toward him, "is I'm going to make love to you gently and lovingly so you won't feel alone, like you have in the past."

How had Stiletto known this? Even I hadn't realized that, yes, that's exactly how I'd felt when Dan and other men had sex with me. Alone.

Stiletto slid the other sleeve off my shoulder and kissed that, too.

"Contraception," I managed to croak. "I know it's not very. . . ."

"Got it covered." His lips traced the tendon of my neck, his soft dark hair brushing my cheek. I closed my eyes and drank it all in—the smell of his shampoo, the heat of his lips against my bare skin.

"And what about if security or someone finds us?"

"We'll just have to take that chance. Can't go back now."

He unzipped my dress and I sat up, startled. I should be doing something. Unbuttoning his shirt or muttering naughty nonsense. I reached for his collar and tried to remember that *Cosmo* article, but Stiletto grabbed my hands.

"It's okay, Bubbles. Relax. We've got all night." My hands still in his, he guided me off the window seat and led me through the candlelight to the bed.

Won't be needing this anymore, I thought as I let the dress fall to the floor, pushing it aside.

Stiletto appraised me, that muscle in his jaw twitching slightly as his gaze drifted downward from my shoulders to my strapless, push-up black bra and matching lace thong. (Hey, it's not like I hadn't known this night was a possibility.)

"If you're the one who's scared," he said, unbuttoning his shirt, "then how come I'm the one who's shaking?"

Lord have mercy on both of us. Seeing him slowly, button by button, undo that shirt and feeling my stomach tighten yet again, I waited for the inevitable choke moment. I am glad to report it did not happen.

What happened was that I rested a knee on the antique wedding-ring-quilted bed and finished the unbuttoning job for him. Spreading his shirt, letting it slip off his back and kissing that incredible hard, tanned chest of his was a very liberating moment.

It was the moment when I acknowledged I wanted this, that I was not going to be sick or scared anymore. This was not Dan, this was Stiletto. They were two different animals, not to be compared one minute more.

"You," he said, lightly touching my bare shoulders with both hands, "are so very beautiful."

I smiled.

"And you," he said, bringing me to him, "are the love of my life."

That knot in my stomach twisted once more until it exploded and bubbled up, not as what I feared, but worse. A huge, blubbering sob. "Oh, Stiletto."

He wiped away my tears and, if I didn't know Stiletto better, I'd say his eyes glistened, too. "I have never meant any words as much as I've meant those, Bubbles. You and I are made for each other."

I stopped crying and gave in to the happiness that was now rushing to fill where the tension had been. "Let's do it," I said, laughing.

"You got it, babe."

To explain in step-by-step detail the events that followed would be about as interesting as describing the correct procedure for applying hair color. So let me skip right to the highlights.

Stiletto was a confident sex partner. Not in a show-offy, hang from the chandelier, drip a Fudgicle on her breasts and lick it off kind of way. More like he had been born with superb sexual instincts which he followed with boundless joy.

Confidence, they taught us at Two Guys, inspired confidence, and it didn't take long for me to unsnap that bra, and kick off that thong (it flew up and actually landed on one of the posts), before delving into Stiletto's jeans. They came off with an equally impressive slap.

Not for nothing did women stare at him when he crossed a room.

With this popular guest arriving at the party, I assumed we were roller coasting to a rapid conclusion, but Stiletto ever so kindly stopped me from playing hostess and murmured, "Later." At which point his lips became very creative and I discovered (for the first time, may I add) what *Cosmo* had been writing about all these years.

His lips, those incredible, sumptuous lips of his, were everywhere, up and down my neck, my back, my arms, in my cleavage and straight to my navel, until my thighs started quivering and he had to firmly stroke those to settle them down.

They would not behave, those thighs of mine. They kept opening and closing depending on where Stiletto's lips and hands went. And that was another thing. His hands. Large and soft and outrageously bold in their travels.

I wasn't sure I had given them permission to visit those places, but as soon as I let out a gasp and Stiletto murmured, "Is this okay?" I found myself answering, "Oh, yes," instead of "Oh, no." Though sometimes I did that, too, and it didn't seem to make one bit of difference with the hands.

You may get the impression that we were largely silent except for the gasps and the kissing and sucking, but you would be wrong. Throughout this glorious tossing and turning and stroking and petting, Stiletto would whisper that he loved me, that he loved *us*, and that I was beautiful and soft and sexy and he couldn't get enough of me, until I felt this. . . .

. . . this other tightening that rippled and radiated right out of me, from the center of my being through my thighs and down my legs and up into my chest. I gripped Stiletto and searched his eyes, but he wasn't concerned at all. He just bent over me and grinned.

"What was that?" I said. "Was that . . . what I think it was?"

"You've never felt that before?"

"Not like that. *Never* like that. That was amazing."

Stiletto smoothed my hair. "You've been deprived, then."

Sweet Jesus. I lay down and tried to figure out where I was and why my head was nearly off the back of the bed. Stiletto continued to kiss and touch me gently while I recovered, smiling to myself until I thought, What about him?

And before you know it, we were back at it. Only Stiletto insisted I be on top (on top?) so he could look at me. Stiletto reached into his jeans pocket and pulled out a condom, showing not one ounce of shame in having brought it along or in putting it on. That confidence thing again.

So the big moment had arrived and the honored guest was invited in. I soon found myself behaving not the way a demure hostess would, but as a wanton, wild woman who didn't give a tinker's dam about anyone else at the party. Screw gently and lovingly, I thought. Faster!

Stiletto steadied my galloping hips with his hands, leaned back and let his eyes close for a second as I felt one of those ripples building again, only this one was even more forceful and I screamed gibberish at top volume. They could have heard me in Hellertown.

I collapsed into that warm spot between his neck

and shoulder, sweating and laughing and crying at the same time. His strong arms went around me, hugging me tight and stroking my hair.

"We did it, Bubbles," he said. "We finally did it."

"Yes," I said back. "We finally did."

CHAPTER 21

I don't recall at what point I first thought of Betty Jo Potrushnka.

It certainly wasn't before our fourth, and for the night last, round in bed. It must have been sometime after Stiletto and I, ravenous beyond words, raided the downstairs refrigerator, feasting on bread, whipped cream, strawberry jam, orange juice and other leftovers from the historical society breakfast.

Because after that, and after Stiletto promised a huge donation to the society in tribute to our spectacular night, we crept upstairs and, wouldn't you know it, found ourselves going for round five. (I thought round four would be the last. Honest.)

It was when I was waking to the stream of autumn sunlight breaking through the paned window that I suddenly remembered Betty Jo Potrushnka and her offhand comment that Thursdays were school field trip days.

"Stiletto." I nudged him. "What day is it?"

"Hrmmph," he said, rolling over and wrapping an arm around me. He began to nuzzle my neck, round six on his mind. "Wednesday, I think."

Good enough for me. I settled down to enjoy the nuzzling in our warm bed. Why couldn't we stay here forever?

The answer came in a squeal and squeak of bus brakes outside followed by the shouts, screams, laughter and high-pitched cacophony common to throngs of children.

"Holy shit. It's not Wednesday," I hissed. "It's Thursday. We've got to get out of here."

I gathered the sheet about me as I searched for the odd underclothing. The bra was by the window seat. The dress was over by the bookcase. And my thong. My thong was up high on the bedpost.

I had barely reached it, and Stiletto had barely fastened the buckle of his jeans, when the door opened and a woman in full Moravian historical garb entered. She was wearing a long gray dress, white apron and white cap. A purple ribbon tied in the front meant she was a widow.

"Oh!" Her mouth froze into a perfect oval. "Oh, my."

I hid behind the bed as I pulled up my thong.

"Hi," Stiletto said, extending his hand as though she had arrived at the Sears showroom. "I'm Steve Stiletto. Sorry we made a mess, but it gave us some wonderful memories. Thank you so much."

He was totally cool. Who was this man? I thought as I tried to zip up the back of my one-sleeved zebra dress.

"Here. Let me give you a hand with that, Bubbles." He walked over and zipped me up, the

294

historical society lady seemingly stuck in the doorway.

"I am so, so sorry," I said, patting down my hair. "It's a long story but please don't call the police. We didn't intend to commit a crime."

"Not in this state," Stiletto said, grinning. "About Texas I'm not too sure."

I flashed him a look to behave.

"Oh," she said again.

I peered at her brass nametag pin. Betty Jo Potrushnka. Just my luck.

"I think we met. On the phone." I gave her my hand, too, which she shook as she took in the zebra stripes. "I'm Bubbles Yablonsky from the *News-Times*. I called yesterday looking for Eunice Morse."

Behind me Stiletto was straightening the bed and picking up the place. I cringed at the thought of Betty Jo seeing our dirtied plates, not to mention discarded old condoms. Please may she not have seen the discarded condoms.

I let go of Betty Jo's hand, which she surreptitiously wiped on her apron. Her eyes widened at the sight of our disheveled bed.

"So *you're* the ones who've been sneaking in here?" she accused.

"Us?" I said. "No. This is our first time." My thoughts ran to the high school kids in the cave, their beer cans and cigarettes. Had they found the tunnel and the trapdoor? "Have you been having problems with break-ins?"

"We did last winter and then the break-ins stopped when they had the security system repaired," she said. "At least, I thought they had had that security system repaired. How did you get in?"

I pointed to the revolving bookcase and embarked on a rambling speech about doing a story on Hal Weaver, entering the cave, following the tunnel. Looking for any research Hal Weaver may have left.

"This is to pay for the inconvenience we caused," Stiletto said, handing her a check. "Please consider it the first of many annual donations we'll"—he said *we'll*—"be making to the historical society in the future."

Whatever sum the check was for, it must have been a whopper, because Betty Jo stared and stared at it, back at Stiletto, and then at the check again.

"Heavens," she said, tucking it in her apron. "That's so generous."

"It's my pleasure, and you have no idea how literally I mean that." Stiletto took my hand. "We never had plans to stay the night. It's just that one thing led to another."

Betty Jo, flush from reading so many zeroes, managed a small smile. "Did you say you were looking for research Hal did? Let me go get it."

She left and ran downstairs, where it sounded as though a herd of rhinos were ready to stampede. I shuddered at the possibility that had Betty

Jo not found us first, Stiletto and I might have become the most educational exhibit Mrs. Cafferty's third-grade class had ever seen.

"Did you hear what she said, Stiletto? She said that other people have been breaking in and using this bedroom."

He put his arms around my waist and kissed me. "Yes, but it will always be ours, Yablinko."

"I'm not talking about that. I'm thinking. . . ."

"Here it is." Betty Joe entered holding a large, brown three-ring binder, saw us in the clutch and cleared her throat. "Ahem."

We dropped each other like guilty lovers.

"Hal spent years researching the tunnel you came up," she said, flipping through the binder. "He gathered so many stories about its original use by the local Native Americans, especially the Delawares, the Northington and Unami tribes. Later, of course, the Moravians built the inn here. It fit with their mission to help political prisoners and slaves, persecuted people in general."

Didn't sound like much of a Steel secret to me.

"May I see it?" Stiletto held out his hands and Betty Jo reluctantly gave him the book.

"Please be careful," she said. "It's all we have left of Hal's works. We were very fond of him at the historical society."

"Of course." Stiletto flashed his charming smile. "I promise we will have it back to you by the end of the day."

"The end of the day? You're leaving with it?"

"Photocopier," he said.

"Ah." She patted the check in her pocket as though to remind herself of life's rewards. "By the way, you are familiar, aren't you, with the history of this bedroom?"

At last an explanation.

"No," I said, "tell us."

"Believe it or not, George and Martha Washington slept here on numerous occasions."

I coughed back a laugh. Stiletto clenched his jaw in an effort to stifle a bawdy remark.

"That's right." Betty Jo Potrushnka smiled at what she mistook as our shock. "And it seemed to have worked for them. They were married forty years. In fact George once said," a glint of moral message sparkling in her eye, "'For in my estimation more permanent and genuine happiness is to be found in the sequestered walks of connubial life than in the giddy rounds of promiscuous pleasure.'"

Stiletto and I looked at each other, instantly reading each other's mind.

That's what *he* thought.

I felt kind of crummy retrieving the Donkey Sucking Mobile from where I had left it the night before, in front of Debbie North's apartment. She must have seen it that morning when she went to work and figured it was mine, that I had been with Stiletto all night. Oh, well.

When we got to Stiletto's house, there was a message on his answering machine left by Dan wanting to know if any "funny business" had commenced at Jane's Princeton interview. He was in a tough spot, here, since he couldn't very well admit to having a spy-cam. Yet he must be scratching his balding head wondering what in the hey-ho happened to the last five minutes of his tape that G erased.

Jane also called to say that Professor Smullen had offered her a recommendation to Princeton, even though she'd cancelled the interview, and Lorena called to remind me she was catering Kiera Weaver's shower at 5 P.M. in Saucon, if I wanted to stop by and do some snooping.

Finally, Sandy wanted to know if I could help at the House of Beauty on Saturday. That was a completely bogus call. What Sandy wanted to know was whether Stiletto had done the dirty deed.

While Stiletto took a shower, I called her back at the salon.

"Don't say another word. I can hear it in your voice," she said. There was an eruption of shouts and applause from the clients in the background. "How was it?"

That was kind of smarmy of her to ask, so I answered cagily. "Remember Mel Gibson's wedding night scene in *Braveheart*?"

"How could I forget? It's what I think about when Martin's not in top form."

"My night with Stiletto was braver and had more heart. And even, in a way, more Mel."

"Yeah, but no priest."

299

"You getting religious on me, Sandy?"

"Skip it. What about Bon Jovi?"

"Bon Jovi," I said, lowering my voice so Stiletto wouldn't hear, "is dust."

"Bon Jovi's dust, she says," Sandy announced to the peanut gallery, which responded with further applause.

Getting back on, Sandy said, "On a sad note, we've had a death."

With all the blue hairs in the salon the lucky candidate was a toss-up. "Which one?"

"Mrs. Domenici. Remember her? She was here on Monday getting her hair done. Passed peacefully in her sleep."

Oh, yes. Little Mrs. Domenici. "I thought she was going on a trip to see her daughter Jeanette."

"Yeah, well, turns out Jeanette's been dead for five years. If I had known, I would have insisted she keep the tip."

"How'd you find out?"

"Mrs. Stottlemyer, the one-woman Western Union, called this morning on her cell. She says the funeral's tomorrow at St. Jude's. The wake's tonight at Wysocki and Sons, though I figure you have other plans."

"Can't imagine." I was involuntarily twirling my hair.

"That's okay," Sandy said. "I'll go for you."

My brain was so befuddled with sex and love and sex that after I took a shower in Stiletto's master bathroom I found myself humming and daydreaming, unable to figure out what to wear or what day it was or whether I had work to do. I kept replaying that night over in my mind, getting so hot and bothered by the scenes of Stiletto's arousing prowess that I had to step onto the balcony in my towel to cool down.

It was cold outside, so I settled on my favorite pair of black leather jeans and a white knit turtleneck. Put on the boots. Did the hair up and the makeup (no glitter) and went downstairs.

It was almost eleven. How decadent of us.

Stiletto had his leather coat on, about to go out. "New York AP called. There's a possible hostage situation at a company outside Philly. Some ticked off employee with an automatic blowing his top on payday."

I had seen Stiletto run off to dozens of assignments, but for some reason this one gave me pause, made my palms tingle. "Take care of yourself, Stiletto. I don't like the sound of that. Hostage situations are scary."

He made a face. "You're not going to start worrying about me just because we've . . ."

I kissed him. His mouth brought back those memories, the kind I couldn't afford to savor right now. Stiletto had an assignment to cover. I had a story to write. I had remembered that much.

"Listen." He gripped my shoulders and acted serious. "I know these mornings after can be difficult. You wonder if I meant what I said in the heat

301

of the moment and all that. I did. Every word. You know that, right?"

"I know that." I searched his eyes. "Aren't you wondering the same?"

He took his keys out, tossing them into the air and then catching them. "What?"

"Whether what *I* said was sincere?"

"Hmm. Seems all I can remember you saying is 'Don't stop,' 'Oh, yes' and 'Oh, oh, Stiletto.'"

He fled out the front door before I could throw Hal Weaver's notebook at him.

Hal Weaver's notebook. I carried it to the dining room, now cleared of all Henry Metzger files, and began sifting through it. It was a disorganized mess.

Assorted coffee-stained newspaper clippings and scrawled notes about the Underground Railroad, the Indians, the Moravians and the history of the Moon Inn, and minutes of historical society meetings. It was the kind of collection a crazy man might keep. Certain banal sentences were highlighted in bright yellow, like "The Lehigh Canal began operation in 1829."

I closed the empty book and looked at the spine. In black marker it said, *The History of Lehigh and the Moravians. 1734–1934.* The whole thing didn't make sense. Why would Hal Weaver have crept back to the Moon Inn on Valentine's Day, having just broken up with his mistress, having just learned that his nineteen-year-old daughter was pregnant, to go over these clips.

I folded my arms on the table and rested my head. I was tired. Beat was more like it. I would have loved nothing more than to take a nap, except I remembered that a rough draft of the Carol Weaver story was due by noon.

Forget it. Like Bill Graham had said, I didn't have the story. I was no closer to finding if there was any truth to Carol Weaver's claim that Steel set her up than I was on Monday night when the BB shooter shot up my bed.

What was the most damning, hard piece of evidence I had? The sign-out sheet with Hal Weaver's name obviously forged. The police and Reinhold could easily argue Carol had signed it. Who knew her husband's signature better than she?

As for Kiera murdering Weaver, that was a mystery beyond my capabilities. I wasn't a cop with a search warrant. Kiera wouldn't allow me in her house. And even if she did, what would I look for? The murder trail was a good nine months old.

Unless . . . unless this book wasn't the secret Weaver was hiding. What if the secret were a person? A person with whom Weaver rendezvoused at the Moon Inn on various occasions.

The person would have had to have been a woman, because it was Valentine's Day, after all, and Weaver had just broken up with his mistress. He definitely wasn't with his wife.

So maybe that mystery woman was the murderer, the femme fatale with the killer nails. The coroner's report noted it would have taken hours for death to set in once the cyanide seeped through the skin and throughout Weaver's nervous system.

And hadn't Betty Jo Potrushnka said other trespassers had broken into the inn and slept on that bed?

Our bed, I thought dreamily.

Which is when I saw it. The thin black corner sticking out from a crack in the plastic binding of the notebook. Searching through my purse, I found a pair of eyebrow tweezers and slowly, gently removed the sheet.

Microfiche. No bigger than a credit card. But what did it hold?

There was only one place that could tell me. This called for a trip to the children's library.

CHAPTER 22

You know, where are the helpful sixth graders when you need them? In school, apparently, since the children's library was empty except for toddlers listening to story hour. Turned out the children's library didn't have microfiche machines anyway. So I had to plead with the librarians in Research to permit me one last try.

They relented when a kind Mormon woman, there to do genealogical research, promised to act as my oversight. We slipped the microfiche under the scope and she gasped in horror when the first image appeared on the screen.

I gasped, too.

Morgue photos. The first was of what I judged to be a scientist in a lab coat. The other was of a man in overalls. Instinctively, I knew who they were. The two Mountaintop lab employees. Dead.

"That's awful," my Mormon friend said. "What is this?"

"Medical journals," I lied. "Thanks for your help."

She rolled away in her swivel chair, still frowning at my screen.

The first was a lab technician who looked as though he had died in pain, his face contorted and his mouth open. The second was a janitor whose countenance was much more peaceful, yet far more disturbing. He was so young. A kid. Couldn't have been more than Jane's age.

And they were so pink. Pink from the cyanide that had killed both of them.

I scrolled down to a plethora of information. Toxicology reports. Internal Steel memos. I read it all carefully, taking notes along the way. The terminology was difficult, a lot about cyanide and acid being mixed. Potassium. Sodium. Hydrogen. Eek!

There was testimony from other people in the lab. On January 2 Donald Halstead was the first technician to arrive for work after the New Year holiday. He had just begun a test strip for a new sheet metal compound when he suddenly began to breathe rapidly and his body went into convulsions, finally falling on the floor.

The only person with the guts and soul to attend to him was a janitor named Tucker Zabrisky, who rushed to his side, unbuttoned Halstead's collar and, albeit foolishly, gave him mouth-to-mouth resuscitation. That may have been a fatal act, because, in doing so, he managed to get cyanide on his person.

The effect was equally quick. The janitor also began breathing funny, gasping and clawing the air. When he fell unconscious, no one attended to him. Couldn't blame them, really.

What I didn't understand until I read through most of the file was that the form of cyanide that had proved to be so deadly had been banned at Steel two decades before because of its toxicity and its threat to the environment. That was what the rest of the microfiche was about.

The cover-up. A Steel in-house doctor wrote out their death certificates. He stated that Halstead succumbed to carbon monoxide poisoning resulting from improper use of a Bunsen burner. (How lame was that?)

The janitor's death was attributed to an undiagnosed flaw in the nineteen-year-old's heart valve.

Then Steel paid a million dollars to both families to keep them quiet. It was a pittance compared to a potential jury verdict in an era when juries were prone to handing down wild awards in the multi millions, one memo noted. Both families signed waivers promising not to sue and gag orders promising not to talk.

I spent the next two hours reading pages and pages about Steel's reckless use of cyanide, not only in the lab, but in steel processing. For as long as I had lived in this town, longer even, Steel had been spewing one of the most deadly toxins known to man. Had it poisoned the Lehigh River's fish? Heck. Had it poisoned me and my family?

I sat back. It was too complicated. I needed a real environmentalist to help me with this, a person who could tell me if Steel's use and production of cyanide was beyond public health limits.

Where had these documents come from, anyway? More significantly, how had Hal Weaver gotten hold of them? This was not material normally distributed to marketing and publicity.

After more extensive searching I saw the name I needed. Brian Morse, head of quality control. Susan's husband. Eunice's ex.

I sent the entire microfiche contents to the library printer at ten cents a page.

According to whomever answered the phone at the Moon Inn, where I did not offer my name, thank you very much, Eunice Morse had not come in that morning to volunteer. Nor did she answer her number at home.

I did not know the name of her sister in Philly, so I called Mickey Sinkler down at the police department. He wasn't in, thereby forcing me to leave a message about where I was headed and the number of my cell phone.

South Mountain wasn't too far from the library. All I had to do was cross through the South Side and it was about three miles uphill. I tried dialing Stiletto but he clearly was out of commission. There was that creepy computerized message again.

When I called Mr. Salvo, I found out why. "Bubbles. Where in God's name are you? You were supposed to be in the newsroom by ten."

"I was working, really. I have just found the most incriminating documents, ever." I checked my glove compartment, where the microfiche was stored in my tampon case. The printed pages were wrapped in a rubber band on the seat next to me, inside Hal Weaver's three-ring notebook. "You're going to flip when I tell you about them."

"Where are you?" His voice sounded urgent.

"On the Fahy Bridge"—*our* bridge—"why?"

"Good. You're not far. Get to the newsroom right away."

I moaned. "How about an hour? I have to contact Eunice Morse. It's vital I talk to her before I write the story. I really will get in a draft by six. I promise."

"Bubbles," he barked. "Get here now. It's about Stiletto."

"Stiletto?" My pulse skipped a beat. "What about Stiletto?"

"Just do yourself a favor. Keep the radio off." He hung up.

For the next three minutes as I weaved in and out of traffic on Fourth Street I would not allow myself to think. Get there. Just get there, Yablonsky, and deal with the news as it comes.

Mr. Salvo was waiting on the corner by the parking lot. I almost started bawling when I saw him.

"What happened to your car?" He shielded his vision to read about the donkey sucking. "You get vandalized?"

"Forget about the car." I slammed the door and ran to him. "Something bad has happened. Stiletto's dead, isn't he?"

"No. He's not dead." Mr. Salvo walked around the back of the Camaro and visibly flinched when he read ASK ME ABOUT DONKEY SUCKING. "But he's the biggest fool I ever met."

I let out a deep breath. Stiletto was alive. That was all that mattered. "What? What did he do now?"

"He went down to a biotech company in Malvern where there's an employee holding ten workers hostage and, typical Steve, he broke in to get a photo. Got himself caught by the psycho."

This took a minute to sink in. "Holy crap! Now *he's* a hostage?"

"As long as I've known him he's been a risk taker. You should know that, too. How many heart attacks have you had over his escapades?"

More than I cared to admit, though before last night I could have taken them in stride. Last night changed everything. I couldn't bear Stiletto getting hurt, much less being in danger. We had had eight hours together. I wanted more. I wanted a lifetime.

I looked up to find Mr. Salvo frowning. "Oh, man, oh, man. You did it, didn't you? You slept with him."

The way he said that, the cynical tone to his voice, made me want to slap his disapproving scowl. Mr. Salvo had no idea what sex had been like between Stiletto and me. It was more than sex. Like they say in the Catholic church in which I was baptized and raised, it was consummation.

"Editors have no souls," I said.

"Sorry." He held up his hands. "Wasn't my place. Uh, if it's any help, your story's on hold. We decided you needed more time."

This, too, took a few seconds to sink in. A story on hold was newspaper code for canned. A story on hold never got completed. It was put on the back burner, where it was left to evaporate into dust.

"You're killing it. You're killing the story, aren't you?" Between the news about Stiletto, the excitement of finding Weaver's microfiche and now this, I was a ball of jangled nerves.

"It was a quagmire, like Notch said. Look at it this way, Bubbles." Mr. Salvo patted me on the shoulder. "You gave the tryout the best chance you had, given that you started with a handicap."

"A handicap?"

"Not many reporters would have been left standing after getting involved in a historical society brawl."

"But . . ."

Mr. Salvo threw up his hands. "Who knows? Maybe someday down the road there'll be another opening and you can try for that."

I surveyed his white face for any indication that this was a joke. How could my tryout be over? I was just beginning to roll. "Who made this decision? Notch?"

"Graham," Mr. Salvo said. "Once he told me you were working on a lesbian lover angle, I had to agree with him, that you were in over your head. Where did you come up with that mush?"

"Graham didn't kill the story because of the lesbian lover angle. Graham killed the story because I wouldn't sleep with him, or do whatever else he wanted." I pushed past Mr. Salvo.

"Where are you going?"

"To the morgue."

"It's not that bad, Bubbles."

"I know," I yelled back to him. "It's not that morgue."

The newspaper morgue, a.k.a. Candy's Room, was right off the back stairs, which meant I didn't have to go through the newsroom and face all the reporters who'd heard of my dismissal.

Candy had overseen the morgue for twenty years, maintaining it in what can politely be described as controlled chaos. She was yellow and wrinkly, just like the newspaper clippings she cut, pasted and stored away daily in a filing system that Interpol couldn't unlock.

Take the night I needed background on a Northington couple who'd been convicted of abusing dogs. It was after five and Candy had gone home. I searched under "dogs," then "abuse," then criminal misdemeanor charges and finally the county courthouse files. Nothing. The next day Candy found the disturbingly thick file in a flash—under "pet discipline."

Most reporters were leery of Candy, often not venturing into her windowless cavern until 5:01, when she was out the door like a shot. And if they weren't afraid of her, then they passed her off as dimwitted. Candy wasn't dimwitted, she was employed. The *News-Times* has been unable to replace her by computerizing its archives because no one could understand her filing system.

Candy was at her large wooden desk, smearing mucilage on the backs of clips and listening to AM news radio. A big box of Puffs was at her arm and an even bigger pile of white tissues was on the floor.

"Are you crying?" I asked as Candy blew her nose.

"It's very personal."

"Oh, I'm sorry." I debated what to say. It's so hard to be tactful during displays of public grief. "Loved one?"

She nodded and closed her eyes. "Steve Stiletto," she whimpered.

I froze. Now what?

"See, I *know* the photographer caught in that hostage situation. That's Steve." She tried to compose herself by blinking back tears. "He moved the filing cabinets for me last year. He always makes a point of stopping by my room whenever he's in the building. I'm one of his favorite people."

I let out a breath I hadn't known I'd been holding. Was that all?

Like most women in the newspaper, Candy had a crush on Stiletto, who appeared in the newsroom occasionally to develop film in the *News-Times* darkroom or help other photographers with an assignment.

"He's so nice," she said. "Easy on the eyes, too," she added, giving her beezer one last honk.

Yes he is, I agreed silently, though I could not allow myself to dwell on what was going on in Malvern. "I wonder if I could pull the obit on a man named Donald Halstead who died January 2 in Lehigh. Also on a Tucker Zabrisky. Same date."

Candy pushed back her chair and flipped through the obit indexes. That gave me another idea. "Can you dig out obits by date?"

"I can give you a list of names and then cross reference them."

"I'd like all the obits from January 2 through 5, if possible." That should provide a wide enough range to find the names of any others who might have died in the cyanide spill.

"January 2 to the 5?" Candy's shoulders slumped. "Give me a couple of hours. I'm not exactly working at full speed under the circumstances."

Dear Lord, what would happen to this woman if someone truly close to her were in peril? As I was waiting for Candy to slowly photocopy the Halstead obit, the phone rang. Another delay.

"It's for you," she said, handing it to me. "The police."

My throat tightened. The police? Was this about Stiletto? Had he transmitted one last request to say goodbye? Did I need to fly down to Malvern to plead for his life?

"Take it," Candy said, still holding out the phone. "I don't have all day."

I took it. "Geezum, Bubbles, I had to pass through three people to get to you over there. You got a secretary now or what?"

It was Mickey. "You hear about Stiletto?" I asked.

"What a show-off. See, this is why cops hate the press. You get yourself a juicy sensitive hostage deal with trained negotiators and psychologists and, wouldn't you know it, a macho journalist breaks in and mucks everything up."

I reserved my biting reply. It was not necessary for me to act like a snapping bitch every time someone slammed my man. "Hostage situations are boring to shoot from the outside. My guess is Stiletto didn't want to end up with dull pictures of a biotech building."

"What about the boys in blue who are risking their lives surrounding that boring biotech building? We never get on the front page. Unless, that is, we whack some creep who deserved it. Oh, sure, then we're blasted above the masthead."

No use in getting into a political discussion with

315

him now. "You get my message about Eunice Morse?"

"That's why I'm calling. No need for you to go up there."

"Why not?" Candy deposited the obit in my lap.

"Because she's dead."

"Dead?" This couldn't be.

"Stiletto?" Candy screamed. "Stiletto's dead?"

I waved her off. "Not, Stiletto, Candy. Someone else."

"Oh." She collapsed against the desk and crossed herself. "I couldn't take that."

"According to the report, a guy named Carlton called this morning saying he was worried about his neighbor, Mrs. Morse. He hadn't seen her drive down the hill in two days and her mail was sticking out of the mailbox at the bottom of the road. So we sent someone up there and, you gotcha, dead."

Mickey crunched into an apple on the other end. Cops amaze me in their cavalier attitude toward the deceased.

"How'd she die?"

"Don't have the autopsy back, but from what the paramedics said it might be poisoning."

"Cyanide."

"No. Gosh, you're dramatic. Botulism. Canned beans or some disgusting crap. Like I tell Tiffany, preservatives are not the enemy. They're our friends."

And to think Eunice had offered me those beans.

Why, if I'd eaten them, I'd be . . . "Mickey, do you have twenty minutes to meet?"

"My shift ended an hour ago."

"Mama's pierogi shop in ten." I glanced at the clock. It was almost four. "They'll be closing, so we'll have privacy."

"No venison-stuffed pierogies, though. Those are enough to turn me vegetarian."

CHAPTER 23

"We're closed," Mama yelled as the bell tinkled and I entered the pierogi shop. "Come back . . . Oh, it's the hussy."

"That's brazen hussy to you." I crossed Mama's utilitarian restaurant.

Six tiny tables with uncomfortable metal chairs (Mama didn't want customers sitting too long) were arranged on the white and black linoleum floor. The fluorescent overheads were so bright that you could make out a person's pores two tables away. Mama didn't have much truck with mood lighting and ambiance. You ordered. You ate. You left and went back to work.

That was the Polish-Lithuanian way.

"So you finally hit the sheets with Stiletto." Mama was wiping down the glass cabinet with Windex and a rag while dressed in a psychedelic top and green fluorescent pants.

"How'd you find out?"

She quit wiping. "How didn't I? First Sandy called, then Mrs. Stottlemyer and after that the dam broke. Had to take the phone off the hook. I won't ask how it was, I see it in your face."

She jerked her head toward the TV behind the counter, where CNN was on mute. "You want me to turn off that trash?"

I shook my head, no. "I'm worried about Stiletto."

"He'll be all right, Bubbles." She stood on tiptoe and patted me on the back as we watched the TV together.

It showed images of the low, white biotech building and close to a hundred cops in full black assault gear hunched behind the doors of their cruisers, rifles poised. Inside the plate glass front of the building it was possible to discern hazy figures walking back and forth. One looked an awful lot like Stiletto.

"You know what being in your situation reminds me of? The war. In World War II, on the night before their beaus were to be shipped overseas, women would sleep with their boyfriends, never knowing if they'd see them again. Can you imagine? All for God and country."

I thought about this. "They had sex out of patriotism?"

"That's why they call it the greatest generation." She slapped her rag on the counter. "Such a sacrifice. That's more than your generation ever did."

"How come when I have sex I'm a slut? But when they have sex they're American heroes? How does that work?"

Mama tapped her temple. "It's all in the intent."

"Yeah. The intent to get nookie."

Before we could continue our argument, the bell tinkled and Mickey entered. Mama was about to shout for him to go away when she recognized her favorite cop and sprang into action, ushering him to the counter.

White plates piled high with pierogies were reheated in the microwave and laid before us, as was fresh coffee.

Mickey cut into a pierogie and inspected its contents. You never knew what to expect at Mama's shop. Evidently it was okay, because Mickey bit into it and nodded. "Not bad," he said, wiping his mouth. "What is it?"

"What is it?" Mama put her hands on her hips. She was so short she was barely high enough to see past the coffee cups. "What kind of question is that?"

"Just tell him." I pushed my plate away. I could not eat. Not with Stiletto's life hanging by a thread.

"Roasted chicken, basil and sun-dried tomato."

"You're kidding," I said. "No chocolate venison?"

A super-sharp butcher's knife appeared in her hand. "Watch what I do to brazen hussies who sleep around before they're married."

Mickey's hand froze with his fork in midair. "Aw, Christ." He actually looked hurt, as though I'd insulted him personally by sleeping with Stiletto. "That's it then, isn't it? He's got you."

"And you've got Tiffany," I said to remind him

of our salon's hippy dippy hairdresser whom he'd been dating.

"Tiffany's not you, Bubbles." He shoved the pierogi in his mouth. "Never will be."

"Ahh, get over yourselves, both of yous," Mama said, slipping into the local plural of "you."

While she went to get Genevieve, I brought Mickey up to speed on the Carol Weaver case, including Debbie North's theories about Kiera, the lesbian love triangle and what I had found about Steel.

"Can I see the Moutaintop Lab documents?" he asked.

"Not until I write my story. It's the only power I possess right now. If I give them to you, the assistant district attorney will want to use them to forward his career, so he will end up leaking them to Lawless and the *Call*. No way."

Mickey wiped his plate with the last pierogi. "Then what's in it for me?"

In the past *me* would have been enough for him to be in it. "I thought you'd like to know, is all. In case Eunice's autopsy turns up unnatural. This way you won't disregard foul play."

"Uh-huh." Mickey slid off his stool and plunked his cop's cap on his head. "You want me to play private bodyguard for you again, don't you?"

I was speechless. What had gotten into him?

"You're going to risk your life to get this story, and what you want me to do is stand in the shadows and catch you if you fall." He stomped off to the door. "Well, that's Stiletto's responsibility now. I'm tired of being a lackey for you. I'm not just a cop, Bubbles, I'm a man."

I stared as he left, giving the door a good, hard slam. I was stunned. Mama and Genevieve were behind the counter, silent for once.

"Love stinks," Genevieve finally said. "Stinks more than my insoles."

I forced myself to listen to the radio on the drive over to Kiera's baby shower. It was rush hour, slow going. As I sat on Wyandotte Hill, creeping from light to light, I tried to picture what Stiletto was doing. Where he was. How he was coping.

According to the so-called experts, the hostage crisis was at its crucial hour. The kidnapper, who was strapped to several sticks of dynamite, had been at it since ten-thirty. He was hungry, tired and stressed brittle.

Dusk was fast giving way to night, when the police would have a better chance of storming the building. This was the moment when nerves snapped. When it could go either way. The kidnapper could let a few hostages go, all of them or none.

Or he might simply explode himself—taking all the innocent people with him.

That's when I flipped off the radio. I did not need to hear this.

My cell phone's green light beamed in its cigarette charger. I was tempted to pick it up and call

Stiletto. To hear his voice just once. To hear him say that he'd get out of this, or that it was almost over—that could sustain me.

But this wasn't about me. This was about him. And a ringing cell phone when nerves were fraying and night was falling might be the ultimate push for a crazed kidnapper. Nope. I'd have to sit tight.

I accidentally hit the accelerator when the phone rang.

"Hi, Bubbles. It's me. Rachel."

I slammed on the brakes and caught my breath. "Hi, Mrs. Stottlemyer."

"Say, are you going to Mrs. Domenici's wake this evening?"

The traffic moved and I awkwardly shifted up the steep part of the hill. As soon as this story was over, I was kicking this phone into the Lehigh.

"I don't think so, Mrs. Stottlemyer. I'm going to Kiera Weaver's baby shower."

"She hasn't had that baby yet? Lordy, she has to be about to burst."

"You know her?" I crooked the phone and shifted into fourth as I headed down the other side of the hill.

"Of course, I know her. They go to St. Jude's."

That was interesting. I would have pegged the Weavers as more of your North Side St. Anne's parishioners, if not converted Episcopalian. Then again, St. Jude's was famous for having the shortest Mass in town—fifteen minutes, tops.

"Is Kiera married?" I asked.

"Not that I know of. Her boyfriend's a real druggie. What's his name again?"

Drugs. I hadn't thought of drugs, but that made sense. That would explain Kiera's demands for money. Along with her nasty personality and her motive for murder.

"I don't know his name." I was in Saucon now and had to pay attention to where I was going. I wished Mrs. Stottlemyer would get off the phone.

"Where are you now?" she asked.

"I'm taking a right onto the Weavers' street." In a flash, a pair of bright headlights appeared in my rearview.

"On Rock Creek? Hey, they get good reception out there, say? I'm on the Fahy. Listen, I wanna tell you about these calls I made from my cell this afternoon. You should have heard the reception I got on those babies."

The headlights were getting closer. "Not now, Mrs. Stottlemyer." I had to hang up.

I let the phone lie in my lap as I parked in front of the Weavers. The pair of lights stopped behind me. And then dimmed.

Hot damn. I was in trouble. Shoving the Steel documents under the passenger seat, I grabbed my purse and clutched my phone. It was my only weapon.

I opened the door and stepped onto the curb. The doors on the car behind me also opened and two figures stepped out. One short. One tall. I'd hit the tall one first. Take the midget later.

The cell phone flew through the air and hit the tall one with a *clank*.

A *clank?*

"Hell's bells, Sally." Genevieve appeared under the gas street lamp. The musket was at her shoulder. "What're you tossing phones about for?"

"It hit Genny's musket and broke." Mama bent to the sidewalk and retrieved some of the pieces. "You'll never put that back together. Not even with Krazy Glue."

I was furious. These two had frightened me out of my wits. "What do you expect?" I said, gathering up the pieces of Stiletto's cell phone. "Why didn't you warn me that you'd be following?"

"'Cause you wouldn't have let us," Genevieve said. "Remember coal country?"

"When Mickey said he wasn't going to be your backup anymore, we decided to sub." Mama handed me the pieces she'd collected. "You're not firing on all cylinders tonight, Bubbles. What with Stiletto about to be blown up and. . . ."

"Enough." I dumped the phone pieces into my purse. "Now he won't be able to call me if he gets out."

"That's okay. Mrs. Stottlemyer has his number."

I teetered slightly on my heels. "Tell me she hasn't been calling him."

"Oh, she's been calling him all right. Once she even asked to speak to the kidnapper or—what do you call people who take hostages, Genny?"

"Hostage taker?" Genevieve suggested.

"That's it. Hostage taker."

Adrenaline shot through my body faster than a triple espresso black. I tried to compose myself. "Mrs. Stottlemyer spoke to the *kidnapper?* The guy strapped with dynamite?" What had she asked him, how the reception was in Malvern?

"Twice." Mama brushed off her knees. "She told him not to be so darned hard on himself. To call it a day, take off the dynamite and go home already."

Vintage Mrs. Stottlemyer. All of life's problems could be solved by putting your feet up and watching TV.

"And what did Stiletto say?"

"I dunno." Mama shrugged. "I told her to call you and tell you what he said. Didn't she?"

"She called. We talked about the wake and Kiera Weaver's druggie boyfriend and how good the reception was in Saucon. Not once did she mention Stiletto."

"The reception's good in Saucon?" Mama asked, completely missing the tragedy of my situation.

"It's always good where rich folk are," Genevieve observed.

It was all I could do to keep from getting in the car and driving over to Wysocki's and shaking Mrs. Stottlemyer upside down. I didn't, though, because I had noticed something was very wrong.

There were no other cars in front of the Weavers' house. There weren't any people here, either. Nor was there any music, laughter, voices or even many lights on.

"This is where the shower is?" Mama asked, inching up behind me. "'Cause it don't look like much fun inside. Where are the pink and blue balloons on the mailbox?"

"Maybe she had the baby already," I suggested, ringing the bell.

There was a low grumbling of voices inside and then footsteps. The door was flung open.

"Party's cancelled," Lorena announced, a cigarette dangling from her mouth. She was back in her chef's outfit. White coat, black pants. Hair in a ponytail.

"Shame on you." Mama reached up and yanked the cigarette out of Lorena's mouth, tossing it onto the grass. "Smoking in the presence of a pregnant woman. Tsk. Tsk."

"Pregnant woman's upstairs taking a nap and don't you ever, ever tsk, tsk me again, old lady, hear?" Lorena came onto the front step and was about to grab Mama by her white Peter Pan collar when Genevieve put a musket to her forehead.

"Make my retirement," Genny said.

Lorena's brown eyes went wide. So wide that she could see me out the corner of them. "You're with these two?"

"Meet my mother and Genevieve." I pointed to them respectively. "Mama and Genevieve, meet Lorena Ludwig."

"Lorena the slugger?" Mama sidled away from

her. "Don't hit me. I'm on an aspirin a day. I'll bruise faster than a banana."

"I'm not going to hit you," Lorena promised. "Not now that I know you're Bubbles's mother."

Genevieve lowered the musket, though she kept it at the ready.

Lorena rubbed her head where the musket had left a big O. "Does everyone you know pack heat? I haven't seen so many guns since the racetrack closed."

I jerked my head toward the Weavers'. "What gives with the party?"

"Susan Morse cancelled at the last minute." Lorena closed the front door and folded her arms in the chilly air. "Said she couldn't make it. Sick or something. We're almost done cleaning up and then I'm outta here."

Sick made me think of Eunice. So sick that she had died at home, her body not found for days. If I hadn't been so preoccupied with Stiletto, I could have focused on her more. I feared that my visit had prompted someone to retaliate. Had Eunice said too much about Brian? Had Steel killed her for talking to me?

Or had she simply fallen ill because of her own sloppy canning?

No matter the answer. I couldn't wait any longer. I had to find Carol Weaver.

I surveyed Mama, Genevieve and Lorena. Three very different (okay, odd) women with very different talents. Mama with the lungs, Genny with the gun and Lorena with the fists.

"How would you guys like to go on a mission?"

"Impossible?" Genevieve brightened.

"Yes." I said. "Probably."

Our group of dysfunctional superheroes marched silently across the wide back lawn belonging to Susan and Brian Morse. We passed the in-ground pool, bedded for the winter, and the tennis courts and headed toward the back patio, our designated point of entry.

Leaves stuck to my feet and my arms had goose bumps, it was so cold.

We arrived at the back door and studied the house. It was mostly dark except for a light in the attic. That's where Carol was, we suspected. There were no cars in the garage, leading us to believe the power couple was out.

"Let's get this over with so I can breathe again." Mama yanked Genevieve's queen-sized knee-high, which she had stretched over her head. "Genny. You really gotta start wearing foot powder."

"It's genetic," Genevieve said. "I got a condition."

"Snap your traps, you two," Lorena said. "I have to think."

Lorena and I were in charge of the inside job. Lorena had used her skills learned during her life of crime to plan most of the operation, which centered on the two of us breaking in and grabbing Carol while Mama and Genevieve patrolled the perimeter.

"LuLu," Lorena said, "give us the high sign you'll use if you see headlights."

Mama leaned back, opened her mouth and yelled, "Heyyy Abbbbottt."

Lorena covered her ears. "Hey Abbott? What kind of lame-ass signal is that?"

"Avoids confusion," Mama said. "I yell, 'Oh, my God they're here' and you'd think, who's here? I yell 'Hey Abbott' and you'll know to skedaddle."

"My mother loves Abbott and Costello," I explained. "She thinks they're a laugh riot."

"How about 'Scram, the bitch is back'?" Lorena suggested. "Or maybe your butch buddy there fires her rusty rifle."

"Butch?" Mama asked innocently. "What does she mean, 'butch'?"

"My rifle ain't rusty," said Genevieve, checking around the corner. "What are you girls standing around for like a bunch of sissies? We gotta get cracking."

"That's what she means by 'butch,'" I said.

Mama and Genevieve spread out while Lorena and I fiddled with the back door. Locked. Damn.

"Suburbanites always leave keys under flowerpots," Lorena said, lifting a mum and finding a key. "It's like, they invest fifty grand on a security system and then leave the key right there. How dumb is that?"

She stuck the key in the lock. It sprung right open. A security system blinked in response.

"What do we do about that?" I asked, pointing to the pad of numbers and lights.

"Screw it. Let's get Carol."

We flicked the lights on and took the carpeted stairs from the kitchen two at a time. The idea of back stairs intrigued me. In a house like this you could descend the front stairs in a flowing evening gown and quip wittily, "Fasten your seat belts. It's going to be a bumpy night."

But if you didn't want anyone to see you, you could run up and down the back stairs in your ripped sweats and stained shirt. The rich really do have life down to a T, don't they?

Lorena was panting when we reached the third-floor landing.

"Cigarettes," I said. "They'll kill you."

"Buzz off, Blondsky." Lorena gasped for more air.

I opened the landing door to a short hallway, off which were two doors. Right away I heard it.

Crying.

"What's that?" Lorena whispered.

"Sounds like someone's crying."

"Let's go, then." She tiptoed into the hallway. "This is one nice attic. You should see my attic, crammed with old beds and junk. Fire hazard."

Lorena was right. The hallway was carpeted with a heavy duty wheat-colored Berber. The walls were painted beige and trimmed in white. Tidy as a pin.

Lorena put her ear to both doors and finally

decided on the left one. As soon as she tried the handle, the crying stopped.

"Go away!" a woman's voice hollered. "Leave me alone."

Lorena made a *hmm?* face and removed a bobby pin from her hair. It really was helpful to have a reprobate in our group, I thought as she wiggled the pin in the lock.

The lock released and Lorena opened the door carefully, narrowly missing a sneaker aimed at her head.

"Now, let's calm down here, toots," I heard her say. "Hey! What are *you* doing here?"

Carol? I ran in after her, right as Lorena and this woman fell to the floor, rolling and scratching and swearing. It was like déjà vu all over again.

"Stop it. Stop it." I grabbed Lorena and pulled her off. "Gee, you have a problem."

"No, I don't." Lorena pointed to the other woman. "She's the problem."

The woman sat in a heap, black and blue marks around both eyes, her brown hair tangled over her face.

"Lorena! What did you do to her?"

"I didn't do it." Lorena struggled to get up. "She came that way."

Susan Morse pushed back her once shiny, perfect hair. Her lips were swollen and red, making it difficult to understand what she was saying. "Wowena's wight. She didn't do this to me. He did."

"Who?" What was going on? I was completely confused. Where was Carol?

"Gosh darnit, Bubbles. You really are a dumb blonde, aren't you?" Lorena cuffed me gently on the head. "Don't you see what's going on? Susan's a battered wife."

Committing an act I never would have imagined in a million years, Lorena leaned down and helped Susan to stand. "Come here, hon. It's okay. We'll get you out of this."

"I can't." Susan's lip started to bleed. Lorena pulled off her black shirt (which she had worn under the white chef's coat) and stemmed the bleeding.

"Yes, you can. I know it seems impossible now, but there are counselors who are ready day and night to help you relocate. We'll get you a lawyer to protect your assets and a safe house where you can stay. There's a whole system in place that can get you out of here right now. Forever."

Susan started to cry again. Lorena put her head to her bare shoulder and patted her back. "Now, now. It's all over, hon."

It was like I had entered an attic to bizarro world. Black was white, white was black. Susan was battered. Lorena was nice.

"Lorena," I started, not really knowing where to begin. "How did you. . . ."

"Five years I was beaten, Bubbles," Lorena said, still comforting Susan. "There were mornings I couldn't go to work because he had bashed both my knees with a baseball bat. If it hadn't been for the battered women's shelter on the South Side, I'd be dead by now."

"I don't want to go to a shelter," Susan said. "It's . . . humilweewating."

"Shhh." Lorena put her shirt back on. "We'll talk about that later. The important thing is where is the son of a bitch now?"

"Brian?" I asked.

Susan nodded. "Out."

"You know when he'll be back?" Lorena asked in the soft tone of an kindergarten teacher.

Susan shook her head.

"But both cars are gone," I said. "Why?"

"Typical batterer trick," Lorena said, knowledgeably. "Get rid of all transportation and probably the telephone, am I right?" She peered into Susan's blackened eyes.

"He wocks the phone," she said, touching her bleeding lip.

I harkened back to when Susan had called me at Stiletto's. I hadn't a clue then, of course, that she was a beaten woman. Brian must have thrown a fit after he caught me snooping around. That's why she couldn't meet me until her husband was asleep. Or perhaps he had brutalized her so violently that night that she hadn't been able to leave the house.

At which point I had an awful thought. "How long have you been here? In this room."

A tear rolled down Susan's cheek. "Since that night Bwyan found woo."

"Shit."

Lorena and I looked at each other. Every action causes a reaction. I should follow the Buddhist philosophy Jane espoused—that to not act is to not cause pain. By visiting Eunice I had condemned her to death; by spying on Susan I had gotten her hurt.

"Bwyan knows evewything," Susan said, turning to me. "He knows what you've found and where've you been. He told me. He told me he's going to stop you. Tonight."

"Is he really." Lorena was getting hot again, her hands turning into fists. "I'd like a piece of his—"

"What," I interrupted, "what does Brian know exactly?"

"I don't know. He wouldn't tell me. All I know is you've made him vewwy, vewwy mad."

"Clearly," I said.

"Come on." Lorena retrieved Susan's sneakers from the floor. "Let's get you out of here."

"Hold on." I blocked their exit. "Before we go, I have to ask you a couple of questions, Susan."

"Bubbles," Lorena whined. "We don't have time. Ask later."

"Did you send the molasses cookies to the Jonathan Frakes?"

Susan shook her head. "No. Cawool called me from jail and said someone had tried to poison her with those cookies. That's when I told her to find a way to get out, maybe through the prison linen, that I was on my way to get her."

"So you helped Carol escape?"

"I was worried. I was afwaid she'd die. That's why we came to you. We had to find out who was behind her almost poisoning. When Cawool said you didn't believe her, we panicked. We had to get you involved."

"Which is why you fired shots at me Sunday night."

"I shot your bed. And it was only a BB gun." Once again she was on the verge of tears. "I didn't want to huwt you. I wanted to make you vested."

There were other ways to make me vested, but this wasn't the place to argue. "One last question."

"Oh, come on." Lorena started hopping up and down. "You can interview her later, Bubbles."

"This can't wait." I squared my shoulders. "Did you kill Hal Weaver?"

"No, I did not," she said firmly, licking the corner of her lip. "And Cawool didn't either."

"Then who did?"

She blinked her swollen eyes.

"Kiera?" I said.

She blinked again and then nodded slowly. "Yes. That's what we think."

I wanted to ask her more, like how and why? But from outside the window, somewhere on the back lawn, came an ear-piercing bellowing.

"Heyyy Abbbotttt."

Brian was back.

CHAPTER 24

"Quick!" Lorena grabbed Susan's hand and pushed past me. The three of us hustled down the back stairs as fast as we could, not an easy task in these high-heeled boots of mine.

When we got to the back door, Susan pointed to the black box on the wall. "Awarm." The green lights had turned to red and were blinking madly. "It went off."

"I didn't hear anything," I said.

"It's silent, you ninny." Lorena tried the door. It was locked.

"Automatic," Susan said. She moved her swollen fingers stiffly over the pad.

"Hurry," Lorena hissed. "I hear them outside."

Indeed, there suddenly seemed to be a lot of shouting and scrambling. There was the pound, pound, pound of someone running. Someone heavy. Like Genevieve.

"I know the combination," Susan mumbled. "I've watched Bwyan do it when he wasn't wooking."

Boom!

Susan lifted her fingers. "What was that?"

"Just a musket going off," I said. "Are you almost done?"

She pushed a four and the light turned from red to green. Lorena opened the door and we dashed outside.

A tiny figure churned past us in the dark. "Heyyy Abbotttt!"

I ran off the porch and snagged her, my heels sticking into the hard ground.

"Get off me!" Mama yelled, about to set her choppers into my arm.

"Owww. Knock it off. It's me. Your daughter."

Mama lifted her dentures and inspected me. "So it is. What's the meaning of this, you grabbing me around the neck?"

"You're acting nutty. What's going on out here? Why are you shouting 'Hey Abbott'?"

"It's the high sign, remember?"

"I know *that*. What I want to know is what sign are you highing?"

Mama pointed to shadows by the pool. "There."

"Got her!" Genevieve yelled. "And she ain't going nowhere with my stockings around her wrists."

"Where's Bwyan?" Susan and Lorena approached us.

"Who's this?" Mama asked.

"That's Susan Morse. Brian's been keeping her locked up in the attic. He's a batterer."

"Poor baby," Mama said.

"Then who does the bull dyke got?" Lorena asked.

"Bull dyke?" said Mama. "What's a bull dyke?"

"It t'ain't a pretty picture, ladies. But she got what's coming to her." Genevieve joined us, pulling someone by the ear. As they got closer I could see the unfortunate victim had one leg of a panty hose tied around her mouth and another around her wrists.

"Cawol!" Susan exclaimed.

"Hmmphmm," replied Carol, bending closer to check out Susan's injuries. "Mdt bewrd."

Which I took to be "That bastard."

"Let her talk," I said.

"She'll scream," Genevieve said. "When I found her in the pool cabana she threatened to scream until the cops came."

"Noomymph," protested Carol.

"No, she won't," I said. "The last people she wants to show up are the cops. This is Carol Weaver."

Genevieve got an a-ha look on her face and pulled down the stocking.

Carol spit something out and said, "This is whacked. Who are you people?"

"Well, you already know me," I said.

"And *me* you couldn't bother to say hi to," Lorena said, pouting.

"The woman who caught you is Genevieve."

"I saw an intruder at nineteen hundred and one hours moving east, northeast," Genevieve reported. "After asserting that said intruder was our designated target, I moved in on her, deploying munitions only to avoid collateral damage."

"Which is when I screamed, 'Hey Abbott,'" Mama added.

"And this is my mother," I said to Carol. "LuLu Yablonsky. We came here to find you, which we did. We also found Susan locked in the attic."

Carol turned to Susan. "What are you going to do?"

"Weave," Susan replied thickly.

"Leave," I said. "We're taking her out of here."

Carol, who was still in Genevieve's firm control, agreed. "Finally. How long have I been telling you to pack up and go?"

"No time to pack up," Lorena said. "We need to just go. That alarm went off, which means Brian's coming back."

"This is it, then," Carol said. "I'm going back to jail."

"Not necessarily." A pair of headlights swung around the corner into the driveway. "That's him. Let's hustle."

We jogged through the backyard, into the woods and to the other street, where our cars were parked.

"Where to?" Genevieve practically threw Carol into the backseat of her Rambler.

"To the Weavers' house. For a little question-and-answer time," I said.

"*Jeopardy?*" said Mama. "We'll have to hurry. It's almost over."

Kiera Weaver was lying on the family room couch, her multicolored maternity sweater giving her pregnant belly the appearance of a beach ball. The TV was on, some cop thing that I turned off when we came into the room.

"Who are you?" Kiera asked, struggling to sit up.

"Bubbles Yablonsky, the reporter you wouldn't talk to." I scanned the room, with its big stone fireplace, beamed ceiling and natural wood paneling. "Nice digs."

"Get out," she said to me. To Lorena she said, "The caterers are gone, so why are *you* still here?"

"Me? I'm here to take pictures." Lorena took out her camera and focused it on Kiera. "Bubbles is here to ask you some questions." Flash! Lorena's camera went off.

"I'm calling the police." Kiera leaned over and reached for the phone.

"No," whispered Carol, coming from the kitchen. "Please don't."

Kiera looked as if she'd seen a ghost. Her thin face, framed by dark hair, became chalky white and her eyes seemed to sink into their sockets. "Mother?"

Genevieve led Carol to a brown leather chair. "Sit," she commanded. Carol sat.

"What did they do to you?" Kiera asked.

"They found me at Susan's. That's where I've been hiding all week."

Kiera's eyes narrowed. "Figures you wouldn't come to see me, your pregnant daughter. Figures you'd want to hang out with your best friend."

"I didn't see you because I didn't want to put you in danger," Carol pleaded. "Everything I've done, I've done for you. Why can't you understand that?"

Flash! Lorena took another photo.

"You did all what for me?" Color returning to her small face, Kiera put a pillow behind her back, which she arched in discomfort. "You killed my father for me? Give me a break."

Mama and I slumped into a love seat and watched the Kiera and Carol exchange like it was a tennis match. We had decided to keep Susan in the living room so as not to exacerbate the situation further.

"For the thousandth time, I did not kill your father. I loved your father. You know that."

"What I know is that you found out he was having an affair." Kiera grimaced and readjusted the pillow. "And so you murdered him."

"No." Carol was close to crying. "I didn't. I never would have. Why would you think that?"

"Because you were afraid he'd do what Brian Morse did to Eunice, dump you for a younger woman. You couldn't stand to lose your house and your country club life, your Volvo and Talbot's charge because Daddy wanted to be happy. So you killed him instead."

"Bull." Susan Morse came to the doorway. "We all know who killed your fawther and it wasn't your mowther, Kiera."

"What's she doing here?" Kiera bent over slightly, her eyes shutting for a second. "And what did she do to her face?"

Time to intervene. "Kiera," I said gently. "Perhaps you don't understand a key fact. Your mother did not kill your father, but she went to jail anyway." I paused to make sure I had everyone's attention. "To cover for you."

"Me?" Kiera slapped the couch. "Why does everyone keep saying that? I didn't kill Daddy."

"Don't lie," Carol said in a way that, had I been her daughter, I would have found to be very irritating. "I know what a bad influence Doogie" (Doogie?) "was on you. He got you into drugs and so messed up you didn't know up from down."

Kiera's face reddened. "I may not have known up from down, but I knew better than to kill my own father. And anyway, Doogie and I have been clean since the pregnancy test." She inhaled sharply. "You can't understand why I don't believe you. But how is it that you don't believe *me*? What exactly . . ." Kiera closed her eyes again.

Mama nudged me and cocked her chin to Kiera's belly, which was visibly contracting.

"Kiera?" Carol inquired. "Are you okay?"

"Braxton Hicks." Kiera sucked in another breath, cringing at the so-called "practice" contractions.

"Untie her, Genny," Mama said. "Let her mother feel."

Genevieve did as she was told. Carol shook her hand and placed it on her daughter's taut middle. "That's very strong for Braxton Hicks."

"I'm not due for another two days," she said innocently.

Mama snickered. "They're not trains, dear. Babies rarely come on schedule."

"We have to get you to the hospital or at least call your doctor," Carol said, reaching for the phone.

"Wait. It's over." Kiera sat back. "I want *this* over before the baby comes, too. I have to know who killed my father before I bring his grandchild into the world."

Ditto, I thought, vaguely wondering how Stiletto was doing.

"What I was trying to say was," Kiera looked at her mother, "what exactly had I done that would make you think I murdered him?"

Carol's jaw clenched. "Nail polish. I found it in your downstairs bathroom cabinet. It was right next to the bottle of potassium cyanide. That's how you killed him. You mixed potassium cyanide with nail polish."

"Did not," Kiera said.

"Did too," responded Carol.

Lorena put her fingers in her mouth and whistled. We all looked at her. "Cyanide?" she said. "Who keeps cyanide in their house?"

Carol raised an eyebrow at Kiera.

"Not me." Kiera put her hand to her chest. "I wouldn't know where to get the stuff."

"How about that prince, Doogie?" Lorena suggested. "Don't druggies cut cocaine with cyanide?"

Gee, it was good to have Lorena on board.

"I've never heard of that," Kiera said. "The only thing cyanide's in that I know of is cigarettes."

"Oh well." Lorena shrugged. "Thought I'd give it a shot."

"And then there was that awful fight you two had when Daddy came home that night," Carol continued. "I heard it from the other bedroom and prayed that you would stop."

I'd forgotten that Hal and Carol had been sleeping in different bedrooms, not to mention under different roofs at times.

"What I assumed," Carol said, her voice shaking slightly, "was that Daddy came home, you fought and you scratched him with your poisoned nails. I didn't know what to do . . . so I put the cyanide on my own nails. In case they tested us."

Tears were streaming down Carol's cheeks and her shoulders were shaking. She said, "A couple of days later, during my umpteenth interrogation, a police officer hinted that they were prepared to arrest either you or me. They were trying to decide. That's when I confessed. To save my baby."

Kiera's jaw dropped. "Oh, Mom." She leaned over and patted her mother's leg. "Oh, Mom."

"There is no love like a mother has for her child." Carol slid her knuckles under her eyes to wipe away the tears. "Steel was cruel to their executives' wives. I had to be perfect, on the right committees, in the right clubs, throw the right parties or my husband would lose his job." She straightened. "Steel took my individuality. Steel took my husband. I sure as hell wasn't going to let them take my daughter."

Kiera was now weeping openly, too. Mama was sniffling. Susan's swollen eyes were puffy, and even Genevieve was snorting back something in her nose. Only Lorena remained unmoved, letting out a big yawn as Kiera awkwardly hugged her grateful mother.

"You do believe me, don't you?" Kiera asked. "That I had nothing to do with Daddy's death?"

Carol nodded, smiling at her daughter. "I do. I did before, too. I've always felt in my bones that it was Steel that killed Daddy. That's why I hired Bubbles to investigate."

I really wish she'd quit using the word *hire*.

"Pop," Mama said, taking my hand. "It brings back memories of how Steel was responsible for killing your own father."

Steel had murdered my father through its safety oversights. His story was far from uncommon. Making steel was dangerous work. Hands were severed. Eyes were blinded. Skin was burned and the extreme temperatures caused heat strokes and heart attacks. Men fell off bridges and narrow walkways.

Or they were poisoned by cyanide. Like lab technician Donald Halstead or janitor Tucker Zabrisky, just nineteen.

I glared at Kiera, who would have been his age when he died. And I thought about the father of her child, who wasn't with her on a night she might very well be in labor. I thought about young love and nineteen-year-old men who can't go long without having sex.

"Kiera," I said so sharply the women stopped hugging. "Did Norma Lubrecht have a boyfriend?"

"Norma?" Kiera winced again. "Oh, yeah. Her. I don't know. She was awful."

Carol squeezed her daughter's hand. "Don't you remember? That's why Daddy brought her here."

"Hal brought her to your home?" I asked. Geesh. Did the cops in this town ever do their jobs?

"We knew her from church," Carol explained. "Very sweet girl. Norma does the Christmas pageant. Her boyfriend died right around the holidays and I guess they'd been living together and Norma was hard up. I forget. Hal felt sorry for her and suggested we hire her to do housework."

"And did Norma clean the bathrooms?" I asked.

"Of course," Carol said. "Though not well."

"She refused to pick up my room before she cleaned," Kiera added. "She expected us to do all the picking up."

Kiera bent over in another spasm of pain. Carol

scooted beside her, rubbing her daughter's back and cooing with concern.

"Where did Norma's boyfriend work?" I asked.

"Come on, Bubbles," Lorena said. "Can't you see these two have other stuff on their minds?"

"We should call a doctor," Susan suggested. "Kiera. Who's your doctor?"

Recovering from the contraction, Kiera said, "No. Let Bubbles ask." Pant. "She's after something. Mom, where did Norma's boyfriend work?"

"I have no idea," Carol said quickly. "All I know is that he died of a heart attack or something freaky. It was genetic."

"And of course you don't know his name," I said.

Both women shook their heads no.

"Oooh." Kiera looked down. "Why am I all wet?"

"Oh, dear," Mama said.

Carol clutched her daughter's hand. "That's it. Your water broke."

"Yuck," said Lorena. "That's gross."

"No, it's not. It means she's going to have the baby." I said to Mama, "Call Dan. Tell him he's got a new client on his hands, Carol Weaver. Tell him to meet her in the labor and delivery room of St. Luke's Hospital."

"Not Dan, your ex?" Carol asked, nervous.

"At least he's up to speed on your case. He'll take care of you."

I stood and pointed to Lorena. "You can take

them and Susan to the hospital. You know what to do."

"Been there. Done that. Come on, Susan," Lorena said. "I'll shoot a roll of your bruises there, with doctors and nurses as witnesses."

"Bwyan will kill me when he finds out," Susan moaned. "He's probably looking for me right now."

"No, he's not." I said. "He's looking for me."

CHAPTER 25

Before I left the Weavers' I made two phone calls. One was to Lieutenant Heller at the Lehigh Police Department. Lieutenant Heller was a smart cookie in my book, and I thought she was someone I could trust to detain Norma Lubrecht on suspicion of murder.

The case would be hard to prove since it would be largely circumstantial. My theory was that Norma, motivated by either hate or greed (Who cares? Motive doesn't have to be proven in court.) engaged in a six-week affair with Hal Weaver conducted at the Moon Inn.

There on Valentine's Day, in a fit of passion over the wrongful death of her beloved boyfriend Tucker, Norma scratched the back of Hal Weaver with nails dipped in cyanide. The cyanide would have been procured from the Weaver house, possibly brought home by Hal, who stole it from the Mountaintop Lab on February 5 to back up the incriminating documents he had procured.

Norma had discovered it while cleaning and planted it in Kiera's bathroom. She tainted the nail polish with it to give the impression that Kiera had killed her own father. Later, I assumed, she mailed the poisoned spice cookies to Carol in jail.

Pure revenge.

The second phone call was to the *News-Times*. Considering the events of last week—the fight with Susan on the floor of the Moon Inn, the botched tryout and Bill Graham's lecherous advances—it was by far the hardest phone call I had to make.

Lorena, Susan, Kiera and Carol had left by the time I hung up. Mama waited by the door.

"Where are you going?" she asked.

"To see my father," I said.

She put her hands on her hips. "You need to do that now?"

"Let's say I'm feeling sentimental."

We started walking toward our cars. "So what do you want Genny and me to do?"

"Tell Mrs. Stottlemyer where I'll be. She should be getting out of the wake right about now."

"The wake. I forgot about the wake." Mama clapped her hands. "You're a good girl, Bubbles."

I planted a kiss on the top of her midget head. "Thanks."

"Even if you do sleep around."

I watched as Genevieve's Rambler pulled out and around my Camaro, heading pell-mell to the wake they were dying to get to. (A sort of play on words, in case you didn't notice.)

I felt alone without Stiletto's cell phone. Odd how you become attached to gadgets that months before you had peacefully lived without. Odd, I thought, my heart swelling, how you get attached to men like Stiletto.

I pressed my foot to the accelerator as I careened over Wyandotte Hill, back to the South Side. There'd be nothing gained by wringing my hands over what might never be. If Stiletto did not survive the hostage crisis, I would go on. I would go on as I had after the other most important man in my life had died.

My father. He had been a hardworking, larger-than-life man I never really knew, who put in long days tamping down sand in the ingot mold into which molten steel was poured. Henry Metzger hadn't been terribly concerned about the safety of men like Yablonsky. Laborers, like the reporters at the *News-Times,* were a dime a dozen.

Though, with union wages, they were far more expensive than that.

The only memory I had of the day my father died was of my mother coming through the door with groceries, the phone ringing off the hook to tell her the bad news and her collapsing. Cans of beans and corn, falling to the floor. Broken eggs and spilled milk.

He hadn't escaped the mold in time. I used to say, jokingly, that Steel had turned my father into a human trophy. But, really, it wasn't possible for anything but ashes to survive hot, red liquid steel. And I never knew what they had buried in the coffin we placed in Hillside Cemetery, the cemetery where most of Lehigh's working class enjoyed their final rest.

That's what I was thinking—what's in that coffin—as I stared at my father's grave the night Kiera was giving birth. Save for the gentle lights that framed the twisting roads through Hillside, the cemetery was dark and quiet. Leaves blew around the headstones and my ankles as I hugged my rabbit fur coat to keep warm.

"How did he die?" a man's voice asked.

Mr. Graham trudged up the hill. He was wearing a black wool coat with a white silk scarf around his neck and a gray fedora on his head. He was very handsome. I wondered if that was why I was slightly attracted to him—because he was such a father figure.

"He died in the ingot mold," I said. "I was just a kid."

Mr. Graham put his arm around me and gave a reassuring hug. He was still panting from the climb. "Tough."

"Yes," I said. "Tough."

I looked up at him. "Why did you decide to come?"

"I wanted to." Under his arm he was holding a set of white pages. I knew those pages. They had come from underneath the passenger seat of my car.

I closed my eyes and said a quick prayer to my father, wishing him peace and asking for a little help from beyond. Then, referring to a map drawn by Hillside's caretaker—who knew me from my many visits here—I strode down to the road and up, taking a left at a large, bare oak tree.

"Where are we going?" Mr. Graham asked.

"I wanted to check out another grave." I carefully counted headstones. "It should be right around here."

When I got to the ninth tombstone I took another left and walked to the seventh, the one with a large angel on top. The caretaker certainly knew his territory. Tucker Zabrisky's grave was right next to his father's. Tucker had died young. Age nineteen. On January 2, son of James and Emmaline. His grave was new; he'd been buried just this spring, after the ground thawed.

A large gold cross hung from the angel's wing. I took a tissue from my purse and picked it up. It glinted in the cemetery lights, somehow more meaningful than when it had hung around Norma's neck at Schoenen's.

She's split, I thought. She's on the lam.

"Hmmph," Mr. Graham said. "Mean something to you?"

"It does." I gestured to the pages he held in his hands. "Do *those* mean something to you?"

Mr. Graham took a step back. "It's not worth it, Bubbles."

"Why isn't it worth it, Mr. Graham?" I wrapped the cross in tissue and put it and my freezing hands in my pockets. "When is it not worth it to expose a crime, an ongoing crime that has killed at least two people, including one innocent kid?" I touched my toe to the grave. "This one."

"Progress." Mr. Graham held on to his hat to keep it from blowing off. "Progress is built on risk. And without risk there is no progress."

"Steel doesn't have to risk the life of a teenage janitor to progress," I said. "Steel doesn't have to risk the lives of the people who live in this town in order to progress."

"The people who live in this town do so because of Steel. Steel feeds them. Clothes them. Sends their kids to the dentist and to college. Without Steel, this town is a dustbowl."

"Without Steel," I clarified, "this town has no newspaper."

Mr. Graham pressed his hat and came forward. "Do you know what would happen if this cover-up got out?"

"Steel would be reformed?" I suggested.

"After the billions of dollars in lawsuits, legal fees and payouts, Steel would yank anchor and sail," he said. "Do you know the story of Johns-Manville?"

"Who's Johns Manville?"

"Not who, what."

So Mr. Graham told me the story of Johns-Manville, an asbestos company based in New Jersey that was socked with so many lawsuits from workers and nearby residents who suffered a fatal lung disorder caused by its product that it declared bankruptcy, closed up shop in Manville, New

Jersey, and moved west, where it turned to making wholesome wood products.

"Have you ever been to Manville, New Jersey, Bubbles?"

I'd heard there were Yablonskys in Manville, though they spelled their name differently. One used to run a strip club out of a chicken joint.

"Can't say that I have."

"If you had, you'd have seen what the uprooting of a manufacturer can do. Manville has suffered, Bubbles. Suffered to the point where it will be decades before it ever returns. Do you want that to happen to Lehigh?"

"Of course not."

"If we publish a story based on these documents you illegally procured, that's what you can expect. Lehigh will be another Manville. And don't kid yourself into thinking your neighbors and friends and other townspeople will be grateful to you for exposing the fact that Steel's misuse of cyanide accidentally killed two people."

"Many more, I suspect. And injured," I said. "And I got a problem with that word *accidentally*."

He ignored this. "They will end up blaming you or, to be more precise, the *News-Times*. That's right. Our hometown newspaper, the newspaper that prints the obits and the weddings and runs the high school football photos, will be responsible for taking away thirty thousand jobs. Is that what you want?"

It really wasn't what I wanted. What I wanted

was for the truth to be published and for changes to take place. Oh, and I also wanted Lawless's courthouse beat.

"So," I said, "guess you're not going to run with the story."

"What do you think? Why do you think I've been hounding you on this one? Private sessions in my office. Dinner invitations."

"Because you liked me? You thought I was kind of cute?"

Mr. Graham laughed. "I don't like you any more than I like the others. What I like, Bubbles, are shareholders and profits. And that's what Garnet, the chain that owns the *News-Times*, likes, too."

"So why did you let me work on the story? Why didn't you fire me like Notch wanted?"

"Because, knowing you, you would have kept on digging and sold the damn thing to the *Call*. This way, I own your work product. This way," he jeered at me, "I own you."

I stared at him, feeling helpless as the night wind flapped the tails of his coat and blew my hair over my face. My plan hadn't worked at all.

Or had it?

"Newspaper profits are made on more than high school football stories and Hess's ads," Dix Notch said, walking down the row of graves. "Newspaper profits are made on hard-hitting stories that win awards and get us recognition. Controversy sells, Bill."

Mr. Graham nearly stumbled over a metal

veteran's marker and had to catch himself on a granite slab. "What are you doing here, Dix?"

Mr. Notch, my arch enemy, pointed his elbow my way. "Yablonsky called me. It was the last thing I wanted to do on a freezing November night, come up here, but she talked me into it. And if there's one thing I've learned since she's been freelancing it's that this broad may have lousy taste in clothes, but she's got a great nose for news."

I was bursting with pride, though I took exception to that lousy taste in clothes comment.

"We can't run the story," Mr. Graham said. "You agree, of course."

"No," Notch said. "I don't agree. Nor do I have a clue as to what's in that document. But if it was enough to bring you here, if it was enough to get you and your buddies on the Steel board to tail Yablonsky for a week, it'll be enough to put on the front page."

Yes!

"Sorry." Mr. Graham patted the pages. "As publisher, I've got the final word."

"That's a crock of shit and you know it. Excuse my French, Yablonsky."

"Oh, please," I said, waving him away.

"Twenty years ago you could have gotten away with that, Bill. That is, when you still owned the paper outright. But you sold it to Garnet and Garnet left you with the title. Not much more. Every action you've taken, including demoting me and running with Yablonsky's other stories,

358

was done only after Garnet signed off. Isn't that true?"

Mr. Graham said nothing, which meant that it was true.

When no one spoke for a while, I piped up. "What about Brian Morse? He's really mad at me. He might do something rash."

"Not likely," Notch said. "As I was leaving the newsroom, Salvo told me that Brian Morse had been picked up on allegations of spousal abuse. He's got other fish to fry right now."

Notch turned back to Mr. Graham. "So, what do you say? You hand me those papers and you get to keep your cushy job, your lunches at the Union Club and your paneled office. No more is said."

Mr. Graham hesitated. "This is a big mistake, Dix. You'll pay and pay dearly. Revenue will go down and heads will roll."

"I'm ready to bear the brunt of it," he said.

"Take it." Mr. Graham tossed the papers to the hard, cold ground. "Screw you. Screw all of you."

And with those final crude words, he went from a strong father figure to a selfish old man. Mr. Notch picked up the Steel document as I watched Graham stroll away, tripping as he zigzagged among the gravestones, back to his large luxury car.

It felt strange, all of a sudden, to be alone with Mr. Notch after such a heady encounter. I brushed away some leaves with my boot and Notch thumbed through the pages. I wondered who would get to do the big write-up. If it was Lawless, I was going to go get drunk on peach schnapps.

"Appears as though I've got some heavy bedtime reading," Mr. Notch said, trying to make light.

"Yes," I said, suddenly interested in the contents of my pocket. Gum. Lipstick. Matches. Norma's cross wrapped in tissue.

"Course now," he cleared his throat, "I'm going to want to see you in the newsroom bright and early at the computer."

I looked up. Hopeful. Please don't say to write obits.

"We won't be able to get it in Sunday's paper. It'll have to be vetted, I'm sure. The police will need a copy in order to arrest Hal Weaver's real murderer."

"Norma Lubrecht," I said. "His maid. She got herself hired as his housekeeper so she could get her pound of flesh for Steel poisoning her boyfriend. How cliché is that?"

"Not that cliché. If Steel had killed someone I loved and tried to cover it up, I might be tempted to commit murder, too. Though, I wouldn't have gone for the flak."

"She was young," I said. "She didn't know. She hit on the man whose name was always linked to Steel on the TV news."

"How did Weaver get the documents?"

I shrugged. "From work, I suppose. Or from Eunice Morse, Brian's ex-wife. My thinking is that

Norma was the one who planted the notion in Hal Weaver's mind that Steel had poisoned Tucker, her boyfriend. He went looking and, sure enough, found the cover-up. Along with the cyanide."

"That answers my next question," he said.

"It must have been exciting, even arousing, for Hal to lead a double life of espionage with a pretty girl like Norma, the two of them on a mission to uncover this secret. Only Hal wanted to use the secret to blackmail his way out of Steel and Norma was waiting for the right opportunity to exact her revenge."

"Interesting." Notch looked off, not quite able to make eye contact with me. "What do you think the prosecutor's going to do with Norma?"

"If he finds her." I opened the tissue and showed him the cross. "This is hers. It was around her neck on Monday. I think she left it on Tucker's grave as a message. She's gone. Long gone. She's had a head start of almost four days."

Mr. Notch thought about what I said. "Well. Seems like you know your stuff. I'll let you write the story."

"Oh my God. Thank you, Mr. Notch."

He put up a finger to stop me from getting too excited. "There will be follow-up calls and more research to do, but if you work steadily all next week, we might be able to get it in the next."

"But," I said, trying to keep my voice professional. "But my tryout ends tomorrow."

"Hmm. That is a problem." Notch leaned on a

tombstone and thought about this. "Oh, well, I suppose we'll just have to put you on the staff."

I couldn't believe it. Was he serious?

"How about thirty thousand? With benefits. That's better than our usual starting salary, but, then again, you've had more experience than most J-school grads."

"Oh, Mr. Notch." I flung my arms around him and kissed his sunburned cheeks.

"Uh, Yablonsky." He removed my arms. "About your overly effusive mannerisms. That's not what professional journalists do."

"Yes, Mr. Notch."

He smiled. A first.

"Can I ask you something?" I said.

"If it's about getting Thanksgiving off, no way. Last one to join the staff gets all the holidays."

"No. Not Thanksgiving. It's about Steve Stiletto. Have you heard what happened with the hostage crisis down in Malvern?"

Notch let out a deep sigh. "The good news is that it's over. The bad news is that there's one dead. All we know is that it's a man. They're not releasing names until next of kin have been notified."

I fought back a wail of pain.

"Stay brave, Yablonsky." He reached out and patted me stiffly. "It's one of your best traits."

I watched as he went back down the hill, leaving me alone with the dead.

One of whom I prayed was not Stiletto.

★　　　★　　　★

I don't know how long I sat on my father's grave. Hours. My butt was frozen beyond sensation and my face was numb. I think I may have slept a bit, or dozed between crying jags, my heart breaking in two to think that I almost . . . almost had had it all.

Jane would get into Princeton, I could feel it. I had reached my goal of a staff position on the *News-Times*. Thirty thousand dollars a year with benefits. More than twice what I made at the House of Beauty.

And yet it would be nothing, it would be dirt, without Stiletto. "Why," I moaned to my dead father, "why couldn't life just hand me a break? Why did it fight me so?"

I felt like I'd been paying for that one sin on the floor of that dirty Lehigh fraternity for as long as I could remember. Since then I'd married a man I didn't love, given birth when I should have been dancing, quit school and worked hard—waitressing, shampooing, getting my GED, going to beauty school, then Two Guys—for eight years.

Eight years!

Not to mention, raising a daughter essentially alone, all the while battling to get a job on this stupid newspaper.

Then Stiletto comes along, and my life, my life feels like it could soar. Like I could wake every day singing. Only to turn around and find that he's been extinguished by a kidnapper who doesn't even know his name. Poof. Lights out.

I remember what Mama used to tell me, that God never tests us beyond our abilities to cope. "Well," I said out loud to no one, "I can't cope, God."

There was a rustling of leaves. I looked up to see a figure coming through the gravestones. The caretaker, probably. Or maybe Notch. Or worse, Norma.

"You know," he said, looking at his watch, "it's after two in the morning."

I felt dizzy. Hallucinating.

"I get home and you're not there. I call around and can't find anyone. Your mother, Genevieve." He knelt down. "They've all disappeared."

"They're probably at the hospital," I said, still not sure if I was talking to Stiletto or his spirit.

"Tried there, too. Nope. No Bubbles Yablonsky. I call Tony Salvo out of bed. He says he hasn't seen you since he fired you this afternoon. I start to worry. I can't sit still. I have to find you. Finally, I'm going out of my mind."

He sat beside me. "You know, this doesn't happen when you're single. When you're single and you come home exhausted after working fourteen hours, you just collapse on the couch, pop a beer. You don't pace, worrying about whether the love of your life's dead in a ditch by the road or if she's been bumped off by a prison escapee."

"Stiletto, that's changed. . . ."

"You're not the love of my life?"

"No. I'm not fired."

"Congratulations. Sounds like you pulled quite a coup."

"Are you alive?" I touched his jeans to see if they were real. "Or are you a ghost?"

"Hmm." He put his living, warm hand in mine. "I'm dead on my feet, but I guess I'm alive."

He smiled at me, his blue eyes filled with feelings he couldn't express, feelings that were beyond words. The joy that I had cursed all night began to reemerge as he leaned down and kissed me, pressing me against my father's headstone.

"How did you survive?" I asked when I got a chance to breathe.

He laughed. "It was the most fucked up story I've ever worked on. Your mother's friend, that phone-mad Rachel Stottlemyer, saved the day. She called me on the cell phone and insisted on talking to the creep. Talked the guy's ear off, so long he finally shot himself in his other ear, just to end the misery."

It was dark humor, but I felt a giggle coming on. "I know how he felt."

"She's also the one who called to tell me you had gone to your father's grave." He turned and read the tombstone. "This it?"

"This is it. Dad, meet Stiletto. Stiletto, meet Dad."

Stiletto saluted.

"So the man who died in Malvern, that wasn't you?"

"Not me." Stiletto played with my hair again. "Don't tell me *that's* what kept you here?"

"I didn't want anyone to find me, to tell me the bad news. So I stayed with my father."

"What about your cell phone?"

"We broke it."

Stiletto looked alarmed.

"Actually, *I* broke it by throwing it at Genevieve's musket. Anyway, that meant there was no way for anyone to reach me, which was good because," I swallowed hard to keep from crying, "because I didn't want to go home and get the call my mother had, that the man she loved was dead."

"I see." He twisted a strand of my hair around his finger. "So you love me, do you?"

"I do. Don't you know?"

"You never said that last night. I assumed you were just hedging your bets in case the sex turned out to be so-so." That amused tone was back in his voice. Does Stiletto take anything seriously?

"The sex wasn't so-so. It was fantastic. I didn't want it to end, ever." I studied his Adam's apple. Why is that thing so sexy? "That's why I was crying, because here I had almost everything I wanted, . . . except you."

"You mean me in bed. Because you'll always have me, wherever I am, Bubbles. You know that, right?"

I knew what he was trying to slide by me in the smooth way he likes to introduce sticky subjects. "You're talking about England."

He kissed me again. "Yeah. England."

"And if I don't go, I don't have you . . . at least in bed."

"I'd be damn tired taking eight-hour flights every day just to satisfy you, my love."

"So what are we going to do?" I ran my finger along the inseam of his thigh, eliciting a very satisfactory moan in response.

"I think," he said, helping me to stand stiffly. "I think we should go back to bed and talk about it."

"Talk?"

He unzipped his leather jacket and put it around my shoulders. "Why? Did you have something else in mind?"

"What I have, Stiletto, has nothing to do with my mind. My mind needs a rest. I'm going to let my body take over for a few hours."

He smiled that great Stiletto smile. "Great. And while it's at it, I'll let your body take over mine, too. Deal?"

"Deal."

EPILOGUE

J ust a quick note to fill you in on what happened over the next few days.

Dan was able to win bail for Carol while Reinhold reviewed her case. George Thomas, the assistant D.A., immediately quit his post and has been making such a big stink over the handling of Hal Weaver's murder that I'm positive Carol will go free.

It would have helped both Carol and Susan if the cops had been able to find Norma. But, as I feared, Norma was gone. I, for one, wasn't about to go looking for her. In fact there was a part of me that whispered for her to run. Run and don't look back.

Susan was charged with harboring a prison escapee, a count that could be thrown out if the D.A.'s office determines that Carol had no part in her husband's murder. With the help of counselors and Lorena, she has returned to her home, reprogrammed the security system and is beginning to recover from her wounds.

I have no idea if Carol and Susan are lesbian lovers. It doesn't matter to me, really, since they aren't killers. Anyway, as Stiletto says, their personal life is none of my business.

Brian Morse continues to sit in jail, unable to post a two-million-dollar bond. Reinhold was able to portray him in court as a flight risk, especially in light of the possibility that Morse could face more serious charges down the road, relating to the Mountaintop Lab deaths.

So far Bailey's death appears to have been truly accidental. Dan doesn't believe it was murder. He is more disturbed by the cruel irony of a slip-and-fall lawyer slipping and falling on his own driveway. No one to sue but himself.

The Mountaintop Lab story hasn't been published yet. I'm waiting for it to be lawyered. In the meantime, I filled out all the personnel forms, had my official press pass made up and picked a desk that is way too close to Lawless. I can't seem to get away from the smell of Ho Ho's.

Kiera gave birth shortly after 1 A.M. on that Friday, to a seven-pound, five-ounce boy named, appropriately, Halsey Buchanan Weaver. The Buchanan was Lorena's idea—a permanent link between Llanview and Lehigh, PA, I guess. I was very glad Carol had drawn the line at Asa.

Doggie or Doogie, or whatever the name of the druggie father, breezed in and out of the hospital, much to Kiera's distress. I assured her that she would survive and made her write down all her frustrations so she could read them eighteen years later, when she had graduated from Two Guys, gotten a kick-ass job, an even hotter boyfriend and when Halsey had finished his Princeton application.

Because if there's anything I've learned from this amazing week, it's that Gloria Gaynor didn't get it quite right. Not only will we women survive. We can do better.

We can have it all.

Susan Morse's Easy Beer Rinse

Susan Morse has beautiful, thick hair, made so by the application of a flat beer rinse. Brunettes might want to add a few drops of calendula oil to bring out the deep, rich colors. The lavender oil helps to neutralize the beer smell, though make sure you test this on a day when you'll be hanging around the house. Nothing turns off a blind date faster than a woman who smells like a Lehigh fraternity.

1 ounce distilled water
1 ounce flat beer
2 tablespoons lemon juice
3 drops lavender essential oil

Mix all the ingredients and use as a rinse. Rinse well with water.

The Miracle of Borax

An excerpt from the Two Guys Community College M.R.S curriculum

Borax, otherwise known as sodium borate, is a naturally occurring mineral that is an inexpensive, nonpolluting, indispensable tool for the clean household. Not only does it soften water, brighten clothes and deodorize, it can also be used to make a favorite summer project—drying flowers.

Chemical Free Scouring Powder

Mix equal parts Borax and bicarbonate of soda. Stir and use the mixture to scrub tubs, toilets and other surfaces where you would ordinarily use Comet.

Drying Flowers

Sprinkle a thick layer of Borax at the bottom of a shoe box. Lay the cut flowers. Top with more Borax. Tape the box shut and wait one week. You may reuse the Borax.

Humidifiers

Dissolve one tablespoon per gallon of water added to your humidifier to eliminate odors. Be sure to rinse out that solution with pure water prior to use.

Bubbles's Nail Conditioner

After weakening her nails with acrylic overlays, Bubbles searched Steve Stiletto's cabinets and found enough ingredients for an emergency treatment. This nail conditioner will help keep your nails from becoming dry and brittle, and your cuticles, too. Unfortunately, if your natural nail has been filed paper thin, only time will grow it to its original strength. And, oh yes, it will grow.

4 vitamin E gelcaps, broken open
2 tablespoons olive oil
2 teaspoons honey
1 drop lavender oil

Soak nails in warm water for five minutes. Remove and pat dry. Mix ingredients above, massaging deep into the cuticles of hands and feet. Wipe off excess.

Tapioca Face Mask
(It's not just for breakfast anymore.)

The acid of the grapefruit juice combined with the starch of tapioca and soothing elements of honey and vitamin E will smooth wrinkles and refresh the skin. Make sure to *cool* the mask before putting it on your face.

½ cup grapefruit juice.
1 tablespoon Minute Tapioca
2 vitamin E gelcaps, broken open
1 tablespoon honey
½ teaspoon vanilla

Mix ingredients in a saucepan over low heat. Boil for one minute, stirring. Cook until thickened, about five more minutes. Remove from heat. Cool. (This is very important.) Spread on face and neck and let sit for fifteen minutes. Rinse and remove.

ABOUT THE AUTHOR

Sarah Strohmeyer is the author of the Agatha Award–winning mystery series that includes *Bubbles Unbound, Bubbles in Trouble,* and *Bubbles Ablaze.* A former journalist whose work has appeared in the *Boston Globe,* the *Cleveland Plain Dealer,* and on Salon.com, she lives with her family outside Montpelier, Vermont. She can be contacted through www.SarahStrohmeyer.com.